FOR BETTER, FOR WORSE

BOOKS BY LAUREN NORTH

My Word Against His
She Says She's My Daughter
The Teacher's Secret
I'm Her Mother

All the Wicked Games
Safe at Home
One Step Behind
The Perfect Betrayal

FOR BETTER, FOR WORSE

LAUREN NORTH

bookouture

Published by Bookouture in 2025

An imprint of Storyfire Ltd.
Carmelite House
50 Victoria Embankment
London EC4Y 0DZ

www.bookouture.com

The authorised representative in the EEA is Hachette Ireland
8 Castlecourt Centre
Dublin 15 D15 XTP3
Ireland
(email: info@hbgi.ie)

Copyright © Lauren North, 2025

Lauren North has asserted her right to be identified as the author of this work.

All rights reserved. No part of this publication may be reproduced, stored in any retrieval system, or transmitted, in any form or by any means, electronic, mechanical, photocopying, recording or otherwise, without the prior written permission of the publishers.

ISBN: 978-1-83618-629-8
eBook ISBN: 978-1-83618-628-1

This book is a work of fiction. Names, characters, businesses, organizations, places and events other than those clearly in the public domain, are either the product of the author's imagination or are used fictitiously. Any resemblance to actual persons, living or dead, events or locales is entirely coincidental.

For Merry Anslow

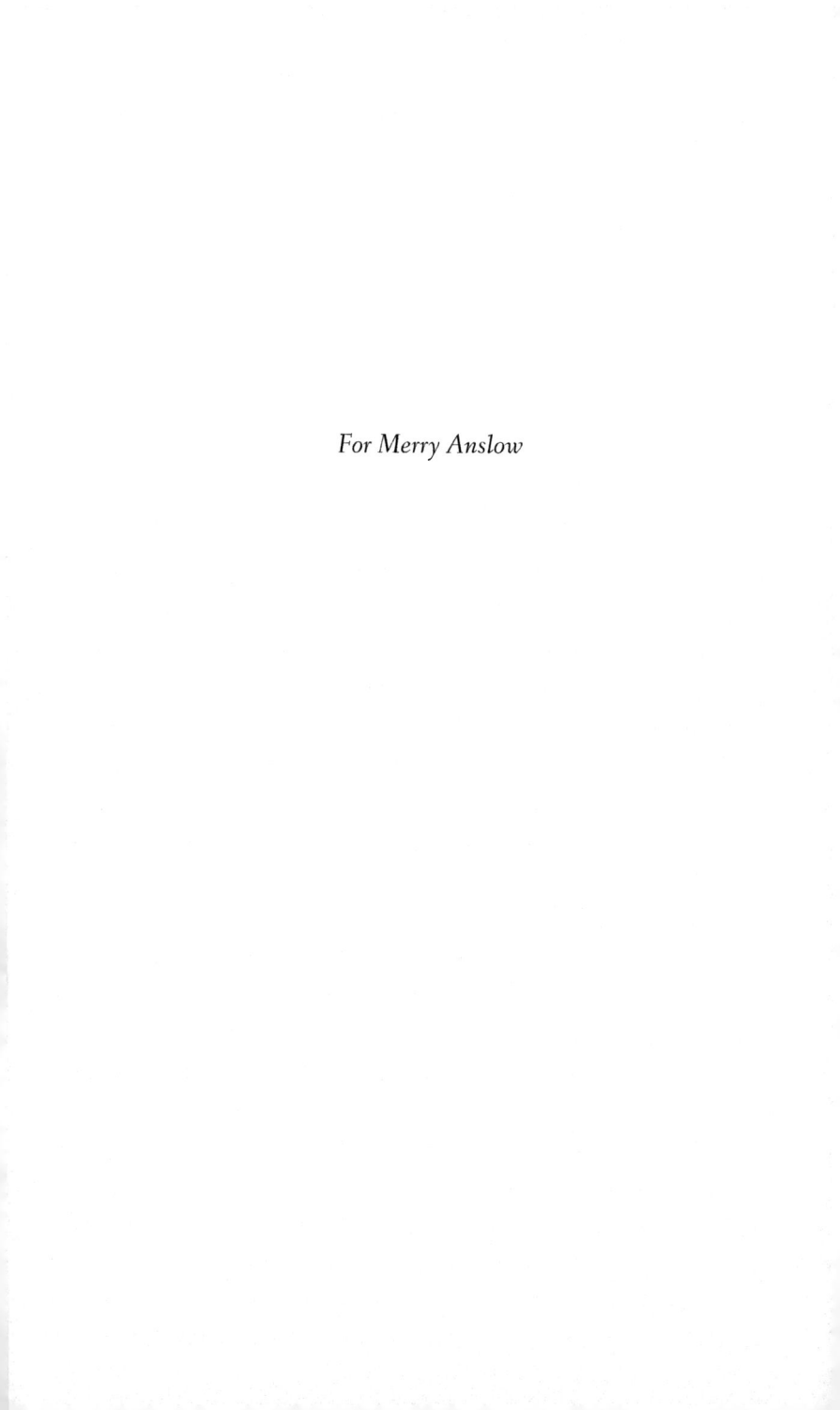

14 DAYS UNTIL THE WEDDING

PROLOGUE
HANNAH

We're laughing as I push open the heavy farmhouse door and see the foot lying on the rug. I see it, but I don't see it. Somewhere in my thoughts I register pale skin, toes and a leather sandal. The whole thing twisted at an unnatural angle. But Jake's lips on my neck are distracting, and my mind is skipping ahead to wriggling out of our clothes and jumping naked into the pool again. Acting like teens with the house to ourselves for a day instead of the thirty-somethings we are. God, we needed this break!

Three nights in a restored eighteenth-century limestone farmhouse in Southern France, just the two of us. Six bedrooms, four bathrooms, a pool – and lying on a red Persian Heriz rug... one foot that doesn't belong.

'I really thought my route was quicker. Are you sure you didn't run?' Jake's teasing voice murmurs in my ear. His Ohio accent is always stronger when he's turned on. His lips press against my neck again, hot and enticing. I wonder if my skin tastes of salt and sun cream from our walk in the midday heat.

'Are you calling me a cheat?' My laugh is so easy I can't believe it's only been four days since I was standing in the middle of our London apartment, shivering with fear, thinking I'd never be happy again. 'And I was only thirty seconds ahead of you,' I add.

'You still beat me.' He grins, and I take the rare win. It was only a silly bet on which path back from the lake was quicker. No different from the dozens of others we've made in our relationship. Jake took the road, whereas I wandered the narrow paths through the vineyards covering the Languedoc-Roussillon region, two hours from Montpellier. I'd let the vines tickle my fingers, taking a moment to myself, feeling home for the first time in forever. I'm surprised I made it to the driveway first.

The door opens another few inches and still the foot is there. Not just one foot now but two. And legs and a body and a head with white hair I recognise instantly. Black shirt, corduroy trousers. Face down. Not moving.

Finally, it registers. Finally, a piercing alarm trills in my head. Reality shoves all thoughts of the pool and Jake's naked body out of my mind. I make a noise – an involuntary yelp – and stop; fear roots me to the spot.

'Hannah?' Jake's voice sounds distant. From his position behind me, he hasn't seen the body yet. 'Han?' he says, shortening my name like he does sometimes.

No words come. None at all. I can't voice the horror. Everything about the body screams dead. It's not just the stillness of it. It's the blood. So much blood. A huge pool soaked into the intricate, petal-like pattern of the rug. And the smell – rust and iron, like old pennies, mixing in the air with our own sweat. My stomach heaves and I gag, but I'm empty from our hike and there's nothing to bring up but the bitter sting of bile in the back of my throat.

Then Jake's moving into the hall. 'Oh, God.' The word comes out in a husky exhale. 'What the...?' He doesn't finish.

Time slows. I don't know how long we stand there. The only sound is the lazy buzz of a fly, throwing its body against the window. Neither of us rush forward to check for a pulse. There's no need. We don't scramble to call for an ambulance on the antique black telephone that sits on the entrance table either – used when the signal drops and our mobiles become useless, as they often do here.

Finally, I speak, the words landing somewhere between a croak and a sob. 'He's dead.'

Jake nods slowly, eyes wide like the shock is rattling in his soul just like it is in mine.

'Oh my God.' My teeth chatter but I lurch forward, reaching for the phone. 'We have to call the police. We need help.' My fingers are already wrapping around the cool plastic casing of the receiver when something catches my eye. A glint of metal. I stop.

Is that...? No!

Another gasp. It is! My thoughts race back to the melon we bought in the village this morning. The easy way the sharp blade of the Le Creuset carving knife slid through the ripe fruit as we prepared lunch. The distinctive wood handle. The same knife now lying discarded by the body.

For the first time since I registered the man on my rug, my tunnel vision lifts and I see beyond it to the pool of blood around him. Then other things – more details. Red footprints on the flagstone floor. The blood so thick every swirl of the tread is visible, as though it was painted on. I have a flash of memory to early childhood. A classroom. A spilled pot of bright-yellow paint. The trail my shoes made. My mother hissing angrily at the teaching staff. The shoes ruined.

Another alarm rings inside me. Loud. Urgent. But I can't believe it. I won't. I want to stay hiding in the thick layers of shock and keep out the new thought trying to take root. And yet I don't pick up the phone.

'Jake?' My voice is a whisper.

He doesn't reply, and I turn towards him. His hands rub his

face in the way he does when he's stressed. My fiancé is smart, organised and brilliant at so many things, but he doesn't like sudden changes, doesn't cope well with the shift. But I have to get this pulsing new thought out of my head. I need him to tell me the reasons I'm wrong.

'Give me a second,' he replies. But I can't. This is too important to wait even one more breath.

'Jake, is that' – my hand shakes as I point to the rug – 'the knife I used earlier?' I know it is. It's the only carving knife in the house. Part of the matching set of ten in an ornate wood block on the kitchen counter. Except this one – the one I used – which I placed in the dishwasher.

'What?'

'The knife. I left it in the dishwasher, remember?' I think I might be sick. The smell of the blood is roiling in my stomach.

His eyes find mine. Wide and fearful. 'What are you trying to say?'

It hasn't hit him yet. 'I...' My head spins. 'Look,' I say, half shouting suddenly to hear myself over the thudding of my heart in my ears.

He shakes his head. Not getting it.

I point to the footprints and the tread marks of the shoes I'd know anywhere. Men's size twelve. The Brunello Cucinelli trainers I'd bought Jake for Christmas. The soles have a distinctive circular tread pattern that spreads out across the bottom of the shoe and into an oval. I stare at each red print made in blood and a sob catches in my throat.

'Look around you. That's the knife I used earlier. Someone took it from the dishwasher instead of using any of the other knives sitting out in the block. And... those shoe prints are from your shoes.' My gaze darts to the space behind the door where Jake left his shoes after our trip to the village earlier. They're sitting neatly together just as he left them, except now the white and blue leather is covered in blood. Not just the treads on the bottom but fat droplets splattered on the tops. I scrunch my eyes shut. Not wanting to see. Not wanting to believe. But when I open my eyes again, the shoes are still there, the blood splattered like someone was wearing these shoes when they dug the dirty knife I used out of the dishwasher and stabbed this man. Murdered him. Inside my mind, a part of me screams.

Jake makes a noise in his throat, and despite the nightmare unfolding before me, I'm relieved he's caught on to the same place where my thoughts are dragging me.

'Oh God,' he says again, making a move towards his shoes – one step then stumbling, righting himself, like he wanted to reach them and changed his mind too fast for his body to catch on. 'I... I was with you,' he says, and it feels ludicrous and unnecessary that he would even need to voice those words. Of course he didn't do this. But I nod because it's true. We were together on the hike, only separating on the way home. It's his shoes covered in blood and it's the knife I used at lunch. It's the body in this house, on this rug. There's no way Jake killed this man. No way I did either.

I look at Jake. His wide eyes blaze with the same fear coursing through me with every thundering beat of my heart.

'I don't know—' he starts then pauses, gaze flicking to the man, the knife, the shoes, as though checking – not believing what we both already know. 'I don't know what's going on here, Han.'

I shake my head, my ponytail swishing at the base of my neck. My mind blanks. I can't process this. I can't find the words. 'This can't be happening,' I whisper, voice trembling. 'Someone must've come to the house while we were out...' I swallow down the rising nausea.

Jake's face pales. 'But who would do this?'

We stand there in silence for a long moment before he heaves in a shuddering breath. 'My shoes – they look like...' He trails off.

'Like someone was wearing them when they did this,' I finish.

'And the knife—'

It's my turn to nod. 'Will have my fingerprints on it. The only knife in this place that does.'

Jake's mouth gapes open as he looks at me again. 'Did... someone do this and... want to make it look like it was us?'

I swallow again, fighting to keep control of my body.

'But why would they?' I ask. Then another question comes and I feel sick, unsteady on my feet. 'And who would do this?'

Jake's eyes find mine, and I see the next question form in his mind, dragging its dark shadow over his face. He doesn't voice it. He wants to shield me from it, but it's there to read in the furrow of his brow and the grimace of his lips. Someone came to my family home while we were hiking by the lake. They put on Jake's shoes. They went to the trouble to find the knife I used earlier. They stabbed a man to death and made it look like we did it.

We're in the middle of nowhere. A mile to our nearest neighbour. A twenty-minute drive to the village. We're alone out here, and the afternoon sun is sinking towards evening and night and darkness. And there is the question on Jake's face that he doesn't ask but jumps between us anyway, landing in my head. Are we next?

The sharp trill of the antique phone shatters the silence and I scream.

1 DAY EARLIER – 15 DAYS UNTIL THE WEDDING

ONE

HANNAH

The moment the car turns into the sweeping driveway my exhaustion lifts. I even smile as the headlights bathe the outline of the farmhouse, standing tall and proud with pale-yellow stone, restored to all its former glory. There's an imposing wood door and quaint wood shutters on the windows, painted the same terracotta as the roof tiles currently lost to the night like the gardens and vineyards surrounding us.

The 5 a.m. alarm in my London apartment and the ferry crossing – the nine long hours spent in this car – fade into nothing.

'Home at last,' I say, scooping the silky strands of my light-brown hair into a ponytail as Jake parks to one side of the house and cuts the engine. He leans forward in his seat, peering through the windscreen with a comical frown that makes me almost laugh.

He shoots me a look and even in the evening gloom, in this car that smells of crisps and sweets and our bodies from the journey, he steals my breath. Dark eyes. Dark hair, short on the sides but longer on top. He's somehow managed to tan in the few days of English sun we've had this month, and his beard is that perfect more-than-stubble length I love. I can already see him in his new grey suit, waiting for me in the church. Two weeks to go! I still can't believe it. This man is everything to me.

He smiles, and it's that amused, teasing smile with just a flash of those perfect white teeth he gives me on Saturday mornings when he asks which London tourist hotspot I'm going to drag him to that weekend, because in the six months he was living in the city before we met, he never went to any. I think of the photo in our apartment of us posing in gallows at the London Dungeons, barely able to stop laughing for the picture to be taken.

'So,' he says, 'I guess the English definition of a farmhouse is not the same as an American one.'

'Really? What were you expecting?' I ask as I open the passenger door, climb out and stretch my aching back. The air is still warm from the sun's heat, and scents of lavender and rosemary carry from the gardens. Not like the too-sweet fragrances I buy sometimes, trying to capture a memory or a feeling from my past.

I close my eyes and breathe in the air and the silence. I think of London again. I think of the feeling of rushing. Of always having somewhere to be and a mountain of work to do – the life of a corporate lawyer in the city. I think of the constant rattle of trains coming and going from King's Cross station. People everywhere. Locals. Tourists. Commuters. Blending in. Standing out. Night buses roaring by on the road by my loft apartment. Car horns. The beeping of reversing vans. Shouts. The soundtrack of my life.

The driver's door opens then closes. Feet crunch on the stones. 'I was expecting a brick cabin,' Jake continues. 'This is a mansion.'

'It's not a mansion,' I say, smiling.

'Really? How many bedrooms does it have?' he asks in his teasing voice.

'Six,' I admit.

He takes my hand and I see the tension of the last few days unknotting in him as it has done in me. He blames himself for what happened. I'm trying not to. It's not his fault his ex-girlfriend is... I search for a nicer way to think of Neve. Something that isn't 'unhinged psycho'. I'm trying to move my anger to pity. It's hard but sometimes I remember that deep down we both want the same man. The only difference is Jake chose me.

I push thoughts of the busted lock and the mess in our apartment and Neve away, and focus on Jake. He didn't want to do this – a mini break two weeks before our wedding. Too short notice. Too much still to organise for the wedding. Not enough time for his usual detailed planning. But I had to get away, even just for the long weekend.

'Remind me never to take you to my old neighbourhood in Westlake,' Jake says.

I shake my head. 'Don't say that. You know I'd love to see more of the States and where you grew up. Ohio sounds so beautiful.'

'One day,' he says, pressing his lips to the back of my hand. 'And you grew up here?' Jake asks. 'For real?'

'Sort of. My mum would bring us for six weeks every summer, and sometimes Easter and Christmas when Dad could get the time off.'

'We should've done this months ago.' He pulls me into his strong arms and we kiss. It's soft and searching and makes my heart lurch. God, this man! 'Come on. Let's leave the bags for now. Show me around.'

I unlock the front door, pushing my weight against it until it opens into a spacious hallway with a flagstone floor and a handwoven red Persian rug. We explore the downstairs first. Every room has been meticulously restored. I run my hands over the cool, rough stone walls, left unfinished to add to its rustic charm.

I show Jake the living room with brown leather sofas in

front of a log burner. Then through an archway to a dining room with an oak table and a dozen high-backed chairs with embroidered cushions, sitting below a grand chandelier with dozens of delicate crystals sparkling in the light.

I smile as I tell Jake about a game of Monopoly my brother and I had at this table that lasted the entire summer. He laughs at the two framed photos on the wall of me standing in a garden in a white dress, and another of William when he was three, posing in a three-piece suit.

The kitchen at the back of the house is dominated by a large black Aga, surrounded by off-white cupboards and hand-painted blue Damask tiles. I find the switch I'm looking for, and a moment later the garden lights turn on, illuminating a veranda covered in vines and surrounded by thick lavender bushes. Beyond it is the rectangular shape of the pool. The water so enticing that Jake pulls me outside like an excited child.

I haven't even shown him the basement with the sauna and gym or the upstairs and the bedrooms with the four-poster beds and standing baths with the views that look out to the sloping vineyards.

'Race you in.' Jake pulls off his T-shirt, showing his toned torso.

I laugh. 'What about our swimwear?'

'Who cares?' He runs back and grabs two towels from the stack in the mud room we passed on our way out. I'm swept away in his delight and kick off my shoes, tug at my top. A moment later, we're naked, the warm night air tickling my bare skin. He takes my hand and grins, and together we jump in.

The water is cold and all-consuming, and as my head sinks beneath the surface, I know I'll be OK. Maybe the police officer who took our statement after the break-in was right. We can move on. I force myself not to think about his shrugged apology when he told us there was nothing they could do. Neve claimed the lock was already broken when she'd come looking for Jake.

Like it wasn't her who'd ransacked my apartment searching for... what? I don't know.

'You said nothing was taken,' the officer reminded us – a man in his early twenties with copper-red hair cut close to his head. 'We've suggested to the woman in question to stay away. I recommend purchasing a doorbell camera and a better lock and trying to forget it happened.'

Like it was that easy.

'What does she want?' I asked Jake after I'd stopped crying.

He shook his head. 'To mess with us, I guess. I didn't even know she was in London. Last I heard she was still living near her parents in Westlake. I'm so sorry, Han.'

Later, he said, 'We'll be OK.' I wanted to believe it, but I looked at the mess – books thrown from the shelves, papers scattered, my clothes – my underwear – tipped out of drawers, and I cried and told him how violated and scared I was. The words didn't feel enough.

In the pool, my lungs start to burn and I come up for air, pushing the loose strands of wet hair away from my face.

I open my eyes and Jake is beside me, his arms reaching for me. I wrap myself around him, closing the gap between our bodies so we're one instead of two. Gently, he pushes me against the side and moves his mouth towards mine. The kiss is deep and exploring. He draws away, eyes searching my face. 'I love you, Hannah Fitzroy. I can't wait to be your husband.'

'I love you too.' I grin, feeling so lucky that Jake is mine. After those hollow years of loneliness, I'll always be grateful we found each other. The connection Jake and I have is like nothing I've felt before. He seems to intuitively know what I need and when. A hundred little things every day to show me he loves me. Like putting a coffee by the bed in the morning when I'm still half asleep after my shower, even though it's early and Jake doesn't have to get up.

He shifts a little and I feel him harden against me, and I smile as his lips find mine again.

Afterwards, Jake wraps a large fluffy white towel around us and we lie in each other's arms on a lounger, listening to the insects and the soft sounds of the night.

'This is the first time since the break-in I feel safe,' I say.

His arms tighten around me. 'I'll never let anything happen to you.'

I lean my head against his chest and think of tomorrow when we'll drive to the village for supplies and I'll show Jake my favourite walk around the lake a few miles away. We'll eat fresh fruit, and baguettes with thick slabs of cheese. We'll drink wine and we won't talk about the table plan for the wedding. We won't talk about the break-in the police could do nothing about. We'll just be us, and it will be the perfect getaway.

14 DAYS UNTIL THE WEDDING

TWO

JAKE

The morning sun is hot in a way it rarely is in England. British heatwaves are like those back home in Westlake – stuffy and humid. But there's a coolness on the breeze here, a lightness to the air, making the sun's heat pleasant, Jake thinks, as they park the car outside a small village twenty minutes' drive from Hannah's family farmhouse.

The warmth seeps into his body, unravelling the tangled knots of the last few weeks. With running his business, the wedding plans and now Neve turning up in the UK, Jake has felt under constant pressure. He worries about Hannah too. It's not just the stress of the break-in this week; it's how hard she works, running herself into the ground, desperate to prove herself, and, he suspects, prove to her parents she doesn't need them.

It worries him he's still not met them. Hannah's father is a crown court judge, her mother a socialite, whatever that means. He'll be marrying their daughter in two weeks and yet they've cancelled every dinner plan and Hannah's dress fitting her mum was supposed to attend. Putting the wedding aside, he and Hannah will have been together a year in June. Lived together for almost as long. Engaged since Christmas. Yet her parents have shown no interest in meeting him. He understands Hannah's relationship with them is strained. It's not like his relationship with his own parents is any better, but Hannah is their only daughter. Surely they'd want to know she's happy and loved. He desperately wants to reassure them that his relationship with Hannah might seem fast, but she's his one. His soulmate. Something he didn't even believe in until he met her. He knew he wanted to marry her the second time he saw her.

He hates that Hannah isn't their number one priority; that they sent her and her brother, William, to boarding school at the age of twelve – the cliché of the elite – and insist she call them Julia and Marcus instead of Mum and Dad. It makes him want to prove even more that no matter what, he'll always put her first.

They walk slowly towards the village – a holiday stroll that would have them barged and tutted at in London. The air is fragranced with flowers, the sky impossibly blue. He takes Hannah's hand, and she pushes her sunglasses onto her head and smiles up at him in that playful, inviting way she does. He drinks her in. Can't believe she's really his. Those feline eyes that have no business being so blue against her brunette hair, but somehow he can't imagine them any other colour. She has a slim face with high cheekbones and lips a pale pink.

At home, she accentuates her features with make-up, adding contours and layers to her beauty she doesn't need, but he understands. The law firm where she's a senior associate is cut throat, and her make-up, along with her designer shoes and tailored dresses, are her armour. He respects it, but he prefers this Hannah. With her hair in a high ponytail and just a brush of mascara.

'Are you glad we came now?' she asks.

He makes a face, cringing as he remembers his reaction

early Thursday morning when Hannah stepped out the shower and first suggested the trip.

'We can't just pack up and go to France tomorrow,' he said.

'Why not?' Hannah asked. Demanded. 'HR have been bugging me to take some holiday and you work for yourself.'

'We just can't. What about the wedding stuff and—' He'd wanted to tell her it wasn't a good time for him. His software – the pinnacle of his business – has interest from a buyer at last, and he needs to prepare for the biggest meeting of his life. But the words didn't come.

'I need this, Jake,' Hannah cut in anyway. 'I can't be in this apartment right now.'

Tears welled in her eyes, and even though it half killed him, he found himself booking a last-minute ferry crossing from Dover and setting his out-of-office email. And he really is glad.

'It wasn't that I didn't want to come,' he says, trying to explain. 'It was just so last minute.'

'Not in the schedule,' they say in unison, and Hannah flashes him a teasing smile.

'I know. I need to be more...' He waves his hands in the air.

'I'm sorry, what is this?' She laughs, copying the movement. 'Dying bird? Angry chicken?'

He tips his head back and laughs too. 'Yes. I need to be more angry chicken about last-minute plans.'

She moves close, slipping her arm around his waist and standing on tiptoes to kiss his cheek. 'I get it. You like to plan because you want everything to be perfect. I love that about you.'

He kisses the top of her head, and as Hannah guides them down a narrow road of old stone cottages with window boxes overflowing with bright geraniums, Jake wonders like he always does how he got so lucky. No one has ever understood him the way Hannah does. No one has ever loved his quirks and his need to plan. He knows it's one of the reasons they fit so well.

Hannah puts so much of herself into her work, the last thing she wants to do at home is make decisions, and that's what he's best at – planning.

He wants their life to run smoothly, but he likes to know what's around the corner too. He likes to make plans and stick to them. Successful people always talk about how important it is to adapt, but Jake owes his success to an ability to stay one step ahead in business and in life, and he does that by making plans and sticking to them.

But maybe he does need to be more adaptable. After all, changing plans is the only reason he and Hannah are together. It's how they met last June. Well, that and a silly bet, something their competitive natures are both drawn to.

It was a sunny Saturday morning and the day of the 55 mile London to Brighton bike ride he'd been training for when his life changed forever. He'd bet himself he could complete the race before Kev, one of the cyclists in the club he'd joined when he'd moved to London six months earlier. Jake liked a bit of competition but only when it was friendly and fun. Kev always took it too far, and so Jake had something to prove.

London hadn't been like Manchester, where he'd first lived for four years after he'd moved from Ohio. In Manchester, everyone wanted to be his mate. He'd joined a fantasy football league and been adopted by the lads. Pints after work. Football in the pub at weekends, not to mention the banter on their WhatsApp group.

When he moved to London to grow his software business, he'd joined a cycle club in Putney to make friends and fill his evenings and weekends, but hadn't gelled with the other men in the way he'd hoped. Still, he'd been looking forward to the ribbing Kev would get from Jake beating his cycle time.

Despite the three-hour staggered start on race day, there were still hundreds of cyclists setting off in Clapham. All going the same way. It was chaos. Someone trying to get ahead.

Someone braking suddenly. An accident was inevitable. On a sharp turn, a pedal from a bike caught in Jake's wheel spokes and he'd felt the other rider wobble and knock against him, sending him careening into a third cyclist. They fell in a tangled heap of bikes and limbs.

The cyclist who'd caused the crash gave an apologetic wave but didn't look round as he sped off.

'I'm so sorry,' they said at the same time, and Jake looked down to find a beautiful brunette lying beside him.

'I'm the one who should apologise,' he replied, pulling himself free and helping her up. 'I crashed into you. Are you OK?' He looked her over, taking in her toned body and the scrape on her calf.

She nodded. 'Aside from a bruised ego, I'm fine. It's my own fault. I never should've taken the bet,' she said. Jake wasn't great with English accents, but he thought she sounded like she might be from Kensington or one of the other nicer areas of London.

'What bet?' Jake found himself asking, fighting the urge to get going. How long had he stopped for? Two minutes? He could still catch up.

They picked up their bikes, moving to the edge of the road as the hoard of cyclists continued to whizz by.

'It's so stupid. I wasn't supposed to be doing this event at all. To be honest, I'm a terrible cyclist.' She laughed, waving a hand at her scraped-up bike and grazed leg. 'But my colleague at the office got pulled onto a last-minute case and couldn't do it, and she'd already raised a ton of money. I said no way when she asked, and she said, "Yeah don't worry, I bet you couldn't do it anyway." And' – she shrugged – 'I'm a sucker for a pointless bet. Sorry. I'm rambling. You should get going.'

'You're not carrying on the race?' he asked, and in that moment their eyes connected and he felt a bolt of something shoot through him. Longing and desire and so much more.

She laughed again. 'The only place I'm going is to hobble

over to that pub for a coffee.' She pointed to a corner building with hanging baskets and picnic tables outside. 'You're welcome to join me, but I don't want to spoil your ride. Anyway, nice to meet you...'

'Jake,' he said, watching the stragglers pass. Four minutes. Still time to catch up.

'Hannah,' she replied, already wheeling her bike away with a final wave.

Jake climbed onto his bike and started to pedal. He made it half a mile before he realised how stupid he was being. He'd just met the woman of his dreams and was cycling away from her. He ditched the race and looped back to the pub, praying Hannah was still there. He can't describe the feeling of relief he'd felt when he saw her sitting at one of the outside tables. It was the second time in his life he'd seen her, and yet he'd felt an instant connection. That was the moment he started to believe in soulmates. That was the moment he knew he wanted to marry Hannah.

Their coffee became a bottle of wine, which became a Thai takeaway in her converted loft apartment. A stunning open-plan space three minutes' walk from King's Cross station.

He stood to leave after dinner and she walked him to the door, all tussled hair and that smile again, and even though he wasn't usually the forward type, something made him kiss her.

He liked the way she felt in his arms, and, to his delight, she kissed him back. He never went home that night. Or the next. A month later, he sublet his place in Putney and moved in to her loft apartment, living on top of each other with too many things and no space, and it felt utterly perfect.

Now they spend every spare moment they're not working together. They visit tourist places in London on Saturdays and join Hannah's old university housemates and their partners for a pub quiz on Thursday nights when Hannah finishes at the office in time. An American among a group of posh lawyers, he should feel out of place, but he never does.

Deciding to follow his heart instead of his plans to finish the race that day was one of the best decisions he's ever made. That and leaving Ohio for England when he was twenty-six. Six years on, he's never looked back.

They turn the corner and a small village square comes into view. There's an old fountain in the centre, the stone dry like the water hasn't run for fifty years. It's surrounded by cobblestones and then stone buildings with shutters painted in pastel colours, faded from the sun. Beside the fountain is an artist on a fold-out seat with an easel, painting a bell tower rising up behind the low buildings. They pass a café with red awnings where a group of older men sit in companionable silence, smoking cigarettes and drinking black coffee.

'Is this place for real?' he says. 'I feel like I've walked into an old French movie.'

'I know, right? It hasn't changed since I was a kid. Same café, same deli, same people. Come on. Let's get some bread.'

'And wine.'

'And cheese,' they say at the same time before laughing.

Hannah grins. 'I love the cheese here.' She disappears into an open doorway, and he's about to follow when something catches in the corner of his vision.

A flash of ice-blonde hair. A darting run.

He spins towards the movement, gaze scanning the gaps in the buildings across the square.

It can't be her. Not here...

THREE
JAKE

For a second, he could've sworn he saw Neve, but as he scans the buildings and road, all is still, and he realises how stupid he's being. Of course she hasn't followed them to France. The break-in has rattled him too, that's all.

Six years since he left the States.

Six years since he escaped his ex.

How can she not see it's over?

It's infuriating, but there's no way she's here. And yet even as he tells himself this, a chill runs down his spine. He knows what she's capable of.

'Jake?' Hannah's voice carries from the doorway.

'I'm coming,' he replies, pushing thoughts of Neve to the back of his mind. One final glance across the empty square then he turns, ducking his head under the low doorway Hannah disappeared through.

He finds himself in the cool interior of a small shop that smells of sweet pastries and bread. Wooden shelves display rows of fresh produce – ripe red tomatoes and plump grapes double the size of anything they have in the supermarkets in England.

Hannah is by the deli counter, talking in French to the assistant, her basket already full.

'You're fluent,' he exclaims when they've paid and he's carrying two full string shopping bags into the bright morning sun.

She starts to shake her head when a man calls her name from across the square. His French accent is thick so instead of 'Hannah', it comes out 'Han-ner'.

Her face breaks into a bright smile as she dashes across the cobbles and hugs a stocky man who looks to be in his sixties, with a head of white hair and a round belly straining against his black shirt.

Jake follows, already smiling at how happy Hannah looks. He places the shopping by his feet as she and the older man talk in French. The smile drops from Hannah's face and a sudden tension descends which he doesn't understand. Jake doesn't know what they're saying, but the words are coming fast and furious now.

There's a small squirm of something in the pit of his stomach. An inadequacy he hasn't felt for a long time. Maybe he'll learn French. It would be useful if they decide to spend more time here, something he hopes they'll do if Hannah gets the promotion she wants and can finally ease up a little.

Hannah shakes her head, taking a step back. He touches her arm gently. 'Han, is everything OK?'

'Oh, Jake,' Hannah says, noticing him beside her for the first time. 'I'm so sorry.' She motions to the man as a frown pinches her forehead. 'This is Claude, our nearest neighbour. Claude is like an uncle to me. Claude, this is my fiancé, Jake.'

'*Bonjour*,' Jake says, hating how inauthentic the word sounds compared to Hannah's French, but he paints on a bright smile and holds out his hand.

There's a pause. A moment when Jake's hand is mid-air and left hanging. Claude's eyes rake over him, assessing with a critical gaze. The silence stretches uncomfortably. Jake huffs a laugh of surprise then wishes he hadn't when he sees Claude's narrow-eyed glare. He drops his hand.

'Claude, please—' Hannah starts to say.

'Who do you think you are?' Claude's accent is strong but his English perfect, and there's no mistaking the malice in his tone as he steps forward and jabs a finger at Jake. 'I should kill you.'

Two things happen at once. The first is a thought elbowing into Jake's head. People don't act like this. They shake hands. They smile. They might inwardly seethe, but they remain polite. They don't threaten to kill perfect strangers. He doesn't like it. Doesn't know how to react. A heat creeps over his cheeks. He hates that he doesn't understand what Claude and Hannah have said to each other. It makes him feel stupid, like the teachers at school back in Westlake, always picking on him to answer questions just because his mom was the principal.

That's when the second thing happens – a coiling anger wraps itself around him at the memory from his childhood and at this moment. He swallows, trying to push it back.

'Claude!' Hannah's cry cuts through the tension. 'Please leave it.'

'I won't do that. Julia and Marcus are very close friends, and this American boy,' he sneers, 'is breaking your parents' hearts with this ridiculous wedding.'

Jake hears the words but they don't make sense. What does this man know about him and their wedding? What does he mean about breaking the hearts of Hannah's parents? He starts to speak, but before he can explain there's been a mix-up, Hannah and Claude launch into another heated argument in French. Jake's rooted to the spot, feeling a fool. Anger simmers, but the last thing he wants to do is escalate the situation and be the cause again of Hannah's hurt.

Her wide-eyed shock from the apartment the night of the

break-in flashes in his thoughts. The mess and damage caused by *his* ex-girlfriend. What was Neve thinking? Of course he blames himself.

Then there's a call from across the square. They turn, and the shop assistant from the deli is in the doorway, waving a pair of sunglasses. Hannah taps her head and with a surprised, 'Oh,' and another firing of words to Claude, she backs away, leaving Jake alone with a man who just threatened to kill him.

Jake clenches his jaw, heat still simmering beneath his skin. 'Sir,' he says, 'if I've offended you in any way, then I can only apologise.'

Claude steps forward and with the tip of his index finger, he pokes Jake in the chest. A hard press. Jake jumps back. His hand flies up, and before he can stop it, he's slapping Claude's hand away. An automatic reaction that comes with a surprised, 'Hey.'

'Save your apologies,' Claude growls. 'If you loved Hannah, you'd call off this ridiculous wedding and leave her alone.'

'Please don't touch me.' Jake's reply is strangled. The anger is no longer a simmer but a burn. 'I can assure you, I had no idea Hannah's parents weren't happy about our wedding.' Even as he says it, he wonders if it's true. They've made no effort to meet him, and the wedding is in two weeks. But why hasn't Hannah said anything? He looks at her from across the square, deep in conversation with the shop assistant. He can see her trying to back away without being impolite.

'You expect me to believe that?' Claude's voice drips with disdain. 'I know your kind. You're only after her money.'

In the back of his mind, Jake wonders what money Claude is referring to. Hannah might come from a wealthy family, but she's always said she supports herself when it comes to her finances. Perhaps Claude doesn't know this.

'That's not true.' Jake takes a ragged breath, forcing the anger from his voice. This is just a misunderstanding. 'I love

Hannah. She's my soulmate. I've never met anyone like her. I can assure you, sir, I only want what's best for her. I've always said if she wants a prenup, I'll sign one, but Hannah has always said no.'

'I highly doubt Hannah said no to a prenup. She's a smart woman, but she's easily led. You're manipulating her.'

Then it comes – another hard jab of Claude's finger; a sharp pain in Jake's chest.

'Someone needs to smack some sense into you, boy. Cancel this ridiculous wedding.'

Jake shakes his head; steps back. His anger is jagged and sharp, ripping through him. He feels sick. His control is slipping, and he can't keep hold of it.

'Get away from me.' His pulse thunders in his ears, a relentless pounding rhythm.

But Claude is in his face again. 'You like picking on innocent women? You get a kick out of this?' He pushes him. Two hands on his chest – a firm shove causing Jake to slip on the smooth cobbles, knocking into his shopping bags. He watches a bright-green watermelon roll towards the fountain and feels something snap inside him; the fury blinding. He no longer sees the perfect blue sky or the quaint village square. He no longer feels the sun burning the back of his neck or hears the chink of cups from the café. He's consumed instead by this rude man with flushed jowls and narrowed eyes standing before him, pushing and poking him. Accusing him.

'Don't touch me,' Jake shouts again. Adrenaline pumps with every furious beat of his heart.

The next second is a blur. Claude lurches forward, but this time Jake's ready and his clenched fists are rising, his right arm pulling back then cutting through the air, and before he can stop himself, he's punching, and now it's Claude who's slipping, falling, landing on his ass.

The world pulls back into focus. The sun, the sky, the

square. Shoppers stood watching. Hannah's shout – distant but there. 'Jake, no!'

Out of nowhere, a firm hand grips his shoulder, and Jake spins towards it, the anger pushing to the surface. That once familiar feeling that he could take on an army – a world – and beat them all. It's been a long time since he felt that. But then he blinks and takes in the tall, narrow-faced man in his thirties wearing a light-blue polo shirt and an old-fashioned Navy cap with a yellow rim. His other hand is resting on the handle of a gun on his belt. Jake catches a single word in the angry spiel that comes from the man. '*Policier.*'

Regret floods his body, bitter and squirming. It's been years since he lost control. He'd even begun to think he'd outgrown the temper that defined his childhood and teens; the whispers of it stretching into adulthood.

Hannah arrives by his side, pushing between him and the police officer who's talking in rapid French.

'I don't understand what you're saying.' Jake's words come in a loud rush. He's still breathing fast, blood rushing to his head. He needs to calm down, get control, plan his next move. He looks down at Claude. The man is pressing a hand to his face, but there's no blood at least.

Hannah says something to the policeman, gesturing between Jake and Claude. Even though Jake can't understand the words, he sees the sentiment Hannah is trying to make. A silly misunderstanding. Nothing to worry about. The officer nods, and Jake's relieved to see his hand drop from the gun. The policeman exchanges a few words with Claude and helps the man to his feet. There's a cut on his foot where it's scraped the ground between the straps of his leather sandals.

Claude waves his hand away as though shooing a fly. He says something to Hannah, and then without so much as a glance at Jake, he turns and strides away.

'You're English?' the officer says when he's gone.

'American,' he replies. 'I'm really sorry. He pushed me first. I was defending myself.'

'You think punching a seventy-one-year-old man is defending yourself?'

Seventy-one? Another squirm of regret. A part of him wonders what difference age makes. Claude is strong and bullish. Even in Jake's thoughts, the excuse sounds pathetic. He should never have lost his temper.

'It was a misunderstanding,' Jake continues. 'I'm very sorry. It won't happen again.' It's not the first time he's said those words, but he really means it this time.

'Be sure it doesn't. I suggest you stay away from Monsieur Dubas.' And with that, the policeman walks away. The villagers in the shop doorways watch for another moment before turning back to their Saturday shopping. Hannah picks up the bags of food and without looking at him, she says, 'We should go.'

She strides out of the square, and he hurries after her, suddenly desperate to check she's OK. To beg for forgiveness.

'Hannah, wait up. I'm sorry. I'm really sorry. He—' Jake stops. Takes a breath. Sweat prickles his face. The adrenaline is still jittering through him, but he needs to shut up with excuses. He hates how pathetic it sounds. 'I shouldn't have hit him. I'm so sorry.'

Hannah doesn't break her stride, but she does look at him at last. He wishes he could see her eyes behind the sunglasses. 'Jake, I was there too. I saw Claude push you. This is my fault, not yours. I should've done more to make him see he was wrong.'

'Is he though?' Jake asks as they reach the car. 'What was he talking about with your parents? You never told me they didn't want you to marry me.'

Finally, in the shade of an olive tree by the parked car, she pulls off her sunglasses. Her eyes are glassy like she's close to tears. 'I didn't want to worry you, but my parents are being' –

she pauses as though searching for the word – 'difficult. It's nothing.'

Jake takes the shopping bags from her hands and places them in the boot of the car before turning and pulling Hannah into a hug. 'I love you. I will do anything to make you happy. But whatever is going on, it isn't nothing if one of your parents' friends says he wants to kill me.'

He feels her nod against his chest before she pulls back. 'Claude has always been a hothead. He once picked a fight with the café owner because he said his coffee wasn't hot enough. But he's right. Julia and Marcus don't want us to marry. My parents still see me as a little kid and they think they need to protect me. They're refusing to meet you, which is just making everything worse because if they met you, I know they'd fall in love with you like I have, but they're saying we've rushed into this relationship and the wedding, and they won't listen to me when I tell them that's not how it is with us.'

'So they don't want us to get married at all?' His chest tightens, the air not reaching his lungs. He can't not marry Hannah. She's the one! She's everything.

A sadness sweeps over her face as she shakes her head. 'They want us to cancel the wedding. They think you're not right for me—'

'They haven't even met me.'

'But they know you're American and not from the same circles, and that's enough for them. They've always had this ridiculous idea that I'll marry the son of one of their friends, give up my job and pop out a couple of kids. It's ridiculous.'

'You should've told me,' he says, swallowing his own disappointment. This is bigger than him.

'I know. I'm sorry,' she says, wiping away a tear. 'I thought they'd come around by now.'

'Is it about money? Claude seems to think I'm only after you for your money.'

She rolls her eyes. 'No! It's not my money anyway. It's my family's money. I don't own the farmhouse or even my apartment in London. It's all in their names. That's what I was trying to explain to Claude. All I have is my salary.'

'Well' – Jake sweeps a stray lock of hair away from her face – 'that and an impressive shoe collection.'

She huffs a laugh and reaches up, wrapping her arms around his neck. His joke has eased the tension, and he holds her close, taking long breaths, trying to steady himself. Steady them.

'I'm sorry I didn't tell you any of this,' she says after a beat. 'And I'm sorry for how Claude treated you. None of this is your fault.'

Jake tilts her chin up and kisses her lightly on the lips. 'It's not yours either, and I still shouldn't have hit him. I'm sorry.'

She shakes her head. 'You were defending yourself. I get it.'

He desperately hopes she means it. The bond and trust they share is like nothing he's ever felt before. He can't lose that. 'We'll figure this out,' he says. 'All we need is a plan.'

He'll get them back on track. He'll figure out a way to win over her parents. They can even postpone the wedding if it makes things right. Nothing else will go wrong. He won't let it.

FOUR
HANNAH

We drive home in silence. Unpack the food and make lunch in silence. I can't stop replaying the moment in the square when I stepped away to retrieve my forgotten sunglasses. The deli assistant asked me a question about London. Something to do with her niece who was studying there, and I tried to step away, get back to Jake's side, but I wasn't quick enough. Then seeing Claude poking and pushing, and the jolting, horrifying moment when Jake's fist flew into Claude's face.

It would be so easy to blame Jake. To say 'of course he should've kept his cool'. But I know him too well. I know how much of his life is about balance and routine. How he likes to lie in bed on Sunday mornings, our hands entwined, and make a plan for the day. Every step thought of. *'I'll pop out for croissants and you make the coffee. And then we'll walk through the city to the river and we'll go to that little Greek place by London Bridge for lunch.'* Every minute accounted for. Maybe there are people who would find it stifling, but I like it.

I work so hard. Long hours. Relentless tasks. Never fully switching off. Having Jake think about all the little things means

I don't have to. But Jake is the first to admit he's thrown by the unexpected and that he needs a few extra minutes to process the change before he's regrouping. Adapting.

In September, we spent a weekend in Windsor to celebrate our three-month anniversary. I'd taken him to the Tower of London the month before, and he'd wanted to see Windsor Castle and more of the quaint Tudor England. He spent three weeks researching the best hotel, where we'd eat and what we'd do. I jokingly said he hadn't scheduled any time for sex, which made us both laugh, and he added it to the plans. It was a perfect weekend. All I had to do was pack my bag and allow Jake to take care of me.

Today, with Claude in the square – it was so unexpected. There was no time for Jake to adapt to Claude's anger, to make a new plan. Claude provoked him, and Jake's response was to lash out. So I don't blame him for throwing that punch. I blame myself. And I wonder if Jake blames me too, after learning from Claude that my parents don't want us to marry.

'I think we should postpone the wedding until your parents are happy,' Jake says in the silence as I grab the large Le Creuset carving knife and cut the watermelon – the blade slicing easily through the ripe fruit.

His words grab my chest, squeezing tight. I can't stop myself crying out. 'Jake, no.' I look up, and his expression is determined but sad too. 'My parents will never be happy with anything short of me walking up the aisle to someone they choose. They can't see that I don't want that. Please don't start ignoring me as well. I want to marry you in two weeks, more than anything. Surely our happiness is all that matters?'

'Are you absolutely sure?' His brow furrows, casting a shadow over his handsome features.

'Yes!' I shout the single word as loud and as adamant as the '*yes*' I gave Jake when he dropped down on one knee on the pavement by the Thames last December and asked me to marry him six months into our relationship. He'd planned to propose under fairy lights with champagne and exquisite food at a restaurant in Butler's Wharf. But we'd been walking back from the Tate Modern and we'd been laughing about one of the exhibits reminding Jake of a derelict building site back in the States. He'd stopped walking, turning serious, and told me as he pulled the ring from his pocket that he couldn't wait another second. And I couldn't wait to say yes. I hadn't realised how empty my life was before Jake. How lonely. I never wanted to feel that again. Not when Jake was everything I could ever want.

And just like that proposal, the relief in Jake's face now is instant. He smiles – the one where his eyes crinkle. It's the same smile he gave me on the day we met when I wheeled my bike away from the event, ego bruised, wondering if I'd ever again see the gorgeous American who'd crashed into me.

'Is this seat taken?' he asked, finding me at an outdoor table with a coffee and a half-eaten chocolate muffin.

I remember the warm delight I felt at seeing him. 'It is now.'

He sat and checked his watch. 'Eight minutes.'

'Is that how long you've got before you need to go?' I asked lightly, fighting a wave of disappointment.

He shook his head. 'It's how long it took me to realise I was riding away from the most beautiful woman in the world, change plans and come back for her. When we tell people this story, I want you to remember it was eight minutes. Not twenty. Not an hour. Just eight. And that still makes me the biggest fool, but in my defence, I don't change plans easily.'

I laughed and that was it. It never felt like dating. We were strangers and then we were together. I told Jake about the intensity of corporate law at Jenkins, Wyatt & Ross. The long hours I worked. How little I had left to give at the end of the day. I told him about the wealth of my upbringing but how lonely it was.

How every day was a fight to forge my own path rather than the one my parents wanted for me – something in the arts or publicity. A marriage. Children. Country clubs. A carbon copy of the life my mother seemed to love. None of it was for me, but unlike my brother, William, I hadn't escaped to another country, out of their watchful gaze and meddling.

Jake didn't shrink away when I bared my soul. He never tells me to slow down. He never complains when I cancel plans to work late. Not only does he understand my drive, he shares it. He rarely talks about his software business, but I know succeeding means everything to him too.

After lunch, we change into shorts and T-shirts and our hiking boots, and we set out towards the lake. We listen to the crickets humming and the birds calling, the crunch of the gravel with each step. And slowly, as the heat of the afternoon sun prickles our faces, the tension of the morning fades and we become us again. The us where we tease and we joke and we laugh. And it's easy and it's everything.

We walk for nearly an hour until we reach the top of a steep cliff and a sloping footpath. I'm already smiling as we turn the corner and see the first view of the lake below. It's just as beautiful as I remembered. The oval shape of the water is surrounded by dark green trees and weathered rocks. The water is crystal clear. I know when we reach the edge, we'll be able to see the soft sediment and rocks below the surface. But from this far up, the water is a perfect mirror to the blue sky and the leaves and the brush of purple from the wild thyme that adds a herby sweetness to the air.

'Wow,' Jake says as a buzzard hovers above our heads, close enough to see the different shades of brown in its wing feathers.

I smile. 'It's beautiful, isn't it?'

'Stunning,' he says. 'I can't get over how quiet it is.'

'It's quiet because no one comes here,' I reply.

We start to walk again, slowly navigating our way down the narrow footpath.

'Why not?' he asks.

'This place actually used to be a limestone quarry, but it was closed a hundred and something years ago and now it's part of nature again. My dad used to say the lake was cursed. When the quarry closed, it put a lot of people out of work and made life hard in the community. A man died, and they say his widow was a witch. The story goes that she put a curse on the mining company and the land so all who come here will have bad luck.'

'Now you tell me,' he quips, and we laugh.

'It's just a story. There's no way we can have any more bad luck,' I say, thinking of the break-in and the fight today.

I slip my hand into Jake's as we reach the bottom of the slope and the water's edge.

'I want to show you something.' I pull us through the trees and point to a small ledge that sits at hip height. I pull myself up as though I'm climbing out of a swimming pool – two hands either side and jump. Jake copies me, and we're shuffling around the corner of the ridge until we're sitting directly over the lake, legs dangling down.

Wild flowers on vines hang from the cliff edge above us, and all we can see is water and beauty. It feels like we're the only two people left on the earth. We sit for a long time, drinking in the beauty and the peace.

'It's stunning,' Jake whispers. 'I wish we could get married right here, right now.'

I smile. 'I'm not sure a vicar would fit on this ledge.'

'True. We could bungee jump him from the top.'

'And have the guests balanced on paddle boards on the lake?' I ask, thinking of the small group of people who came to our engagement drinks last month and have RSVP'd yes to our wedding. The boarding-school and university friends I've stayed in touch with. Our Thursday night quiz team. And my family, of course. My parents and their friends I'm expected to invite.

Jake's invited his football friends from Manchester too.

Fifty people in total. Not too big. Not too small. Intimate, I think. The only people who haven't RSVP'd are my family.

Jake huffs. 'Might ruin the view a bit.'

'Just a bit.' I laugh. 'Here, look at this.' I shuffle round and push back the vines to show a small cave. 'I used to crawl in here when I was little and pretend it was an entrance to a hidden world like Narnia. I used to love pretending and acting out scenes from the book.' I smile, losing myself to the memory. 'We did Narnia in a play once at drama club. I really wanted to be Edward, but I got the White Witch.' I do my best evil cackle.

'I didn't know you went to drama camp as a kid. You're a constant surprise, Hannah Fitzroy.' He throws an arm around me, and I lean into his body.

'How far back does it go?' Jake asks, peering into the darkness of the small cave.

'Not much further than we can see. But I don't think anyone else in the world except us knows this ledge even exists. Cool, right?'

'Very. Talking of cool, how about we go back for another swim in the pool?' There's desire in Jake's gaze, and I grin.

'Fastest one back?' I ask.

He raises his brows in question. 'You seriously think you can beat me?'

'Is that a bet?' I sing-song.

'Yes,' he says, and we both scramble down. Then he kisses my lips, and with a final grin, he strides up a path to the right. It will lead him through the woodland and out to the road. I turn left and make my way back up the slope. At the top, I stare at the view a final time and feel myself shiver.

I don't believe in superstitions or curses, but I can't shake the feeling something is coming for us. Jake would laugh if I told him. He sees the world in the black and white squares of a chessboard. Each move leading to another and another. The right strategy, the right plan, and you win. But he assumes everyone is playing the same game. I think of Neve and then I think of the fight in the square earlier. Not everyone plays by the rules.

FIVE
JAKE

An hour later, Jake turns the corner by the neatly trimmed hedges and onto the driveway, and there it is, the stunning restored house, so grand and inviting. And there is Hannah, five paces ahead of him. His heart is still racing in his chest from the exertion. A fine layer of sweat clings to his body. He licks his lips, pushes away the emotions threatening to overwhelm him and focuses on Hannah.

He loves the challenges they set each other. He likes the edge of friendly competition between them. Never serious and always ending in laughter. Like dividing the shopping list and seeing who can reach the checkout first. Or which of them can get the most correct answers on the quiz shows they watch. And racing of course.

'First one back wins.'

'Last one to arrive pays.'

'Loser cooks dinner.'

'Winner chooses the restaurant.'

It's one of the many reasons he knows she's perfect for him. His 'one'.

He's glad they separated on the walk back. He needed time

to himself to regroup and find a way to fix what he did. The morning in the square is a distant memory. He doesn't need to dwell on what happened in the village. He was provoked. He lashed out. Made a mistake. It's over. He'll never see Claude again. All he wants now is to focus on how much Hannah wants to marry him. Nothing can stand in the way of them.

In the distance, the sun is creeping lower in the sky. He checks his watch. They've been out all afternoon. It's nearly 4 p.m. and still just as hot. Hotter even. But he can't resist jogging the last few metres to catch up to Hannah.

'Hey,' he calls, and she turns. Her skin shines with sun cream and the exertion of their walk. Her ponytail swishes, and she's already grinning triumphantly. 'I win.'

He laughs, his hands snaking around her waist as they walk the final steps of the driveway together. Hannah finds the key and unlocks the front door as his thoughts jump to last night in the pool. He feels himself harden.

'I really thought my route was quicker. Are you sure you didn't run?' His lips graze her neck. He wants her so bad he thinks of pushing her up against the doorway and having fast, furious sex right here. Except he wants to take his time too. He wants to worship every inch of her.

'Are you calling me a cheat?' Hannah laughs and he feels the joy of it humming against his lips. 'And I was only thirty seconds ahead of you.'

'You still beat me.' He runs a hand down her back and over her perfect ass.

Then Hannah stops suddenly. Her body stiffens as she makes a noise. She's blocking the doorway and his view into the house. His pulse quickens and the first whisper of unease brushes over him.

'Hannah?'

She doesn't reply, and he says her name again before stepping around her and into the hall. Reality rushes at him with the speed of a bullet.

Claude is lying face down on the rug in a pool of blood.

Still. Lifeless. Dead.

'Oh, God,' Jake hisses, desperate to look away, to turn and run and pretend he was never here, never saw, never knew, but it's as though his eyes are glued to the body.

'What the...?' he starts to say but can't find the words to finish.

'He's dead,' Hannah mutters over the pounding rush of blood through his veins.

He nods, unable to form any words.

'Oh my God,' she says then, louder now. 'We have to call the police. We need help.'

Yes, they should call the police. Hannah stops in her tracks, but he's not paying attention. His breathing is ragged, and suddenly the smell of blood fills his senses and he's hit with a wave of nausea.

'Jake?' Hannah's voice trembles, and he wants to comfort her, but how, when he can't process this for himself?

'Give me a second,' he says, rubbing a hand over his face.

'Jake, is that' – Hannah's voice trails off as she points to the large carving knife with the wood handle he remembers her pulling from the knife block over lunch – 'the knife I used earlier?' It's no longer just a knife but a murder weapon.

'What?' he asks. He can't think straight. He can't understand how the late afternoon sun is still shining outside as it sinks lower in the sky. How everything was perfect during the hours they've spent hiking. And now it's all gone so very wrong.

In a distant part of his mind, he knows they're in shock. He forces his eyes away from Claude's body and looks at Hannah. Her face is pale, her eyes wider than he's ever seen them. Why isn't she picking up the phone and calling the police? He should do it, but he doesn't even know which three numbers to press for emergency services.

'What?' he asks again.

'The knife,' she cries. 'I left it in the dishwasher, remember?'

A new kind of fear is snaking through his body, but he doesn't want to know what it is or why it's there. 'What are you trying to say?' he asks.

'I... Look! Look around you. That's the knife I used earlier. Someone took it from the dishwasher instead of using any of the other knives sitting out in the block. And... and those shoe prints are from your shoes.'

His eyes flick to the place behind the door where they left their trainers earlier. There's a ringing in his ears. His throat closes. He can't breathe.

His shoes! The white and blue leather is splattered with bright-red blood.

'Oh God.' Jake staggers back. Hannah is staring at him, her mouth open.

'I... I was with you.' The words tumble out, and she nods and he's grateful. Then it clicks. What she's been trying to tell him. The knife she used. His shoes. This house.

'I don't know—' I mutter, unable to tear my eyes away from Claude's body. 'I don't know what's going on here, Han.'

'This can't be happening,' she says, shaking her head. 'Someone must've come to the house while we were out...'

He swallows down the bile burning his throat. 'But who would do this?'

Jake can't stop staring at the distinctive oval shoe treads from the trainers Hannah bought him for Christmas. His favourite shoes. Not just the style but because they were a gift from her.

'My shoes – they look like...' he says, trying to grab hold of the thought.

'Like someone was wearing them when they did this.'

'And the knife—'

'Will have my fingerprints on it. The only knife in this place that does,' Hannah whispers.

He looks to her then, unable to stop the dawning horror from hitting him. 'Did... someone do this and... want to make it look like it was us?'

'But why would they?' she asks in a quiet voice. 'And who would do this?'

He can hear Hannah's teeth chattering and it's enough to stir a primal need in him to protect her. He steps close and pulls her into him, drawing back to look at her face. It's etched with fear, and he knows she's not thinking of why but who? Jake's thoughts jump ahead. Are they next? Are they in danger? The thought is one of the fairground rides that spins and spins until everything is blurred and the sky is down, the ground up. He wants off. But this is no thrill ride. He moves suddenly, whipping round, slamming the front door shut and turning the lock. The walls close in. The smell of blood overwhelming. The fear doesn't diminish.

They need a plan.

Think.

Claude is dead.

Do something.

It looks like he did it. Or Hannah. Or both.

This is bad. Really bad.

Jake's mind flashes back to the village square. The man Jake was seen fighting with earlier is now dead in their house.

Then out of nowhere the ringing is no longer in his ears but shattering the silence as the phone on the side table trills, sharp and intrusive. Hannah screams and reaches a shaking hand to answer.

He pulls her back. Shakes his head. 'Don't answer.'

'Why not?'

He can't explain. 'It's just' – he looks down at Claude's body – 'what if the person phoning is the person who did this?'

Her eyes widen. She's shaking her head but drops her hand. The phone stops ringing, and Jake realises as an electronic voice tells the caller to leave a message that the phone only looks antique and is actually modern. They stand statue still and listen to the message with growing horror. He didn't think things could get any worse, but they just have.

SIX

HANNAH

I bite down on my quivering lip and wish I was back on the ledge by the lake, pushing into the little cave and coming out into a different world where none of this is happening. A childish, stupid fantasy. Jake's arm is around me, but there's no comfort in his embrace. His body is as tense as mine.

The answerphone message stops, and there's a beep and a pause. And then: 'Hannah? It's Marie Dubas. Is Claude with you? I hope he didn't cause you any trouble. After he bumped into you in the village, he came home absolutely determined to convince your boyfriend to call off the wedding.'

I turn to Jake and even though she can't hear, I whisper, 'It's Claude's wife.'

'She's not French?' he asks, voice just as low.

I shake my head. 'She's English, but she's lived here most of her life,' I reply and wonder why I've explained. What does it matter where Marie is from?

From the recorded message we hear her sigh. 'Please would you call me when you get this. We have plans this evening and I was expecting him home by now.' She hangs up and the silence is cloying. Even the fly has stopped its buzzing.

My eyes pull back to Claude's body. 'Marie,' I say as the first tears spill onto my cheeks. 'She's... her husband... Claude.' I close my eyes, shut out this hallway and this moment, and I sob.

I'm barely aware of Jake guiding me towards the kitchen. I stumble on legs that aren't my own and don't object when he pulls out a chair from the table and I sit.

'I need to call the police,' I say again.

'I can—' Jake starts to say, but I shake my head.

'You don't speak French.'

My eyes dart around the room. The kitchen looks just as we left it. The copper pans hanging from the rack. The intricate royal blue pattern of the tiles on the wall. Our lunch plates stacked by the sink.

I pull my phone from my pocket. 'No signal.' The words come in a rushed exhale. 'We'll... we'll have to use the one in the hall where Claude—' A sob catches in my throat, and I'm shaking so bad I don't think I can stand.

Jake fetches us two glasses of water, and I gulp mine back, the glass clinking against my teeth with the tremor in my hands. The water helps.

'OK, I can make the call.' My words come fast and laced with panic, and I look at Jake, feeling lost. 'But what will we tell them?'

Jake's mouth drops open. When he speaks, it's like he's not sure. Like he's asking a question. 'We tell them the truth. We've done nothing wrong, Hannah.'

I shake my head. 'I know, but it looks really bad, doesn't it? You were fighting with Claude this morning and now he's dead.' My voice cracks, but I push on. I have to. 'In our house. And there are footprints in the blood from your shoes. I know we need to call them, but I just... I don't know what to say.'

Jake's face drains of colour, and I grab for the only piece of hope I think we have.

'There could be DNA evidence that proves we didn't do this,' I say, unconvinced.

'Did anyone see you on the way back from the lake?' There's hope in his eyes now too, but it dies when I shake my head.

'Me neither,' he says.

I think of the kitchen knife and the shoes again, and the water in my stomach sloshes like the waves on a stormy sea. I swallow, and it cuts painfully against a lump forming in my throat.

'It's like you said – we did nothing wrong.' I make a move to stand, but Jake's hand grabs mine and I drop back into the chair, heart thumping in my chest.

'No,' he whispers. 'You were right. It looks really bad.'

'What are you saying?' I start to pull my hand away, but Jake keeps holding on.

He doesn't reply. I can see his mind working, looking at the chessboard he describes as living in his head, working out the next move and the next as an anxious energy surges inside me.

'Jake,' I cry, 'we need to call the police. If anyone comes to the house now, if Marie comes looking for Claude and sees him dead on the rug and us sitting here...'

'Hang on,' he murmurs.

The terror whips through me, morphing into frustration. 'No.' I stand again, legs still shaky. 'There's no time. I'm calling the police before this gets worse for us.'

I'm halfway across the kitchen when he speaks.

'What if...' he starts, and I turn back. His deep brown eyes are filled with desperation. 'What if we call them and they think we did this? You heard his wife! She said Claude was still angry. What if the police look at the evidence in that hallway and believe what they see?'

The horror of his words hangs over us. My heart is still beating so fast it feels like it might crack my chest wide open. I look at the clock on the wall, and Jake's gaze follows mine. Time is racing on. The afternoon has slipped away. We need to make a plan.

'I can't go to prison, Jake.' The words come in a half sob. 'My family. My career. I could be fired for even being questioned by the police. But what other choice is there? A man is dead in our house. Our neighbour... Claude... is dead. We can't undo that.'

He closes his eyes. 'Let me think.'

'There's no time,' I say again, heaving in a shuddering breath.

A beat of silence and then Jake asks, 'How did he even get in the house?'

I think for a second, thrown by Jake's change of direction. I want to scream at him that it doesn't matter. 'They have a key and check on the house while we're in England. He must've let himself in to wait for us when there was no answer.'

The next questions remains unanswered. *Then what happened? Who was here instead of us?*

Jake presses his hands to his face, and I bite my lip, forcing myself to give him this minute to adapt. One thought is charging around and around my mind – a raging bull. If we can't go to the police, then where does that leave us? Panic is clouding my thoughts. Are we really thinking about this?

A minute passes before Jake lifts his head and drinks his water down in three long gulps. I recognise the look in his eyes as his gaze finds mine. He has a plan. A fluttering relief moves through me.

'Calling the police is the right thing to do,' he says, his words now slow and deliberate. He squeezes my hand, his thumb rubbing the square diamond of my engagement ring. 'But if they don't believe us, we'll be charged with murder, and let's face it – everything about this points to us killing Claude.'

Fresh tears swim in my eyes, but I don't interrupt.

'They'll look at the evidence. They'll hear hooves and think horses,' Jake continues. 'No one saw us at the lake. We've done nothing wrong, but I don't think anyone will believe us.'

I shake my head. 'We're normal people, Jake. We're not criminals. We can't—'

'We don't deserve to have our lives ruined, do we?' he whispers, cutting me off.

'But what about the person who actually did this?' I ask. 'Claude was a hothead and an idiot sometimes, but he didn't deserve to die.' Tears roll down my face. I don't try to stop them.

'I know. But, Hannah, this isn't just about Claude. You see that, don't you? We can think about who did this later. Right now, we have to decide what to do, because whoever did this to Claude is also doing it to us. They must be trying to frame us for this murder; it's too coincidental for it not to be deliberate. What if there's other evidence we did this?'

'What do you mean?' I frown.

'We can see the knife and the shoes, but what if there's other stuff? Like our DNA on Claude's body? Someone has gone to a lot of trouble to do this to us. I don't think they'd stop at just shoes and a knife.'

His words make sense, even if I don't want to believe them.

'And you saw the way that police officer looked at me in the village today,' Jake continues. 'I was seen fighting with a man who's now dead in our house. It looks so bad, Han. If we call the police, we risk spending the rest of our lives in prison. And even if we're eventually believed, it could take years of prison and court cases, and' – his voice dips so the next words he speaks come as a whisper – 'it could destroy us.'

'I get all that, but what's the alternative? What are you saying?' My words are rushed. I feel the pressure of time slipping away from us. The knowledge that whatever we do, we have to do it now.

Jake looks at me. 'If we want to protect ourselves and our

lives, we have to cover this up. We have to hide Claude's body somewhere it will never be found. We have to clean the hall and pretend that we came back from our walk and everything was normal.'

I take in his words, and I know he's right, but when I speak, my voice trembles as much as my body. 'I don't know if I can do that.'

'Me neither,' Jake replies. 'But what choice do we have? We either call the police and pray they look beyond all the evidence and that we don't spend the rest of our lives in prison for something we didn't do, or we cover it up and we carry on.'

I wipe away the tears, and it feels like my life is flashing before my eyes. I see all the hard work – the countless hours I've spent building my perfect life. I think of the police and what they'll do if I pick up the phone and beg them to come. Finally, I think of Jake. My whole world.

I know all the reasons why what Jake is suggesting is wrong and crazy and impossible, but they don't stick in my mind. All that's there now is Jake's words. *'What choice do we have?'*

SEVEN

JAKE

Jake's breathing is quick and ragged as he waits for Hannah to say something. He keeps his eyes fixed on the swirling knots of the wood table. Can't bring himself to look at her. What must she think of him for even suggesting they do this? But he's looked ahead. He's seen the police interview room and the accusations – all the ways this could ruin their lives.

'Han?' he says when he can't stand the silence for another beat.

She bites her lip. 'I don't know what to do. We haven't done anything wrong, but if we cover this up, we will have. We'll be perverting the course of justice. It's serious, Jake. If we do this, there's no going back. And if the police find out, they'll never believe we didn't kill Claude too.'

'I know, but I don't think they'll believe us now either.'

She nods in agreement. 'It will haunt us for the rest of our lives. I don't know if I can do it.'

'I feel the same,' he says. And he does. They're not criminals. They're a normal couple. Two people on a long weekend in France. It's crazy to even consider this. But he also knows that one way or another, if they pick up the phone, their lives as they know it will be over. It isn't fair.

'Either way,' he continues, 'we're screwed. But if we cover this up, it buys us a shot at freedom, doesn't it? That's the only way I can see it playing out.'

When he looks at Hannah, the fear in her eyes makes his heart crack, but he doesn't expect the words that come next.

'We could take the body to the cave by the lake,' she says. 'It's completely hidden. No one goes there.'

A feeling rushes through him. The blast of cold wind on a bitter winter's day. It's relief, but it's a sheer, awful terror too. She agrees with him. She wants to protect their future too. His plans have only stretched as far as knowing they can't involve the police. He hasn't considered how they'll do it.

'Shouldn't we bury it?' he asks.

Hannah shrugs, pulling her hair back and tightening her ponytail. 'I don't know. I just don't know. I've never done this before.'

'It's OK.' He reaches for her hand and wishes it was true. 'Let's think about it for a minute. If we bury... the body,' he says, unable to bring himself to use Claude's name, 'where could we do that?'

She thinks for a moment. 'Even if we don't call the police, they'll come asking questions eventually, won't they? They'll notice a newly dug hole in the garden. And all this land around us is vineyards. The owners are proud. They walk their lands a lot. They'd notice disturbed earth in their fields. But the cave is hidden, and it's easier than digging a six-foot grave.'

He nods, fighting the urge to rub his face. He needs to get a grip. For Hannah as much as himself. Think clearly. Make a plan. Stick to it. That's how they'll get through this.

'I...' Hannah starts to say as she slips her hand out of his, 'should call Marie and tell her we've been out all day and haven't seen Claude. I'll tell her we just got home. We don't want her coming here.'

He nods. 'How soon before she calls the police and reports him missing?'

'Probably not until tomorrow. Claude has a habit of dropping in on neighbours, drinking a lot of wine and losing track of time.'

'OK,' he replies, but his heart is still racing, his head spinning with the rush of oxygen. He wishes they could pause time and really think through this. Every angle, every move afterwards, but there's no time.

Hannah swallows and seems to gather herself. 'We'll wrap his body in the rug to carry it out of the house,' she says. 'It's ruined anyway.'

'Won't your parents notice it's gone?' he asks.

She looks crestfallen for a second. A dead-end already. 'I'll tell them I took it back to my apartment as a reminder of my time here. They won't care and they never visit.'

He nods. 'OK. Let's do it.'

'We need some things,' she says. 'Duct tape to hold the rug in place and cleaning stuff. It's under the sink. The duct tape is... I think it's in the pantry where the washing machine is. Bottom drawer. I'll call Marie and then I'll... roll up his body.'

She grimaces as though trying to keep down a bitter pill. He hates this. Her wide smile – those 'take me to bed' eyes he loves – seem far away. A flickering worry pushes at the edge of his thoughts that maybe whatever they do next, this has ruined them.

No!

He pushes the thought aside. He won't let that happen to them. He can't lose her.

Hannah stands, hands gripping the table as though she's not sure her legs will hold her. 'Get the stuff. It's going to be dark soon and we need some light to find the cave.'

'You're right.'

'Get the wheelbarrow too,' she says from the doorway. 'The gardener leaves it by the outbuilding where the tools are kept. Bring it around to the front door. We'll use it to transport the body to the cave.' Her voice cracks but she disappears, and for half a beat, Jake is frozen in the empty kitchen. He thinks this is what it must be like to be drugged. Thoughts scattered; mind spinning.

Get tape.

Move wheelbarrow.

Claude is dead.

They're hiding his body.

The final thought screams in his head. They can't seriously be doing this, can they? He draws in a long, slow breath and forces himself to think ahead once more. To imagine picking up the phone and calling the police. He twists and turns every possible outcome over in his mind and still finds himself at the same reality.

Jake was seen arguing with Claude earlier today by a police officer. Now Claude is dead in their house. Jake's shoes are covered in blood. The knife Hannah used and left in the dishwasher is the murder weapon, covered in her fingerprints. No matter how he turns it in his mind, the police will never believe they didn't do this.

The thought spurs him forward, and on shaking legs, he moves across the room to the utility Hannah mentioned. It's a small windowless space with a sink, washing machine and dryer on one wall, and cupboards and drawers on the other. He drops to a crouch and pulls open the bottom drawer. It's overflowing with clutter. Balls of string and screwdrivers and spare light bulbs and charging cables tangled into a clump. But no masking tape.

He shoves the items aside, pushing his hand to the back of the drawer. 'Have you got your eyes open?' Hannah always asks when he can't find something – his phone, his watch, his tie. Somehow, she locates it in seconds, and it's always exactly where he thought it was but couldn't see it.

He looks again but there's still no tape. He yanks open the other drawers. Place mats and tablecloths. Spare cutlery. No tape. Desperation grips him – claws digging in. His heart starts to race again. He's aware of time rushing ahead of them. Hannah alone with a dead body.

Come on!

He scans the room. Opens cupboard after cupboard, and then, when he's about to give up, he sees the silver roll of tape he's been looking for. Not in a drawer but sitting in the corner of the worktop. He grabs it; starts to run back to the hall before he remembers the other things. Cleaning products under the sink. Cloths. Towels from the pile by the back door for the pool. Fluffy and white, soon to be red. Bile burns the back of his throat.

The wheelbarrow next. He runs past the pool. The pale-blue surface ripples from a jet, the water enticing even in this nightmarish moment. A flash of memory from last night hits his thoughts. Was it only yesterday the world made sense? He turns away, focusing on the thump of his feet on the four steps down to a lawn area. He heaves in breath after breath as he reaches the outbuilding.

He finds the wheelbarrow leaning against the wall where Hannah said it would be. He dumps the towels, cleaning products and tape into the base and wheels it around the outside of the property, going too quick, weaving and out of control. The last of the sun blazes a brilliant orange as it sinks towards the horizon. His mouth is dry. He can't remember ever feeling so thirsty. He thinks he might be sick.

He leaves the wheelbarrow outside the front door, and then he's back in the hall as beads of sweat roll down his back. He finds Hannah kneeling on the floor. The rug is already rolled up lengthways, lumpy from Claude's body. The blood has seeped through to the beige weave on the underside of the rug. A dark, menacing stain.

This is real. This is happening. Claude is dead. He was murdered. Jake doubles over. Can't breathe. Can't think. He rubs his face. He needs more than a minute to process this. He needs a lifetime.

EIGHT

HANNAH

My hands are trembling as I look up at Jake from my place kneeling on the floor. I feel his horror and his fear deep in my core.

'Jake?' I pull myself up, wanting to reach for him. Needing support as much as I need air, but my hands are sticky with the drying blood. I stare down at the red of it drying on my skin and feel sick. Reality is charging through me like the sharp jolts of an electric shock. What are we doing? What have we done? I have a sudden urge to take it all back, to run and run and never look back, but already we're in too deep.

His gaze falls to my white T-shirt and the smears of red. We'll have to burn our clothes, I think, before wondering in what world that thought would've crossed my mind before tonight.

'We should...' Jake swallows and lifts his hands as though he'll rub his face but stops himself. 'We need to put the body in the wheelbarrow and then clean in case Claude's wife comes by. It needs to look like we haven't just murdered someone.'

'We haven't,' I hiss.

He flinches and must regret his words because his tone softens as he says, 'I know. I just mean, it won't look like we have. We can scrub everywhere with bleach when we get back.'

I nod, grateful he's thinking ahead again. Whatever happens, we're in this together. We have each other.

Time loses all meaning as we work side by side, running the roll of tape around and around the rug.

'Hannah?' The urgency in Jake's voice is jolting. 'Are you ready?'

I shake my head. I'll never be ready for this. But I move to the top of the rug and Jake takes the bottom. It's heavy and awkward, but we manage – me moving forward, him moving back. A security light above the front door flicks on, casting a harsh white glow that feels like an inescapable spotlight. We both freeze. Pain stretches from the tops of my shoulders down my arms. I can't hold on much longer. Jake must sense my struggle because he urges us on, and we shuffle and step our way to the wheelbarrow, dropping the rug so it's head one end, feet the other.

We hurry back to the hall and use the pristine white towels from the pool to mop the blood. It takes forever, and by the time we're back outside, the sun is almost gone. Above our heads, the sky is a wash of purple and inky blue. A crescent moon and the first stars shine in the sky, but it's the growing shadows I notice before racing inside for a torch.

When I return, Jake is gripping the wheelbarrow handles so tight I can see the whites of his knuckles. He looks at me with a mix of fear and doubt in his eyes. 'Are you sure about this?' he asks.

A sob catches in my throat. It's raw from the exertion of the last hour. I wave a hand at the bulging rug. 'It's too late to be asking that.'

If anyone comes now and sees us, it's all over. Terror shakes me like a rag doll.

Jake rubs the back of his neck. 'I mean, are you sure we should hide the body near the lake. Anyone could find it there, couldn't they?'

'Can you think of anywhere better?' I ask, voice a hiss that carries too loud in the still of the night. 'The lake is completely cut off by road now. The only way to get there is to walk, and the locals don't go near it because of the curse.'

'We could bury it somewhere around the lake.'

I shake my head. 'The earth is rocky. We'd barely get a few feet down. It wouldn't be deep enough. A stray dog or a fox will dig it up.

Then in the silence there's a sound – a movement then a rustle of leaves. I hold my breath, trying to listen over the pounding beat of my heart.

'Did you hear that?' Jake's voice is barely a breath.

I nod as a dozen scenarios race through my mind in a split second. Only one thought sticks. Someone is out there watching us. 'Do you think... Could it be the person who killed Claude?'

'Why would they stay?' Jake whispers in the darkness. 'Wouldn't they be miles away by now, thinking we'd call the police?'

'I don't know. We don't know what they're thinking. What they're doing. We don't know who did this.'

Jake heaves in a deep breath, his frustration rippling in the air. 'You're right, but we can think about that later. One thing at a time. Right now, we need to hide Claude's body before anyone comes.'

There's another rustle from the bushes in the driveway. Closer this time. And then we see it – a fox emerging from the undergrowth, its eyes glinting in the darkness. Relief floods through me, and all I want is to sink to the ground and never get up. But we have to keep going.

'Come on,' I urge. But as we make our way down the driveway, Jake pushing the wheelbarrow, following the puddle of light from my torch, I can't shake the feeling of eyes watching us.

NINE
JAKE

It's 2 a.m. before they slip beneath the cool white bed sheet. The fruity lemongrass of the bodywash is thick in the air from the hot shower. His skin tingles from his scrubbing, but beneath it, like dirt pushed under fingernails, Jake thinks he can still smell the blood.

Everything they've done replays in his mind like a horror movie on loop. The bumpy downhill struggle with the wheelbarrow, almost tipping constantly. The wheel catching on stones and vines. Then the struggle to lift the body onto the ledge and the awkward push and shove until it was wedged in to the very back of the cave. Then hurrying back by the bouncing torchlight gripped in Hannah's hand. The cleaning of the hall until the skin on his hands stung and the bleach fumes made him cough. Only when every last item of clothing and blood-stained towels were thrown in the metal bin he'd found in the outbuilding and burned with petrol until they were nothing but black grit buried deep in a flower bed did they dare stop and allow the exhaustion and the horror of the night to take over.

They had to do it, Jake tells himself again and again. There was no choice. The police would've taken one look at someone like him and he'd have been thrown in jail for life. Hannah would fare better, he thinks. Expensive lawyers and the right upbringing goes a long way, but if that thought had crossed her mind, she'd kept it to herself and stuck by him. He didn't think he could feel any more for her than he did yesterday, but what they've done together tonight has added a depth to their bond he can't explain. He is unutterably grateful for how she handled everything tonight. What she did to protect them. To protect him.

This was the only way, he tells himself again. But in the panic and frenzy to cover it up, the initial fear of Claude's murder was swept away. He's dead. And if their plan works, his body will never be found. His murderer never brought to justice. The thought knots in Jake's soul.

He sighs in the gloom of the bedroom, lit only by a faint strip of moonlight pushing through the windows. He wishes he could switch off his thoughts. He can feel Hannah's eyes on him.

'Did we do the right thing?' she whispers.

Her question cuts into him. He wishes he had an answer. 'I don't know.'

She bites her lower lip. 'We were panicking and in shock, Jake. What if we've made a mistake hiding Claude's body?'

He stays silent, but he's certain Hannah is thinking the same thought as him. *Too late now.*

'There's no point dwelling on if we've made a mistake,' he says. 'It'll drive us crazy. Right now, we need to get our stories straight.'

'What stories?' she asks.

'In case anyone asks us,' Jake replies with more calm than he feels. Every muscle is tense and aching. Every movement is a reminder of heaving Claude's body into the cave. 'I think we keep it simple. We stick to the truth, but we say we stayed together on the walk. And we got back from the lake a few hours later than we did. It's what you told Claude's wife, so we stick with that. We'll say we had a swim and ate dinner and went to bed.'

Already his mind is racing with anything that might trip them up. 'We ate bread and cheese, and drank a bottle of wine. I'll tip one down the sink so there's an empty bottle on the side.'

He waits for her to tell him he's going too far, but she doesn't. The weight of what they've done lays heavy on them. He isn't sure he'll ever sleep again.

There's a rustle of sheets and the motion of the mattress moving. A second later, Hannah's body scooches into his, and he wraps her in his arms.

'Jake.' Her breath is warm on his neck. 'I'm scared.'

Her hair is damp as he kisses the top of her head. 'Me too. But we've been smart. The police—'

'No.' She pushes herself up and in the dim moonlight her eyes glisten with a fear that cuts into his chest. 'Of course I'm worried about what will happen if the police come looking for Claude, but I'm scared for who did this.'

His thoughts charge forward, mind racing as fast as his quickening pulse. He can't stop his arms tightening around her, wishing there was something he could do to make this all go away.

Her voice falters as she continues. 'Someone killed Claude. They stabbed him and left him to die. It's so horrendous. But they... they wore your shoes. They went to the trouble to make it look like we killed him. Why?'

The weight of the question presses down on him until Jake fears it could suffocate him.

'Maybe Claude came looking for us,' he says, thinking aloud. 'And maybe someone broke in, looking for valuables. Claude startled them and they killed him.'

He senses Hannah's uncertainty. The question only causes more questions. He can see them running through her head.

Like if Claude startled an intruder, then why wouldn't they just run? Claude was big, but he wasn't agile. Why did someone wear Jake's shoes?

There's the fight in the village too. That damning scene witnessed by a police officer no less.

'It feels personal, doesn't it?' Hannah says, and it's like she's plucked the thought from his head.

In the dim light, tears swim in her eyes, reminding Jake of how vulnerable she was after the break-in. The moment he thought he saw Neve in the village earlier flashes in his mind.

A cold shiver runs down his spine, and he grips Hannah tighter, seeking solace in her warmth. Wanting to forget. He knows he should tell Hannah that he thinks he saw his ex-girlfriend yesterday. That she could be behind Claude's murder. The fear that it's all starting again makes him want to scream and cry. He can't bear the thought of going through it all again – everything that happened with Neve six years ago, when the only option he had was to run from Westlake and start a new life three thousand miles away in Manchester. The thought of Hannah having to live through it too fills him with a jagged fear. He's never told her why he left the States, and with everything they've gone through in the last few hours, now isn't the time. He'll tell her. Just not tonight. His fingers brush against the bare skin on her arm, tentative, allowing her time to draw away, but instead she tilts her head and brushes a kiss against his lips.

Desire stirs in him. It doesn't melt the fear or adrenaline still coursing wildly through him, but the raw need for reassurance and connection pushes any other thought out of his head. He's already hard as Hannah's fingers tangle in his hair, pulling him closer in a silent plea for the oblivion they both crave.

The sex is urgent and intense, leaving them both breathless and spent, but later Hannah grips his hand tight and cries as she says, 'We have to get through this.'

'We will,' he says with a conviction he desperately wants to believe.

She falls asleep in his arms, and there's nothing he can do to stop the fear crawling back over him. It's a familiar feeling – a fear he thought he left behind when he moved from Ohio. When he met Hannah, he truly believed he was settled. No more running. No more fear or looking over his shoulder.

It's the fear that keeps him planning – always thinking ahead. Right now, that fear is for the police finding the truth. It's for whoever did this to them. And for Neve and what she's capable of. But it's also for Hannah. She's right. They have to get through this.

13 DAYS UNTIL THE WEDDING

TEN

HANNAH

We wake in the late morning, the sun high, the room hot. We're a tangle of sheets and limbs, and for an uncomfortable moment it's as though we're strangers. Like we don't know the first thing about each other. Then Jake turns towards me and our eyes lock, and I know that whatever happens next, we're in this together. We made a choice and now we have to live with it, and there's no one else I would want by my side.

'Are you OK?' he asks, slipping a hand into mine.

I nod even though it doesn't feel true. Memories from yesterday come at me in a rush of horror. It feels nightmarish and unreal.

Jake runs a hand through his hair, still dishevelled with sticking-up ends from falling into bed after the shower. I remember the water running down the plug hole, red from the blood we'd cleaned. I close my eyes and try to push the image away.

'I'll make coffee,' he says, pulling on a pair of shorts and disappearing from the room.

I dress carefully, wondering how quickly the tall figure in the pale-blue polo shirt and French police cap will be at our door, a hand resting threateningly on his belt. I take extra time over my hair and cover my ashen skin with foundation that glimmers in the sunlight.

The dress I choose is a black maxi dress covered in large yellow sunflowers. I look at my reflection in the mirror and it's as though I'm staring at someone else. I swallow, feeling empty and sick with the dread creeping over me. Questions come. Quick and hard like bullets. What am I doing? What have we done? The walls of the bedroom seem to shift around me.

I heave in a deep breath that hits the bottom of my lungs and lift my chin a fraction. The woman in the mirror does the same and it anchors me. I force myself to think of the life we have in London, waiting for us like a paused film. The boring normality of corporate law. It's not the sexy job portrayed on TV and in films. It's endless negotiations and months of back and forth over the smallest line in a contract. Always it comes down to the wire. Late nights and early mornings blending together. But I like the black and white of corporate law. Right and wrong.

I'm on a roll now, thinking of my life away from this trip and what we've done. My mind takes me to Fitzroy House, outside Bath near the west coast, and Julia and Marcus. She's a fifty-seven-year-old socialite. He's a sixty-six-year-old judge, semi-retired and only taking the easy cases.

Is it normal for parents to encourage mediocrity in their children? To not want their child to succeed? To not want them to be happy? They wanted a daughter who doesn't try for anything but beauty and fun, and leaves the work to a wealthy husband; the same cycle of their lives on repeat. It's archaic and mortifying, but worst of all, they're disappointed.

Jake is not who they'd have in mind as a son-in-law. It isn't just that he's American and not from their social circles. It's that he's building his own business. Jake is the first to say his software company is still growing. There are good months and bad.

He's apologetic sometimes and I hate it. I hate that he thinks this – us – is about money or financial security. It's the last thing I care about, and I tell him so often.

The argument from the village square yesterday leaps into my thoughts.

'This American boy is breaking your parents' hearts with this ridiculous wedding.'

With everything that's happened since, I don't know how Jake feels about the wedding. A new kind of fear tightens across my chest. My same plea from last night echoes in my thoughts. We have to get through this. When I was lonely and trudging through life, Jake saved me. We clicked from that first coffee together, and even now – after what we did last night – I can't imagine my life without him.

Downstairs, I take the coffee Jake's made onto the veranda, certain the acrid smell of bleach has seeped into the stone walls. I can't be in the house. I sit and watch the sun reflect on the pool like shards of shattered glass. The garden is filled with the noises of the morning; of the world carrying on. The chatter of a bird nearby, the chirrup of the crickets, and the gentle lap of water being pumped in and out of the pool. I could almost convince myself this is a normal Sunday morning on the getaway I thought would be perfect. But my body betrays me – every muscle taut.

When a leaf from the vines growing around the veranda posts tickles my shoulder, I yelp and leap up. My coffee spills and my thoughts with it. Before I can stop myself, I'm back in the hall, staring at the foot that didn't belong. My mind leaps forward and I think of standing frozen on the driveway in the dusk. The feeling of being watched by more than just a curious fox. I shiver despite the heat already pouring into the day and stand on Bambi legs, desperate suddenly to be inside once more.

I find Jake in the kitchen. He's moving with a sense of purpose, placing plates and cutlery on the table, the muscles in his arms flexing with every movement. He looks up when I step into the room. Carefully, I smell the air. It's only coffee and the herby scents from the small plants growing on the window ledge. No smells of blood or bleach.

He gestures to the table and the bread and butter and jams already laid out. I shake my head. 'I don't think I can eat.'

There's a pause and then he nods, stepping towards me, his hand finding mine. He always does this. Seeks me out. Finds a way to touch. A hand, an arm, a kiss to my cheek. It makes my heart ache. It's a reminder of just how much we have to lose.

'Me neither,' he says. 'But I thought... if someone comes this morning looking for Claude, it might look strange that we're not eating.'

Jake's right, and I realise we're on different paths. I'm stuck in the horrors of last night. Jake is pushing ahead, making his plans. I'm glad one of us is. 'You're right,' I reply.

The silence falls between us again. It feels like both of us are avoiding asking the obvious question – who? Who would do this? To Claude. To us. I'll ask Jake again later. Right now, just being upright feels like it's taking everything I have. Then I think of something I can do and it feels good. 'I don't think I can just sit around. I'll go into the village,' I say. 'We'll need more bread, and I want to see if there's any news. Claude knows everyone, so...' I trail off, not even sure what I'm trying to say.

'Good idea. It will help to know what's going on.'

He doesn't offer to come, and I'm grateful for the time alone. I wonder if he feels the same. I drop the thought. We should be sticking together. Jake stands at the open front door, leaning against the door frame, shielding his eyes from the sun, and watches me drive away.

He's there again when I return an hour later, as though he's been waiting for me this whole time, except he's dressed in fresh clothes and his hair is styled.

I take the drive too fast, wheels skidding on the stones. An anxious fear is rising in me as I jam the brake and kill the engine.

'They know,' I say to the questioning look Jake throws me as I leap from the car and hurry towards him. I tighten my ponytail, trying to steady my nerves before continuing. 'It's all over the village. Marie called everyone she could think of last night and then the police this morning. There was an officer talking to the café owner. I think he'll be coming here next.' My voice cracks, betraying the fear.

'It's OK. We knew this would happen.' Jake's calm, but I think I catch the same fear flickering in his eyes.

He takes my hand and guides me towards the house, but my feet falter. 'I don't think I can do it.' I look to the open doorway and the shadowy hall. I'm sure I can still smell the blood.

Jake squeezes my hand. 'Do what?'

I throw out my hand to the doorway, fighting back tears. 'Go inside. Lie to the police.' A sob heaves in my chest. 'Carry on.'

'You can, Hannah,' he soothes. 'You're the strongest person I know.'

I tilt my head so our eyes meet. I feel anything but strong. I grab his hands and the words come with the same rushed urgency pulsing through me. 'We could run, couldn't we? We could pack the car and be in London by tonight.'

Jake is shaking his head before I've even finished. 'You have no idea how much I want to,' he says. 'But we have to be smart about this. We booked the ferry ticket for Monday night. It'll look suspicious if we leave a day early.'

He's right, but I push anyway. 'We could say we had a fight or someone is ill or there's been an emergency at work.' Another sob unleashes, and Jake's arms are around me. I lean into his steady warmth. He moves to whisper comfort in my ear, but the words die at the sound of an engine in the distance – a car coming up the road to the house.

'The police,' I cry.

A current of fear courses between us, connecting us in an unspoken understanding. Even if we wanted to run, it's too late now.

'We can do this,' Jake says. 'We're in this together.'

The memory of the blood-soaked rug, the shoe prints, the knife hit me in strobing images. I nod, but my skin prickles with a thousand goosebumps.

Can we really get away with this? I long for an answer. I long to peer into the crystal ball it feels as though Jake possesses sometimes with his certainty and his plans and his confidence. But all I'm left with is the realisation that it's too late to turn back. Too late for the truth. Too late to run.

ELEVEN

HANNAH

Jake tugs my arm as the sound of the car grows nearer. 'Come on,' he says. 'We have to look like we're having brunch and nothing is wrong.'

Nothing wrong? I would laugh if I wasn't so terrified. It feels like the truth is written all over my face. One look at me and it'll all be over. He pulls me into the hall and my gaze lands on the space where a rug used to be. It looks so empty.

In the kitchen, I see Jake's been busy in my absence. There's an empty wine bottle by the sink and the detritus of the breakfast neither of us could stomach.

'Sit,' he says, and I give in to the jelly feeling in my legs and sink into a chair. Then we wait in silence. Jake leans against the counter by the sink, his hands worrying at a knot in the wood. The only sound is the rushing beat of my heart, so loud I think it will drown out the knock at the door. But then we hear wheels on the driveway, an engine cutting out. I stop breathing for a long moment. A car door bangs. The crunch of footsteps.

It's happening!

Jake's eyes find mine. He looks desperate. 'We can do this, Hannah,' he says. 'Remember, we had no choice. They'd never have believed we didn't kill Claude. Hiding his body was our only way for a shot at a future.'

I nod. Not because I agree, but because it doesn't matter. We made a choice and it's too late to undo. Our lives are teetering on the edge of a sheer drop. If we can't pull this next part off, it's all over. The thought causes a panic to grab me in its vice-like hold.

The sound of the door knocker thuds through the house, echoing against the stone walls.

'Smile,' Jake says, his hand slipping into mine, squeezing tight in reassurance or warning, I'm not sure. Either way, it's a silent message to stick to the story. But the panic won't let go. I can't remember what time in our story we said we arrived home yesterday. Did we swim and then have dinner or was it dinner first?

In the steps it takes us to cross the hall, Jake has pulled himself upright, shoulders back, head lifted, and when I look, his face is a mask of calm. I try to do the same, forcing my lips into a smile that feels like a grimace.

On the doorstep, just as I imagined this morning, stands the tall, thin man who spoke to us in the village yesterday after Jake hit Claude. His police uniform is crisp, his badge gleaming in the bright sunlight. Sharp eyes lock on to mine before flicking to Jake. A line forms between his brow as though he already knows everything.

'*Bonjour, ça va?*' he says before moving to heavily accented English. 'I am Stéphane Allard. I'm with the local police. May I come in?'

Jake is all smiles and welcomes as he leads Allard to the kitchen, offering coffee with such warmth it's like this man is an old friend. It's a confidence that draws people in, and I wish I had a smidgen of it right now.

Jake sets about making coffee I can't stomach, and I clear the plates from the table, apologising for the mess of our late breakfast. Now we're here, in this moment, it feels impossible. There's no way he'll buy our story. No way we can do this. My insides are liquid and zipping with nervous energy.

'How can we help you?' Jake asks when we're sat around the table, the air thick with the smell of coffee and the masculine scent of Jake's aftershave.

Allard purses his lips. 'You're aware Monsieur Dubas has been reported by his wife as a missing person?'

'Yes,' I reply. Beneath the table, my leg jitters. I must knock the table leg because a teaspoon rattles on a saucer, drawing Allard's attention. I force myself to be still. 'Marie called us last night to ask if we'd seen him, and I just heard in the village he's still missing.'

'He was here yesterday,' Allard says – a statement not a question.

'No.' Jake's reply comes too fast. Too certain.

An awkward pause follows before Allard continues. 'He's not happy about a wedding, I understand.'

I make a show of rolling my eyes. 'It was nothing. A misunderstanding in the village yesterday morning. And one I'd have cleared up if we'd seen him, but we didn't. We left for a hike straight after lunch and we didn't get back until the early evening. If he did come by, we must have missed him.' I'm surprised by how light and calm my voice sounds. Like it could be the truth.

Allard studies us with those knowing eyes. I swallow, wanting to drink the water on the table but not daring to pick it up in case my hand shakes and gives me away.

'Can anyone confirm your alibi?' he asks. The final word feels like an axe smashing at our lies.

'Alibi?' Jake pushes a hand through his hair, an amused smile twitching on his lips. 'You make us sound like criminals.'

Allard leans back in his chair. He rests his hands on the

table. Steady and patient. 'I'm merely trying to establish if anyone saw you yesterday afternoon.'

I shake my head. 'I don't think we saw anyone. But look, I've known Claude all my life. He's always disappearing to some town or vineyard for a few days. Why is this any different?'

'It's different because he was seen arguing with you the day of his disappearance,' Allard says. 'He set out from his home soon afterwards to talk to you. So I'm wondering if during that conversation the argument got out of hand and became another fight. In the heat of the moment, he was hit or pushed, or banged his head. An accident perhaps.'

I sense Jake stiffen beside me. Beneath the smile and the air of ease, I know exactly what he's thinking. This is why we didn't call the police yesterday. This is proof we've done the right thing hiding Claude's body. Even without Allard's accusation, the suspicion is sharp in the air.

Jake stands and begins to collect the cups. He carries them to the sink, throwing the words casually over his shoulder. 'I can see why you'd think that. I shouldn't have lost my temper in the village yesterday. I feel terrible about it and would've apologised to Claude if we'd seen him yesterday afternoon, but we didn't. We went to that cursed quarry – what's it called, Han?'

'Le Lac Blanc,' I say, and at last I look at Jake. I watch his eyes widen a fraction as though he's just realised what he's done. The lake isn't simply where we walked yesterday afternoon. It's where we've hidden Claude's body. And now Allard knows we were there.

The man's tone carries surprise as he repeats the name of the lake.

'We only went to the top,' I lie. 'To see the view. Then we walked through the vineyards.'

'All afternoon and into the early evening?' Allard frowns and it's obvious he doesn't believe us.

'Yes,' Jake says from the sink, but Allard's eyes never leave my face. It feels as though he's reading my thoughts.

My fingers stray to the square diamond of my engagement ring, rubbing at the smooth jewel – something I do when I'm stressed. It grounds me. A reminder of what Jake and I have. I glance at the ring, expecting to feel the familiar comfort, but instead I almost gasp. There, in a tiny gap between the diamond and one of the claws holding it in place, is a drop of red. Blood.

The jittering spreads from my leg to my body. I swallow again, mouth so dry it's like dragging razors down my throat. I dip my head; the sunflowers of my dress swim before my eyes. I whisper a 'sorry' to Jake.

'Hannah?' There's an urgency in his tone. A 'what are you doing?' question. Can't he see Allard isn't buying a word of our story?

'It's OK,' I reply, shooting him a look. This is it, the moment where everything could come crashing down around us.

Jake remains composed, his features schooled into an expression of innocence, but I swear I can hear his own heart skip a beat.

I look from Allard to Jake. I think of sitting at this table yesterday with a body lying in a pool of blood just metres away from us. The same panic pummels my body now. We were shocked. Under pressure. Terrified. We made a decision in the spur of the moment, but was it the right one?

'It's no use,' I say. 'We have to be honest.' I take a breath and twist the diamond of my ring so it's on the inside of my hand, hiding the blood. And then I speak.

TWELVE
JAKE

Jake struggles to breathe as Hannah fiddles with her engagement ring. Her eyes are teary and she looks so small in the chair beside the police officer. It takes everything he has not to rush forward, to take her in his arms and give her comfort. To pull her away and beg her not to do what she's about to do.

The frenzy of it surges through his veins. He thought they were in this together. He thought they'd protect each other. In that second's pause, his mind sees Hannah confessing. She'll say it was his idea to hide the body. She'll tell the police how scared she was, going along with his plans. It will all fall on him. He'll be charged with murder. He can't believe he's already mentioned the lake they went to yesterday. The location where Claude's dead body is now hidden.

'We weren't just out walking until the early evening—'

'Hannah.' His voice is a croak of emotion as he begs her silently not to continue. The fear of the last twelve hours threatens to topple inside him.

She shakes her head but won't look at him. 'We found a quiet spot in one of the vineyards,' she says, naming something in French. 'And we sat for a while and... one thing led to another.' A blush creeps over her cheeks. 'That's why we were out so long.'

Jake almost laughs with the relief flooding his body as Allard looks uncomfortable and shifts in his seat. If Allard suspects they're hiding something, and Jake's certain he does, Hannah has just given him a reason for it. Very clever.

Hannah pushes her hair behind her ears. She has no idea how self-assured she is. It's her upbringing – an entitlement that could've made her selfish and spoiled, but somehow created someone confident, easy-going and fun. Last night, Hannah asked if they'll be OK, and he told her yes, not knowing if it was true. Now he sees it is. He needs her so much, so fiercely, there is no other choice. They have to be OK. Better than OK. They'll be happy again. He'll make sure.

There's a pause as he waits for Allard's next question, but instead the officer stands.

'If you remember anything else or if you hear from Claude, please call me.' He pulls out a business card from his pocket and places it on the table. 'Could I take a telephone number please? In case I have any more questions.'

A dainty relief dances and skips through Jake's veins as he reels off his number. He feels himself wanting to smile broadly, to share a look with Hannah. He fights it back. Keeps his face calm. Don't get smug. He might be so far out of his depth that the world has tilted on its axis, but he understands people, and Allard is someone who misses nothing, even the briefest of looks.

Jake forces a slowness to his steps. Nothing to hide. No rush. That holiday pace. Jake feels his eyes pulling to the flagstones where they found Claude's body, but he keeps his gaze up.

At the door, with one hand on the handle, Allard turns back. 'When are you leaving?'

'Tomorrow,' Hannah says. 'But I think we'll come back in the summer. I've forgotten how much I love it here.'

Jake nods and places an arm around her shoulder. He feels her trembling. One more minute, he thinks, and this will all be over.

Allard's gaze drops to the floor, staring at the exact spot where the rug used to be. For an awful moment, Jake fears they've missed a drop of blood, fears it's all going to come crashing down in a split second.

The officer sniffs and immediately Jake thinks of the bleach they used last night to clean. He can no longer smell the fumes or feel it scratch the back of his throat, but maybe he's just used to it now.

His mind skips ahead, deciding whether to play dumb or confess to cleaning. Could he say he dropped a bottle of wine? No. There's no pile of broken glass in the bin. It's the kind of error that can trip them up. He'll say they brought mud into the house after the hike and he spilled some cleaning products.

He's about to blurt something out about the smell when the door is opening and the sharp rays of sunlight are pouring into the hall and Allard is wishing them a safe journey home before climbing into his car.

He's leaving. They've done it. The thought comes in another rush of queasy relief.

The second the door is closed Jake sags against the wall. He has a flash to childhood. Standing in front of the principal, being accused of something stupid – hiding the mascot outfit or squirting shaving cream into lockers. It didn't help that the principal was his mom. It made the teachers and other kids wary, keeping their distance. Of course he acted out. But sometimes he got away with it and would breathe the same sigh of relief he feels now.

But he's not that boy anymore. Not the teen who was kicked off the football team for fighting. He's calm. Thoughtful.

Successful. He repeats the words like a mantra, wishing they felt as true as they did yesterday before his fight with Claude.

They wait until the sound of the car engine fades into silence before speaking. Both voices overlap, a mix of relief and fear.

'That was a good idea to tell him we stopped—' Jake remarks just as Hannah blurts out, 'God, that was awful. Do you think he bought it?'

Jake thinks. There was an uncomfortable scrutiny to the police officer. The sense that he knew more about Claude's disappearance than he was letting on. 'I'm not sure,' he says. 'I guess it doesn't matter. It's not about what they believe but what they can prove.'

When he looks at Hannah, her eyes are focused on her engagement ring. She's rubbing at the diamond. 'There's blood in between the clasp,' she mutters, her voice trembling. Before Jake can react, she's sliding down the wall, collapsing to the flagstones and sobbing.

He wants to sink down beside her and cry his own tears of fear and frustration and relief. But Hannah needs him to be strong, and so he crouches in front of her, takes her in his arms and carries her into the garden. He places her gently on the same sun lounger they sat on together the first night.

The moment he places her down, she's sitting up, eyes teary but flashing with something else – anger or frustration, he thinks. She wipes the tears from her cheeks.

'Who did this to us?' She asks the question like he has the answer and has been keeping it from her.

He shakes his head and sits on the lounger beside her, so they're facing each other, knees almost touching. 'I wish I knew.'

When Hannah looks at him, there's a sudden determination to her features. 'Could it be Neve? I thought this getaway would be about escaping, but it feels like trouble has followed us.'

His instinct is to protect Hannah. To say no. To blame some

unknown assailant, but the question he keeps tripping up on is why? Why would someone frame them for murder? He has to be honest. Hannah deserves that at least.

'I want to say no,' he says, 'but...'

'But what?' Hannah pushes.

'But there was a moment in the village yesterday after you went into the shop when I thought I saw her.'

Hannah gasps. 'Oh my God. Why didn't you tell me?'

'Because it was a split second from the corner of my eye and when I looked, there was nothing there. I thought I was just rattled after she broke in to the apartment.'

'I need to know what happened between the two of you, Jake.'

Jake feels his jaw clench. His gaze drops. He can't look at the burning questions in Hannah's eyes. How does he explain everything that happened with Neve? It's part of the past he's tried so hard to forget.

'What do you mean?' he asks, buying himself another moment to get control of the icy fear pushing through his veins, because of course he knows what Hannah is asking.

The same dogged determination that drew him to Neve, when they met in a bar on Main Street in Westlake when he was twenty-four, is the same determination he wants to shield Hannah from now. Neve was like no one he'd ever met. The people around Jake back then – his parents, his sister and her husband, the community college tutors who'd hounded him for assignments he'd never seen the point of completing – were all pushing and prodding, trying to squeeze Jake into the same box as every other twenty-something schmuck.

Neve was the first one who didn't care that he was a college dropout. She saw something in him before he fully saw it in himself. For years, he'd believed the remarks always thrown at him.

'You're lazy.'

'You can't stick at anything.'

'You never think about the consequences.'

'Just get a job and knuckle down.'

Neve hadn't thought those things. She'd loved his business ideas. *'You're going places, Jake. And maybe I'll come along for the ride.'*

When he looks back at the two years they spent together, he wishes he could pinpoint the moment things shifted. When Neve's interest in him became controlling. When she wanted to know every meeting he took. Every decision he was planning. But maybe it had always been there. He'd just been too wrapped up in having someone believe in him to see it.

'Jake,' Hannah says, 'I'm sorry if this is hard for you, but I should've pushed you to tell me about Neve after she broke into our apartment. I guess I was so focused on how awful it was, how violated I felt, that I didn't stop to ask why someone would do this to us. But I need to understand why your ex-girlfriend followed you to England six years after you broke up. Why did she wait all that time? What happened between the two of you? Because people don't just break into homes, Jake. And if she's capable of that, then maybe she's capable of killing a man and making it look like we did it. Is she capable of that?'

A strangled noise escapes his throat. 'I don't know. Neve was always a bit on the wild side. We dated for two years and it was pretty obvious we weren't right for each other. She was always looking for the fun and the chaos while I wanted to plan. By the time I realised the relationship was going nowhere, her grammy died and she was so upset, I couldn't exactly break up with her then.

'The grief changed Neve. She went from wild to completely off the rails. She started drinking a lot and wanting to be out all the time. She became obsessive and needy. She'd come to my office at random times, expecting to find me with another woman. She was constantly calling me and demanding I drop everything and go to her. She started tracking my phone.' He takes a breath. He can feel his pulse juddering in his veins. There is more he should say about the end of his relationship with Neve, but even after all this time, the fear is still raw.

'It was hard to end things,' he continues. 'She wouldn't listen when I said it was over. I moved out, but she kept coming by my new place. She'd turn up when I was meeting clients and start telling them I was a jackass and a cheater. She started harassing my family too. Calling my parents in the middle of the night to tell them what an awful person I was. She felt I'd betrayed her somehow by breaking up with her.

'It sounds so crazy when I talk about it, but that's what it was. What she was back then. Crazy. It was like I'd done something terrible to her. Set fire to her house or killed her cat or... I don't know. But I didn't, Hannah. I swear. All I did was tell her it was over. I'm no psychologist, but I think she poured all of her grief and hurt for her grammy into blaming me for something. I became her focus. Her obsession. It got to a point where moving away and getting a fresh start felt like my only choice.'

'So that's when you moved to Manchester?'

He nods, studying his hands. A sharp lump of emotion forms in his throat. He hates talking about this. Hates remembering the worst time in his life. It all went so wrong so fast with Neve. It's been so hard to rebuild his life twice over – first in Manchester and then in London. He never thought he'd meet someone like Hannah and be able to let his walls down again. And now he's found the one person he wants to spend the rest of his life with, the one person perfect for him. Before Neve broke into the apartment, he was weeks away from having all his dreams come true. Now it feels like it could all go up in flames any second.

'It felt like the last place she'd ever think to look for me,' he continues, remembering his first one-bed studio in a student area of the city. It was tiny and run-down, but it had felt like freedom. 'I kept expecting her to turn up, but she never did. I thought she'd moved on. I thought she'd forgotten about me, but after last week, I think Neve has spent all this time looking for me.'

'And now she's found you.'

'I'm sorry, Hannah. I'm so sorry,' he says, the emotion thick in his voice.

Her face softens and she slips her hands into his. 'It's not your fault. I'm sorry for what happened to you in Westlake.'

They wrap their arms around each other. Hannah cries again, and he rubs her back, wishes he could tell her it would be all right. He isn't sure how much time passes before she lifts her head from his chest and asks, 'What do we do now?'

He thinks she's seeking reassurance about their relationship. 'We find a way to get past this,' he replies. 'We focus on our wedding.'

She shakes her head, wiping tears from her face. Even in her worst moments, her beauty takes his breath away. He has a sudden need to hold her and tell her he loves her, can't be without her.

'No,' she says. 'I mean, what do we do right now? Today. I get that we can't leave early. But I can't think what to do.'

Jake sees her point. When he'd first visualised today, he saw them side by side by the pool, reading the books they bought on the ferry from Dover, drinking wine and stopping to have slow, sensual sex in the afternoon heat. 'Maybe we could swim and see how we feel,' he says.

Hannah looks like she might cry again, but then she nods. 'OK.'

As she steps away to change, his phone vibrates from his back pocket. He doesn't reach for it. Somewhere away from the nightmare they're trapped in, it's a normal Sunday afternoon, the time when his Fantasy Football WhatsApp group jumps into life, sharing scores and banter.

He doesn't really get soccer. It all seems so sedate compared to the football he played in high school. But he joined a Fantasy Football league when he moved from Ohio to England and settled in Manchester.

When Jake moved to London, he kept the Fantasy Football League and the WhatsApp group. He likes the banter and the friendships he's never found in London.

His past in Westlake is nothing. A nothing house. A nothing neighbourhood. He used to think he'd go back one day. He's fantasised so many times about arriving on his parents' doorstep and showing them and his sister how he's made something of his life. But then he met Hannah and the fantasy died. What would be the point anyway? His family made up their minds about him long ago. They'd never understand he's not the same person he once was.

Hannah has mentioned wanting to see the place where he grew up one day. He understands the pull. The same way he longs to meet her parents. It's a connection to a part of their lives they both don't have. He'll keep finding excuses. It's not just his family's opinion of him keeping him from going home.

It's only later when Hannah is pretending to read by the pool and he's pretending to enjoy the wine he opened, and Claude's death and all they did has become a grotesque, shadowy thing they're pretending isn't sitting between them, that he thinks to check his phone. He finds the WhatsApp group brimming with banter, just as he expected. But it's the other message that makes his body tense. He sits up from the lounger, the sun suddenly a searing ball of scalding heat on his skin. He taps on the notification from Neve. His heart stops.

I have to see you!

A new fear burns through him. He taps a hurried reply.

There's nothing more to say. I'm with Hannah now. We're getting married in a few weeks. Please leave us alone.

He wishes there was more he could say or do. How can he make her see there's no going back for them?

Her reply comes a moment later.

I can't do that.

The words swim on the screen. What the hell does that mean? His heart thuds in his chest as he lies back on the lounger and watches the sun ripple on the water. What has she done? What is she planning to do? The questions grab him by the throat and choke him.

12 DAYS UNTIL THE WEDDING

THIRTEEN

HANNAH

It's late Monday evening by the time we're home and parking in the underground car park beneath the apartment. The building is a Victorian red-brick warehouse converted to living spaces as part of London's Urbanisation Project, a few minutes' walk from King's Cross station and twenty minutes to Camden and Regent's Park. There's no lift, so we trudge with our suitcases and our weary tiredness up the three flights of stairs to my converted studio loft. The only noise is the heavy tap of our feet from the extra weight of our luggage.

There have been moments today when things have felt almost normal. Every mile we put between us and the farmhouse and the picturesque Languedoc-Roussillon region has lifted the dark cloud of what we did. We even shared a joke on the ferry – Jake teasing me about a seagull's squawk sounding like my singing in the shower. We both laughed. But any spark of our old selves is interspersed with long periods of silence I don't know how to fill.

But we're home now and things can only get better, I tell myself as we turn the final flight of stairs and there is my polished black wood front door. My home. I'm halfway to sighing with relief when my eyes catch on the shiny new lock and the rectangular doorbell camera Jake fitted last week. I'd forgotten they were there.

Ahead of me, Jake keeps moving, already fishing out his set of keys while my feet stop dead on the final stair. All day, I've longed to be home, but I've been so caught up in what happened in France that I forgot about the trashed apartment and seeing Neve.

Jake senses my hesitance and his tone when he speaks is reassuring. 'It's OK, Han. We've both got the doorbell app, right? So we know no one came to the door while we were away. She hasn't come back,' he adds.

There's a flicker of something in his face. Is he wondering like me if Neve didn't come back to the apartment because she was in France with us. But he's right. There have been no notifications on the app. It won't be like last week when I opened the door after a long day of work, only to find a tall woman with ice-blonde hair standing in the centre of our living room, looking both wild and somehow sheepish. Without a word, she'd walked straight past me and out the door, leaving me among the mess of my apartment, shaken to my core.

The scrape of a key in the lock pulls me away from the memory. Jake steps inside and I follow, dropping my suitcase and rolling away the ache in my shoulders. Remnants of the break-in are everywhere.

Straight ahead is a rectangular living room, running the width of the building. Sloping windows overlook a balcony where I attempt to grow strawberries in the summer, always forgetting to water the plants and being lucky if I get one piece of fruit. Beyond it are more converted living spaces and office blocks, the distant skyline of the city. We're high enough and far enough away not to be overlooked, and I rarely close the cream linen drapes.

We've only been away for three days, but as I step inside,

there's a cool, abandoned feeling in the air. There's a plaque on the wall by the entrance to the building, detailing the history of the warehouse. According to the swirling italics inscribed on the gold square, the warehouse was used to store flour. But sometimes, like now, I swear there is a faraway, barely there smell of coffee beans lingering in the beams that run across our head and in between the brickwork of the exposed walls.

I step further into the apartment, throwing my cardigan down on the brown leather sofa. My eyes catch on the coffee table. It's covered in our wedding paperwork. Menus and schedules and sample invites, coloured fabrics for chair covers, a list of songs our DJ has given us to strike or approve. It's all mixed together. The folder is sat useless on the side, the metal rings broken. Something else for me to organise and tidy.

Against one wall is a huge oak bookcase. The books are back after they were swept from the shelves and flung to the floor, against the walls, all the way to the open-plan kitchen and breakfast bar on the other side of the apartment. But in our rush to tidy, the books are out of order. I like the spines to be arranged by colour in a sweeping rainbow of red, all the way to purple then black. They look a mess, and I'm surprised to find it's no longer fear darting through my veins but anger. It builds in me. A need to lash out. To snap.

'I hate that your ex was here,' I hiss at Jake. Blame carries in my tone. It isn't Jake's fault, but I'm too tired to be reasonable.

Jake's reply is soft. 'My first meeting isn't until ten tomorrow. I can spend a few hours getting the apartment back to normal.'

I grit my teeth. There's no retort I can throw at his kindness. So I draw in a grounding breath. 'I'm going to take a shower.' I turn left around the corner to the bedroom. There's no door to slam, but the apartment curves round the building, the bedroom and kitchen tucked away either side of the living room, so I have some privacy at least. Beyond the kitchen is a small utility room, and beyond the bedroom is an en suite.

Jake has mentioned moving somewhere bigger after the wedding. We're always on top of each other here. Not enough storage for both of us. It means Jake's laptops and computer equipment are always stacked in one corner or another – wires and gadgets I have no clue about.

The space has never been an issue. Neither of us have craved time away from each other. I guess it's inevitable that the feeling will come, but I hope it won't. I like living here. I like that I can be at my desk at the office in Farringdon in twenty minutes, and when the weather is nice and I remember my flats, I can walk home. I think of a life spent packing and unpacking every three months. Boarding school terms then university. I'm not ready to leave yet.

The bedroom has an exposed brick wall on one side and a wall of mirrored doors hiding wardrobes and drawers on the other. I switch on the light and see the smudges of fingers on glass and remember finding my clothes thrown on the bed and the floor. Even my underwear was tipped out. I asked Jake last week if Neve was looking for something. But he shook his head. 'She'll be trying to get under our skin.'

'It's worked,' I replied.

Yesterday, I pushed Jake to tell me more about his relationship with Neve. It was hard to hear the hurt in his voice as he'd described their relationship. But I'm no closer to understanding why she's fixated on Jake or what she's capable of, and those two things terrify me.

I shiver and head for the bathroom. It's modern – white appliances and two large skylights. A glass walk-in shower with three different water systems. I twist the rainfall to hot, strip off my clothes and step beneath the water, hoping it can wash away the swirl of my emotions along with the dirt of the journey home.

My eyes are closed, my hair wet from being washed, when Jake steps into the spray, taking me in his arms and suddenly I'm crying, heaving sobs. 'Will we ever be OK again?' I ask, thinking of the blood-soaked rug and the squeak of the wheelbarrow as we pushed it down the path to the lake.

He cups my face in his hands; his eyes when they gaze at mine are filled with a mix of hurt and hope. 'Yes,' he says with a confidence I'm in awe of. Again, I think of how it seems he has a crystal ball and can see into our future. 'We're home. It's over. The police didn't come back and that officer hasn't called me.'

'Are we supposed to just forget what we did?' I ask.

He looks suddenly sad. 'I think we have to. I think we wake up tomorrow and carry on with our lives. We have the wedding cake tasting Wednesday night, remember? 7 p.m. Will you be able to get away? I can move it to eight?' He turns off the water and hands me a towel. 'That is if you...' His voice trails off.

I turn to look at him and watch the bob of his Adam's apple. His worry cuts into me.

'Because I'll understand,' he continues. 'With your parents wanting us to call it off and after Claude... I'll understand if you want to—'

'No!' I cry. 'What's happened has only made me more certain you're the one, Jake. I want to marry you.'

Relief washes over him. 'I feel the same. Our wedding will be a turning point. I'm sure of it. We can forget all this.'

In the bedroom, I step back into his embrace. I wrap my arms around him, breathing in the smell of soap and water and something Jake-like that can never be washed away. An exhaustion sweeps over me. I close my eyes, feeling as though I could fall asleep right here. Tomorrow, my alarm will trill at 5.40 a.m. and I'll shower and dress, and when I go to the office and my colleagues ask me how my romantic weekend in southern France was, I'll smile and tell them it was bliss. If I pretend for long enough, will it become true?

My stomach turns with a hollow hunger and I remember we've not eaten since picking at a brunch in a roadside café on the way to the ferry port. I'm about to ask Jake if he wants anything to eat. Hot buttered toast sounds appealing. But Jake is stepping out of my arms and reaching for his phone from the side table by the bed. His torso is still bare. Beads of water glisten on his toned skin, tanned a darker shade from our time by the pool yesterday. There's something in the way the colour drains from his face, eyes suddenly wide, mouth slack, that causes a dart of fear to shoot into my chest.

'What is it?'

He turns the screen towards me, showing a message open from an unknown number. There are no words. Just a video, the screen dark and a white triangle in the centre, urging us to press play.

FOURTEEN
JAKE

In a distant part of Jake's mind, he's aware of the dripping of his hair on the skin of his back and Hannah wrapped in a towel beside him. He's aware of his bare feet on the wood floor of the bedroom and Hannah's gaze on him as he stares at the message on his phone.

He doesn't know what it is yet, but there's an instinctive part of him that senses it's bad and he wants to shield it from Hannah. But it's too late and so as his heart hammers a warning drum in his chest, he presses the play icon.

His screen turns black and at first there's nothing. Then only sound – hurried breathing and the rustle of leaves from whoever is recording. Then there's light and blurred figures. The footage shakes as it zooms in, and then Jake can make out the large farmhouse door and the driveway. And then the wheelbarrow waiting outside.

Realisation hits with the force of a sledgehammer. He swallows back a strangled cry. He thinks Hannah gasps, but the roaring in his ears drowns everything out. This was filmed two days ago. The day they found Claude dead on the rug. The evening they... The video gets there before his thoughts do. He and Hannah struggling with the heavy rolled rug, shuffling towards the wheelbarrow.

His mouth turns dry. His head spins. This is a video of them moving Claude's dead body out of the house. He remembers the rustle of noise then the relief of seeing the fox, but someone was there too, and they've recorded what he and Hannah did that night.

A dozen expletives charge into his thoughts as his mind leaps to an excuse, something – anything – he can tell the police if they see this – but it's like throwing himself at a brick wall. There's nothing he could say that the likes of that officer, Allard, would believe. There's no escaping the size of the rug, how they struggle with it.

Allard's accusation rings in his head. *'I'm wondering if during that conversation the argument got out of hand and became another fight. In the heat of the moment, he was hit or pushed, or banged his head. An accident perhaps.'*

On his phone screen, Jake watches himself and Hannah pause on the driveway. Even from this distance they look guilty. Then they push the wheelbarrow down the driveway in the direction of the lake, Hannah's torch light bouncing ahead of them. The video stops and the icon returns, as though asking if they want to watch it again.

Icy fingers trace a line down his spine. He fights the desire to delete it. To smash up his phone. To run.

The hairs on the back of his neck prickle, and even though it's crazy, he can't help looking up, gaze darting around the room as though the same person who hid in the bushes and recorded them is lurking nearby, still watching. The sun has set and the view outside the window is dark. There are lights on in other apartments across the courtyard, but their building is higher. No one can see them. And yet, he still steps to the window and closes the drapes.

'Jake?' Hannah's voice is whispered and trembling. She's

seeking a reassurance he can't give. His eyes dart back to the message, checking for any words he could've missed, but it's just the recording.

Questions pummel his thoughts. Has this already been sent to the police? Will they be arrested? The realisation is crushing. Everything they did was for nothing.

They're right back where they were when Claude was still dead on the rug, except now it's worse. If they'd called the police, there was a possibility, however small, that the police that night would've seen they were being framed. That possibility disappeared the moment he convinced Hannah that hiding the body was their only chance at freedom. If Allard sees this recording, they'll be charged with murder.

He tries to slow his panicked breathing as he turns to Hannah. Her face is pale, eyes wide with fear.

'What do we do?' she whispers.

Slowly, he shakes his head. His tongue sticks to the roof of his mouth and it's an effort to speak. 'I... I'm not sure.'

There is always a plan, he thinks. Always a way forward, a way out. He just has to find it. But the enormity of this video and what it means is pounding in his head and he can't think.

'Could we go to the police first?' Hannah's words rush out.

He drops onto the edge of the bed, pressing his hands to his face. 'And tell them what?' he asks, voice muffled.

'The truth – that Claude was dead when we got home and we realised we were being framed so we... we hid his body,' she replies. 'Confess before we're caught. We'll tell them we made a massive mistake because we were in shock.'

There's hope in Hannah's voice, like she thinks they can walk this back. She doesn't get it. Maybe she's right. Maybe they did the wrong thing that night hiding Claude's body. But right or wrong, it's too late to undo it now. His palms grow clammy and yet he shivers again. 'The police will say we covered it up and then had an attack of conscience and cooked up a story about being framed to get out of it.'

'But this video proves someone else was there,' she says. 'It backs up our story.'

He shakes his head. 'It won't be enough. It shows we did it. That's what they'll focus on.'

He'd felt so certain this morning that if they could just get home, it would all be OK.

'Jake,' Hannah says after a pause, 'why is this happening to us? We're supposed to be getting married in less than two weeks. Who's doing this? Is it Neve?'

His mind yanks back to Neve's text yesterday. *I can't do that*, she'd said when he'd told her to leave them alone. He hasn't told Hannah about the message exchange, but this video has her written all over it. He remembers a time just after they broke up when she'd begged him to meet her. He'd gone in hope of trying to calm her down. She'd tried to rile him, poking at his temper, wanting him to lash out. He'd kept his cool, only later learning she'd been secretly recording him.

He feels the heat of Hannah's gaze on him. She's waiting for his answer. More than that, she's waiting for him to take control and share his plan like he always does.

'It could be Neve, but I'm not sure. It's so extreme. Whatever happens, Han, we'll find a way to get through this,' he says, forcing a confidence he doesn't feel.

'Should we call the number or reply? Ask them what they want?' Hannah asks.

He shakes his head. 'I don't think we should rush into doing anything,' he replies. 'We need time to think it through. Whoever sent this recording hasn't asked us for anything yet. And considering that it's been two days and the police haven't come back, we can assume they've not been sent it either. I think we should wait and see what happens.'

'Do nothing?' Tears pool in Hannah's eyes.

'I don't think we have any other choice.'

The truth is he doesn't know what to do. Hannah's question spins in his thoughts. *'Why is this happening to us?'* He doesn't have an answer. Everything was so perfect and now it's like they're living in a nightmare. He can't see a way forward. Can't think beyond the voice screaming at him to run while he still can.

11 DAYS UNTIL THE WEDDING

FIFTEEN

HANNAH

Do nothing.

Jake's words spin in my head all night as fear steals my sleep. They're still lodged in my thoughts as I slide out of bed a few minutes before my alarm and begin my usual routine. By seven thirty, I'm at my desk with a strong coffee and one question shouting louder than the rest: how can we do nothing? Someone else was there that night. We have to do something, don't we?

The offices of Jenkins, Wyatt & Ross are sleek. Desks of polished wood. Ergonomic chairs. Monitors and laptops alongside binders and folders filled with contracts piled on every desk and in boxes on the floor. This side of corporate law has yet to go paperless. It's quiet this early but not empty. There's always one account with an urgent deadline and a team pulling all-nighters. But it's not the frenzy of activity it will be by 9 a.m. I try to concentrate on clearing my inbox after my days away, but every task feels like I'm wading through treacle.

When Beverly from accounts stops by to ask about my weekend in France, I jump, nearly bursting into tears. She makes a joke about pre-wedding jitters and I force myself to laugh. Every time I close my eyes, it's Neve's face I see. That half-smile she gave me when I pushed open my apartment door and I found her standing in the mess. Jake thought he saw her in the village in France too. Did she follow us?

I struggle to settle as the morning becomes afternoon. My head is a mess of skittish panic and questions I can't answer. I try to concentrate on the contract for a merger between two investment firms, but the words swim across the screen. My mouth feels dry, my stomach queasy, like I'm hungover. My phone is constantly in my hand, messaging back and forth with Jake, checking he's OK. That nothing else has happened. We're both careful to keep our words vague, and neither of us mention Claude or the video sent to Jake last night.

I don't know how I make it through the day. But as I step out of the office, it's gone 8 p.m. and I'm bone-tired and wired at the same time. All I can think about is the steady warmth of Jake's arms around me. I send a message, letting him know I'm on my way. He'll check on the Find My app we use to share our locations too, so he can time dinner perfectly. Giving me a few minutes in the apartment to change and wash the make-up and stress of the day from my face before he's dishing steaming food onto two plates.

When Jake and I first started dating, we took turns to cook or he'd meet me from the office and we'd find a table at our favourite gastropub or head to the tapas place on St John Street we love. It quickly became clear that Jake was the better chef of the two of us, and without a commute and long hours in an office, he took on the role of dinner preparation as soon as he moved in with me. Lasagne, chicken marsala, beef bourguignon. He can cook anything. Always made from scratch. Always delicious. When I asked him where he learned his skills, he told me, 'When I moved to Manchester, I didn't know how to cook an egg. I also didn't know a single person in the country. I quickly got sick of take-out and loneliness, and so I signed up for a cookery class.'

Dinner has become another thing I don't need to think about. Another reason I'm grateful for Jake, I think, as I step out of the Tube exit at King's Cross station and walk the few minutes to my apartment. Even at this point in the evening, there's a warmth to the air, as though spring is finally giving way to summer.

The traffic is heavy with taxis and buses, the air smelling of greasy fast food and petrol. I head along the main road towards the cut-through and the shortcut home. My apartment building is one of three converted warehouses in the complex, facing in a U-shape onto a pretty communal courtyard with a flower garden and benches where people sit in the summer.

There's a main road entrance further up and around to the left, another five minutes' walk. But I always take the cut-through – a narrow pathway between two of the buildings that leads into the courtyard. I long to see Jake. I tell him I love him every day. And every day the same knowledge slices through me – I can't lose him. I rarely think of my life before Jake, but I know I can't go back to that emptiness again.

Jake is my life. His reliability and trust is everything. I know the passcode to his phone and he knows mine. I can open the Find My app and see his location any time I like. Although without an office to head to, he's usually at the apartment working on building his software business, only venturing into the city for the occasional client meeting or to meet me after work. When I look into his eyes, all I see is openness and love.

The emotions I've fought to keep pushed down today rush to the surface. Eleven days until I marry the man of my dreams. The man who makes me feel whole. I think back to the night before the break-in when everything felt so perfect, curled up on the couch with Jake, planning the honeymoon we'll take later in the summer.

'On the count of three, we'll both say our favourite destination choice,' he said, tapping the binder he'd filled with holiday brochures and ideas. 'One... two... three.'

'Bali,' we said in unison before we burst out laughing.

Jake's eyes crinkled with excitement and desire. 'You and me in a luxury cabin and our own private beach and one of those personal butlers to bring us cocktails.'

'That sounds dreamy.' I grinned, my hand running up Jake's thigh. A second later, he'd pulled me onto his lap and slid his hands under my top.

'You're the peanut butter to my jelly, Han,' Jake said as he kissed me.

I laughed. 'I'm not sure if that's incredibly cute or gross.'

'It's cute. And tasty. I'll make one for you at the weekend.'

'No, thanks,' I said. 'I'll take your word for it.'

'Says the woman who likes Marmite,' he replied, crinkling his nose until I leaned forward and kissed him again. That's how it's been with us, right from the start. In sync.

We have to be OK, I think again, my thoughts pulling back to the present. To France. To what we did. To Neve. To the video we were sent last night.

Do nothing.

It feels wrong. But really, what choice do we have? That question again. Instantly, dread is pooling in my stomach, and I quicken my pace and turn into the gloomy cut-through, needing to be home.

Away from the traffic of the road, my heels tap the pavement, echoing around me. A prickling unease spreads over me and suddenly I'm not thinking of Jake or France. I'm breathing fast, alert. Focused. The sun has dipped lower in the sky, and it's dark in this space between the buildings. I glance over my shoulder, back towards the busy road. A rush of buses and cars and vans. People hurrying. Scooters and delivery bikes. No one is there. I'm completely alone.

Two more steps and I pause again, feeling eyes watching. I throw another glance behind me, and my heart stutters, my feet stop. This time there's movement. My gasp is strangled as I draw back, hitting the wall with a jolt. I can't see a face or a body, but there, in the shadows of the cut-through entrance, is a figure.

SIXTEEN

HANNAH

The already narrow brick walls of the cut-through close in. I dig my phone from my pocket, almost dropping it in my panic as I tap a message to Jake.

Can you come meet me in the courtyard?

No time to explain why as I turn and run, stumbling in my haste as the weight of eyes watching from those shadows burns into my back. It's like the moment outside the farmhouse all over again. Holding my breath. Staring into the darkness. I was certain we were being watched, and I was right.

My phone jumps to life in my hand. I think it'll be Jake, but when I look at the screen, the name of the caller is Julia. I reject the call and twist round, certain I'll come face to face with whoever is there, but it's still only shadows.

'Who's there?' I call out, feeling stupid. Fear jitters through my veins.

The buildings close in another inch, swallowing me whole as the shadows lengthen with the setting sun. Panic surges through me. It's no longer just my footsteps I can hear echoing on the pavement but another set. Closer and closer they come. Then I break into the courtyard and the door to the apartment building opens, and there's Jake in a white T-shirt and jeans, a dish towel slung over his shoulder.

I shout out a desperate, 'Hey,' bolting forward, certain with every step I'll be yanked back into the shadows. I watch him take in my distress and the smile slip from his face. He rushes towards me, and we meet in the middle of the courtyard, a clash of bodies and relief.

He pushes my hair away from my face and tilts my head up to look at him. 'Han, what is it?'

'Someone's following me,' I gasp.

Jake frowns, glancing over my shoulder. 'Did you see who it was?' His hands grip my arms, steadying yet urgent.

I shake my head, still trying to catch my breath.

He looks from the empty street to my face. 'I can't see anyone. Are you sure?'

'I...' *Yes*, I want to shout, but in the comfort of Jake's arms, my heart rate is falling and suddenly I'm not sure. I've been so tired today. My head in a fog. Is it possible I imagined someone there? Tears sting my eyes as I shake my head. 'I don't know.'

'It's OK,' he says. 'I've been going crazy all day too. I kept expecting the police to burst through the door.'

'Me too,' I whisper, allowing Jake to guide me inside. As the door to the apartment closes behind us, I shoot a final glance towards the dark cut-through, and even though I'm no longer sure anyone was there, I still shiver and grip Jake's hand a little tighter.

The moment I'm in the apartment, I kick off my heels and breathe in air fragranced with garlic and chicken from the dinner Jake has prepared. I look around the open-plan space, taking in the shine to the wood floors and my bookshelves back in their rainbow order. A new folder filled with our wedding planning sits on the glass coffee table. I don't need to step around the sofa and open it to know everything will be organised just as it was before. Jake has done exactly as he promised – cleaned and tidied any trace of the break-in a week ago. I close the door and lean against the wall for a second, waiting for the relief to come. I'm home. But all I feel is that prickling unease.

Jake steps close, holding me tight against his chest, like we've been apart for a year rather than a day. He smells of the clean scent of his aftershave and the aromas from cooking dinner. We stand in the middle of my apartment, wrapped in each other's arms for a long time. When he finally pulls back, he studies my face, eyes filled with worry.

'Are you OK?' he asks.

I nod, not trusting my voice.

He guides me towards the breakfast bar, and I drop gratefully onto a stool as he slides an empty wine glass towards me, brows raised in question.

'Thanks,' I say, and a moment later he's filled it with my favourite white. I take a long gulp of tangy, cold liquid. 'Sorry.'

He shakes his head. 'Don't be. It's totally understandable after everything that's happened. And we're both OK, right? Nothing has actually happened today?'

There's a hope to Jake's voice I can't swallow, but before I can question it, he's picking up his phone from the counter.

'Did you see the message from Lily on the Quiz WhatsApp about a team for Thursday? Do you fancy...?' His voice trails off as he takes in my expression. The quiz team are my group. People I've known since university. Some even longer. They've adopted Jake as one of their own, and I know he enjoys the nights out more than I do, especially working out of the apartment as he does. He meets potential clients every so often, but he's on his own so much, and I know it gets lonely. But I can't face a quiz and seeing our group of friends this week. I'm not sure I'll ever be able to again.

'Jake,' I whisper, taking a deep breath. 'Even if I was being paranoid just now, it doesn't mean this is over. That video... It shows what we did.'

Jake sets down the dish towel and leans against the counter. 'I know. But we have to carry on, don't we? Otherwise they've won.'

'Won what?' I cry. 'We don't know what they want. Or who is doing this. Or why. This person is holding our lives in their hands and there's nothing we can do about it. How can you be so calm?'

Jake's shoulders sag. 'I'm not calm, Hannah. I'm terrified. But I'm trying to hold it together, for both of us.' He turns away and without another word he starts scooping the dinner onto two plates. I want to tell him I'm not hungry, but he's gone to so much effort. So I smile and say, 'Thank you,' as Jake places a plate of chicken in a creamy sauce in front of me, followed by bowls of buttery new potatoes and steaming vegetables.

We're quiet as we eat. I concentrate on chewing and swallowing. When I take another sip of wine, my hands shake enough for Jake to notice.

Concern creases his features. 'Han, it's going to be OK.'

'How can you know that?' I ask, wanting so badly to believe the confidence in his tone. A jagged lump of emotion forms in my throat. I place my knife and fork on the plate and push my half-eaten dinner away, knowing I won't be able to swallow another mouthful.

Jake reaches across the counter and takes my hand in his, squeezing gently. 'Because I love you and you love me. And when we're together, we're strong enough to get through anything. We have to focus on our future. The wedding is less than two weeks away. Like I said last night, I have to believe it can be our turning point.'

I meet his eyes, seeing the desperation there, the need for me to agree. But I can't. 'What if whoever is doing this sends this video to the police?' I ask.

'I've been thinking about that all day,' Jake replies. 'And I think if that was their plan, they'd have done it already.' His words are steady, reasonable.

I don't answer straight away. Instead, I think of my wedding dress, hanging in its case in the wardrobe. I think of the invites we've sent to our friends and family. The fifty guests who'll be sitting in the pews a week on Saturday.

Neither Jake or I are religious, but we've chosen St Pancras Old Church as the venue for the ceremony. It's one of those hidden London gems, tucked away and all but forgotten between glass buildings and apartment blocks.

The church is a beautiful old grey stone. Inside, the walls are a fresh white, and when the sun hits the stained-glass window in the mornings, the entire church becomes a riot of pink and blue and red hues. But it's the outside I fell in love with. The stretching clock tower and the lawns of lush green grass, bordered by pink rose bushes. It's only a five-minute walk from the apartment, and we walk by most Sundays and check on the rosebuds. They'll be in full bloom by the wedding.

We've booked the ballroom at the Great Northern Hotel by King's Cross station. It's so close, we can walk to it with our guests, hand in hand, husband and wife.

I wonder if Jake is right. If we just carry on. If we pretend for long enough everything is OK, it will be.

'Han?' Jake's voice is pleading.

I give a small nod. 'Maybe you're right,' I say, trying so hard to believe it.

He smiles, the relief evident on his face. 'We'll get through this together. I promise.' He stands and walks around the counter, pulling me into his arms again. 'I'll never let anything happen to you.'

I let myself sink into his embrace, drawing strength from his solid presence. The moment is shattered by the buzz of Jake's phone from the counter.

He steps away from me, leaving a cold void, saying nothing as he stares at the screen. I can tell by the way his eyes widen that it's another message.

My blood turns to ice. 'Jake?'

I stand and move around the counter to be by his side. He shows me the screen. It's another wordless message with a video attached. He hisses an expletive and taps the play icon. The air remains trapped in my lungs, unmoving, as the video starts to play. It's us again. But not at the farmhouse in France. The shaky footage was filmed minutes ago. It's me running into Jake's arms and us hurrying into the building.

Someone was there.

SEVENTEEN

JAKE

Jake's mind races, chasing away the exhaustion. If only he'd slept better last night. His thoughts are speeding one way then the next, searching for understanding or a way forward.

'Oh my God.' Hannah's voice is a breathy exhale. 'Someone was there. They know where we live. Jake, what are we going to do?'

He wants to scream at Hannah that he doesn't know. He doesn't always have the answers, but he has to keep it together. For both of them.

'I'm going to reply.' He taps out three words.

Who is this?

The reply comes instantly.

Wrong question.

What do you want?

Jake fires back as his heart thumps in his chest.

I think you know the answer to that!

'What does that mean?' Hannah cries.

'I don't know,' he mumbles. He swallows, mouth dry. Beads of sweat form on his top lip. He's spent the day convincing himself they'd be fine if they stuck together, focused on the future. But somewhere in the hours in this apartment, trying and failing to work on his proposal for the meeting with Novexia International – the tech business interested in his software – he's also convinced himself this wasn't personal.

Idiot!

Of course it's personal. The messages are coming to his phone. Whoever was in France – whoever followed Hannah – has his number. And there's something familiar about the taunting replies.

'It has to be Neve,' Hannah hisses like her own thoughts have followed his.

Her words cause a sickening chill to race through his body. He rubs his face, suddenly feverish. Hot and cold and not thinking straight. But Hannah is right, and that realisation terrifies him.

His phone hums in his hand with the arrival of a new message.

Ready to see another video?

A new attachment lands, and in a split second the kitchen, the apartment, Hannah, all disappear. The world turns black. All he sees is the new recording now playing on his phone.

He didn't think anything could be worse than the shadowy images of him and Hannah carrying the rug out of the farmhouse in the dusky twilight. But this... it's like a fist gripping his throat, blocking his airway.

He desperately wants to look away, to close his eyes and

escape, but he's frozen in place, unable to control his own body. His legs give way beneath him and he sinks onto the stool. All the while, his gaze never leaves the image on the screen of the rug and the flagstone floor in the entrance hall of the farmhouse.

He watches the rays of sunlight stream in from the window, making patterns on the Persian rug and across the unmistakable lump of Claude's body. The knife is lying beside him. Then the video pans out and there are Jake's shoes, kicked off and covered in blood. This video was taken just after Claude's death. Jake wants to climb into his phone, press his hands to the knife wound, scream for help. His thoughts flash back to the moment his fist collided with Claude's face – the feel of flesh pressing against his knuckles. He didn't mean for any of this to happen.

This second recording of Claude dead on the rug is the final nail in a coffin already buried. If there was even the smallest chance they could've explained away the first recording of them carrying the rug out of the house at night, then it's gone now. This is Claude dead in the farmhouse. If the police see these recordings side by side, it's over.

The world pulls slowly back into focus. He's aware of Hannah's shuddering breath beside him. The tears pooling in her eyes. The pounding of his pulse in his temples. He's aware that he has to do something. Anything.

Without thinking, he taps the number at the top of the message, connecting to a call. He taps the loudspeaker so a ringing fills the kitchen. One, two, three. Then it stops. His phone screen turns blank. The call was rejected.

A split second later, another message appears. *There's more to come!*

More? Jake fights the urge to double over. How can there be more? How can it be worse than this?

There's no time to think before another message arrives. Then another and another.

If you try to call again, the videos will be sent to the police.

If you try to run, the videos will be sent to the police.

If you go to the police, these videos will be sent to them.

And a final message that chills him to his core.

I'll be watching.

Silent tears stream down Hannah's face. 'Why is this happening to us? Who is doing this?'

He stands on weak legs and pulls her into his arms, the gesture automatic. He doesn't reply, doesn't have the answers. He isn't even sure he has it in him to comfort anyone.

When Hannah speaks, her voice trembles as much as her body in his arms. 'What are we going to do?'

Run! The word echoes in his head. Just like it did six years ago in Westlake. But it was just him then. Neve had destroyed the refurbished tech business he'd been just getting off the ground. Calling his clients and telling them all kinds of things about him. He had enough money in his account for a plane ticket and a little set-up money and nothing holding him in Westlake. Running hadn't just been the right thing to do. It had been easy.

But now he has Hannah and the life they share. Hannah has her career and a family and her friends. And his software business is so close to taking off. If the meetings with Novexia International go well this week, it could change everything. Novexia don't just want to license his financial reporting software to use for their systems; they want to buy his company and roll out the software globally. If he can pull this off, he'll finally be able to give Hannah the lifestyle she deserves. She could give up corporate law if she wanted. Although he knows despite the stress, she loves her job and he'd never want her to give up something she loves.

He hasn't told Hannah about the Novexia offer yet. At first, he couldn't believe it was really happening. Then he realised it would be the perfect wedding gift. The best surprise for their wedding night. He can't wait to see her reaction when she learns he's a millionaire.

After messing up school, dropping out of college; after a lifetime of failures and setbacks, he can't let this chance slip through his fingers. Bile scorches the back of his throat. Jake steps back, needing space and air and a moment. He has to think. Has to find their next move.

'Could you contact Neve?' Hannah asks.

His eyes shoot to her face. Hannah doesn't know about the pleading messages he'd sent Neve in France, begging her to leave him alone. He hates keeping things from her, but now doesn't feel like the time to mention it. What good would it do? 'I could, but I'm worried it would make everything worse. You don't know what she's like, Han. She can't be reasoned with.'

They fall silent for a moment.

'What about your dad?' he asks.

'What about him?' She hugs her arms to her chest as confusion draws on her face.

'Your family are pretty well off, right?' He thinks of the farmhouse and the estate in Bath where Hannah grew up.

She shrugs. 'I guess.'

'And your dad's a judge. Could he have connections? Could he help?'

Hannah shakes her head. 'No. He's not... they're not... I don't really know what you're asking, but my parents don't have the chief of police on speed dial or anything. If I thought they could help us, I'd have called them in France. And Claude was Dad's best friend. If he ever finds out what I did...' The rest of her words are lost to a choking sob. 'My family can't help, Jake.

They can't buy us out of this trouble, if that's what you're thinking. And even if they could, I'm not sure they would.'

Jake closes his eyes, biting back the desire to push Hannah further. Surely her parents would do anything to help their daughter? But then would his parents help him if he called? He knows the answer. Whatever they do next, they're alone in this.

'If we went to the police—' Hannah starts.

'No,' Jake is quick to reply.

'Hear me out,' she says. 'If we showed them the video from tonight. Just that one. If we said I had a stalker and gave them the phone number, they could find out who's behind it and stop them.'

He shakes his head. 'And then Neve or whoever is behind this would send the other videos to that French police officer, Allard. We're implicated in Claude's murder, Han. We can't go to the police. The messages made that clear.'

She nods as silent tears roll in two lines down her face. It hurts to see her like this, but his mind is racing, moving him towards a plan. 'But...' He stops; runs a hand through his hair. Thinks. Swallows. 'But finding out who the number belongs to is a good idea.'

'How can we do that?'

'We could hire a private detective.'

'What?' A frown creases Hannah's face. 'This isn't a Hollywood movie.'

'I know, but these people exist. Private investigators are used for all kinds of jobs. Businesses use them all the time for opposition research and digging up dirt on competitors. We could do exactly what you just suggested but with a private investigator. We'll tell them you're being stalked and ask them to find out all they can about the number. Investigators have access to databases we don't, and all sorts of ways of getting information. And they wouldn't approach the person like the police would.'

'Then what?' Hannah asks. 'Let's say we find out who is behind it? Then what do we do?'

'One step at a time,' he says because he doesn't have an answer. 'Finding out if it's Neve means at least we know who we're dealing with. It could give us leverage.'

Hannah opens her mouth to reply but stops. Her face turns deathly pale.

'What is it?' he asks.

'It's just hit me,' she whispers, heaving in a shuddering breath.

'What has?'

She swallows like she's trying to pull herself together. 'This whole time I've been so consumed with the police finding out and the recording last night, worrying about what this person will do with it. But I've missed the obvious thing. We hid Claude's body to protect ourselves.'

'I know,' Jake replies. 'It was our only option.'

'No.' She shakes her head. 'You don't get it. Someone murdered Claude. We've covered it up for them. And now that someone is still out there. They know who we are. They know where we live. They're watching our every move. This isn't just about threatening us with sending that recording to the police. We've helped a murderer go free and now they have their sights on us. What if we're next?'

Hannah's words steal the air from his lungs. For a moment, he's winded. Unable to draw in breath. He opens his mouth to reply, but what can he say that could make this better?

What if we're next?

EIGHTEEN

JAKE

Hannah's words hang in the air, like smoke he could choke on. The walls of the apartment seem to press closer until he feels like he's locked in the prison cell he was so desperate to avoid in France. For the first time he wonders if they did have a choice that day in the farmhouse. If they could've called the police and tried to explain rather than hide Claude's body and clean up all that blood. Would they be in any less trouble than they're in now?

Goosebumps race across his skin. He has a flash again of that moment in the village square where his anger took hold and his fist shot out, punching Claude's face. He pushes the feelings aside. Whatever this is, they're still here. He has to keep looking forward for both of them. Jake draws in a deep breath, makes sure his voice will sound steady and finds the reassurance and love Hannah needs from him. But before he has a chance to voice them, her ringtone shatters the silence. His thoughts leap to the person sending the recordings, but with a trembling hand, Hannah shows him the screen and the name of the caller. *Julia.*

Hannah swears under her breath at her mother's name

lighting up her phone. When she looks at Jake, her eyes are still filled with terror. 'She called earlier and I didn't answer. I should take it. It might be about the police investigation into Claude's disappearance.'

She wipes her eyes, pulls back her shoulders and swipes accept as she steps into the living room with a, 'Hi, Julia.'

Jake stays in the small kitchen. He stares at the half-eaten dinner on their plates and the pans stacked by the sink. He should clear up, but his heart is still racing, thoughts scattered from the messages on his phone and those recordings and who sent them.

I'll be watching!

His gaze flicks to Hannah pacing back and forth by the sofa. He can't let his panic take over. He reaches for Hannah's wine glass and takes a long gulp. It's lost its chill and tastes acidic and unpleasant. He takes another gulp anyway, hoping to calm his racing pulse as he listens to one side of Hannah's call.

Julia doesn't call often, but when she does, it's always at inconvenient times. Like the week before last when they were trying to decide on a honeymoon location. They've decided on Bali in August or September. Hannah wants to wait for her promotion at the end of the summer before taking a long break. They'll book it soon. If this deal with Novexia to buy his company goes through, he can surprise her with first-class seats and the best money can buy.

Hannah makes a noise of agreement on the call. Then silence. Then, 'We saw him in the village on our first morning and he was fine.'

Jake's thoughts cut dead. He holds his breath and listens. They're talking about Claude.

'It's so sad. I hope he's OK,' Hannah says, and Jake realises how much harder this must be for Hannah. To him, Claude was an angry man who provoked him once and now he's dead. To

Hannah, he's a close family friend who was like an uncle to her. He remembers the delight on her face when she rushed across the cobblestones to greet him.

Then he thinks of Hannah's parents. They don't want her to marry him. Claude's words ring in his head. *'This American boy...'* According to Hannah, he's the wrong type. Not born into the right family. There's nothing he can do to fix that, but he's certain that if they just agreed to meet him, he could charm them. He could make them see that Hannah is his whole world. He wants to spend the rest of his life making her happy. Surely that counts for something?

He wishes he knew more about them. They're a private family. When he'd googled them once, he found a photo of them arm in arm at a black-tie charity ball hosted by Kate Moss. The shot made it to the back pages of a gossip magazine. He remembers thinking how much Hannah looks like her mother. The same light-brown hair and petite features.

Hannah's mentions of her mother are rare, usually dropped into conversation as a passing reference.

'Julia isn't the kind of mother who hugs.'

'I've never had a picnic on the grass before. Julia always told us they were common.'

'Julia and Marcus have gone abroad to visit William.' The last was said a few months ago when they'd cancelled another lunch, preferring to fly to Dubai to see their son than have lunch with their daughter and the man she's planning to marry.

Jake takes another sip of the lukewarm wine. He can feel the first trickle of the alcohol work its way into his system. He doesn't want to eavesdrop, but it's hard in the small apartment not to listen. And Hannah is only in the living room.

He hears her sigh. 'We've been through this before—'

Whatever Julia cuts in with, it causes Hannah to drop her head and press her palm to her forehead. A moment later, she continues. 'I'm not a little kid anymore. I'm a lawyer. I have a career. I will never be the woman you want me to be. Why can't you just be happy for me?'

The next pause is longer. He watches the frustration on Hannah's face seep away, replaced with a tight frown and then sadness. Her cheeks glisten with tears. 'What are you saying?'

Jake fights the urge to step across the apartment, snatch the phone from Hannah's hands and talk to her mother himself. Hannah is fiercely independent and strong. He doesn't want to be the kind of man who tries to take that away from her, so he stays where he is and listens.

'Don't say that,' Hannah replies, her tone pleading. 'You don't mean that.'

Another pause.

'Of course I care about you. You're my parents, but I'm marrying Jake in eleven days whether you're there or not. I love you, but this is my life. You have to accept it.'

The floor feels uneven beneath Jake's feet. The disappointment is acute. Her parents are threatening not to attend the wedding. His chest aches for Hannah.

'Yes I do,' she hisses. 'Because I love him and he loves me. I've never met anyone who makes me feel the way he does. If you'd just meet him, you'd—' The silence this time is short. 'There's more to life than money.'

Tears continue to stream down Hannah's face, but her voice is fierce. 'Fine.'

She hangs up and buries her face in her hands as she drops to the sofa. Jake closes the gap between them in urgent strides and sits beside her, his arms pulling her close.

'They're not coming to the wedding,' she says eventually, voice muffled from where she's buried it in his chest. 'Not just my parents but my entire family. My aunts and uncles. Close family friends. People I've know my whole life. None of them are coming either.'

'Why?' he asks when what he's really thinking is, *How can they do this?*

She draws back and wipes her face. 'It's all the same crap. How we've rushed into this relationship and the wedding.'

'I'm so sorry, Han,' he says, kissing her hair. 'Tell me what to do. How can I prove to them my intentions are honourable?'

She gives a furious shake of her head. 'There's nothing. In their eyes, you're not right for me because you don't come from the same social circles they think are important. Nothing will change that. I... I just can't believe I'm even upset about this with everything else going on.' Anguish pulls at her features.

It hurts to watch her pain. Hurts more what he knows he has to say. 'Han—' He takes her hand, rubbing a finger over the diamond that cost nearly everything he had and still didn't feel like enough for this perfect woman. 'I love you.'

'I love you too,' she replies.

'I meant what I said in France,' he continues before he can change his mind. 'I'm happy to postpone the wedding. It has been a whirlwind, and I don't want you to fall out with your family over me.'

'Thank you,' she whispers.

He waits for her to continue, and when he can't stand it anymore, can't draw in one more breath, he asks, 'What are you thinking?'

Fresh tears build in her eyes. 'I'm not sure. I can't think straight. I was followed tonight, Jake. Someone could be outside our apartment right now. A murderer who killed Claude. I just can't think about the wedding. I'm sorry.'

Jake nods slowly, his heart sinking. He hoped she'd say she still wanted to marry him no matter what her family thought or what was going on around them. But he understands.

Her eyes are two deep wells of blue as she looks at him. An ocean he feels he could lose himself in. 'Julia said something else just now. About France.'

His body tenses. 'What?'

'Marie called my mother and told her Claude is missing. The police are retracing his movements the afternoon he went missing. They're looking for any sign he reached the farmhouse, and my parents have given the police access to look inside the house.'

It's a fight to keep his expression calm. He can feel Hannah trembling beside him. He can't let her see his own fears. He has to protect her.

'Don't worry. We were careful. There's nothing to find.' He desperately hopes it's true.

'What are we going to do?' Hannah's question comes in a strangled choke.

Jake doesn't know if she's asking about the recordings and the threat. Or their wedding. Or this new thing – the police searching the farmhouse. He pushes away the panic threatening to swallow him whole.

'One step at a time,' he says again with more calm than he feels. 'We can't do anything about the police investigation in France. All we can do is focus on trying to get one step ahead of whoever is behind these recordings. We think it's Neve, right?'

Hannah nods.

'But we don't know for sure. Let's hire a private investigator like I said. And see what we can find out.'

They stay on the sofa for a long time, going around in circles. Raking over and over the questions they can't answer. Who is doing this? What do they want? And why? The messages on his phone spin in his head, but eventually Hannah agrees to his plan. Tomorrow he'll find a private investigator who can trace the phone number. He wonders if it really will lead back to Neve. The thought makes him feel sick. Hannah's suggestion earlier of contacting Neve weighs heavy. She has no idea how many ways Neve could destroy their lives. If she's behind this... He cuts the thought dead. He can't keep asking himself these questions.

They have a plan. A step they can take. He has to focus on that. The thought is almost enough to stop the dread pooling in his stomach and the knowledge that whatever comes next, this person isn't going to stop. No amount of wishful thinking or looking to the future is going to help them now.

10 DAYS UNTIL THE WEDDING

NINETEEN

HANNAH

I stretch my arm out to the nightstand, my hand feeling for my phone to turn off my alarm. It's another ten minutes before it's set to go off, but I'm awake. Haven't slept. The thought of another day in the office pretending everything is normal after what happened last night fills me with a dark, heavy dread.

My head sinks back into the pillow, and I watch the pearl-white light creep in from the drapes, eyelids heavy with exhaustion, my mind still racing. Every time I started drifting towards sleep, the moment from the cut-through shook me awake and I'd hear those footsteps moving in time with my racing heart.

Jake thinks hiring a private investigator will help. He's fixed on the idea like it's a lifebelt in a stormy sea. To him, it's the next move of the chess piece. To me, it's crazy. Unreal. Private investigators are things for movies and books. This is real life. I don't think anyone can help us right now. But I understand the need to do something. To take back some control.

Isn't that why I told Jake I needed the getaway to France in the first place? To do something to ease the feelings of anger and fear I'd felt finding Neve in my apartment, my things everywhere. Everything touched and rifled through. Nothing taken.

My heart lurches at the memory, and I shut it down. I can't keep raking over these fears.

Beside me in the bed, Jake is still. His breathing even but not deep. I wonder if he's awake too and find myself not wanting to look yet. All night, my thoughts have zigzagged from the terror of eyes watching from the shadows to seeing Julia's name flash on my phone and answering that call. Ten days until our wedding and my family won't be there.

Hurt stretches through me, a physical ache in my chest. I try to imagine stepping into the cool interior of the church, the beautiful silk of my dress hugging my body just right. My smile wide. The pews filled with our guests. Our friends. A small group of Fantasy Football mates Jake met in Manchester. None of them were able to make the engagement drinks we held in The Wilmington one Sunday afternoon in March, but they're coming with their partners to the wedding. Ten of them in total. Then our Thursday quiz friends who know Jake as well as they know me now.

No clients of Jake's. No family either. They've said it's too far to travel. He rarely talks to his parents or sister. Rarely talks of them either. He seems more upset about my parents not attending than his.

Lying in bed beside Jake, it feels like it's the two of us against the world, and right now the world is kicking our asses, as Jake would say.

The images of the church feel dreamlike and unreal. But then I try to imagine not marrying Jake next week. Carrying on as we are. This apartment. Our lives. It feels just as impossible. Whatever else happens, Jake is my shot at happiness. I won't lose sight of that.

For the last few hours, as night rolled slowly towards morning, I've formed and practised, rewritten and repeated in my head the words I need to say to Jake. The realisation of it is thorns prickling and catching my insides.

I turn my head on the pillow and finally I look at him. His beard is still long from the weekend, accentuating his strong jaw and handsome face. There is something about him, even now, even all these months in, that makes me ache when we're near.

He's lying on his back, eyes open, staring at the ceiling, but as my pillow rustles, he shuffles his body to the side so we're facing each other. How many times since we met last June have we lay like this, whispering about our future? Hundreds it feels like. Making plans and sharing our dreams. How we'll move to Devon one day, to an old farm we'll do up. We'll have three children. Two boys and a girl, and they'll go to the local village school and help feed the chickens at the weekend. A whole future mapped out. A wholesome, perfect life I ache for just as much.

He reaches for me, a warm hand taking mine beneath the cover.

'Hey,' he says in his morning voice – husky and not yet bouncing with the energy that sweeps through him once he's counted to five, taken his deep breath and climbed out of bed. 'Are you OK?'

I nod, even though it isn't true. 'I didn't sleep.'

'Me neither,' he replies. I notice the deep lines of his frown and the sadness in his eyes.

My bottom lip quivers. Tears build. It all feels too much.

'Han,' Jake says. 'Please don't be upset. I know what you're going to ask me. And it's fine. We can postpone the wedding or call it off completely. Whatever you want. I understand. I just want to be with you.'

His soothing causes a knotty lump to form in my throat. 'It's not...' I pause. Swallow. Try to get hold of my emotions. 'It's not that I want to postpone or cancel our wedding. I love you, Jake. I want to be your wife.'

I watch my words sink in and a tension lift.

'I feel the same,' he says. 'But I feel like there's a "but" coming.'

I nod. 'But when I think about getting married in front of our friends but not my parents or family, it feels wrong.' My voice cracks, but I push on. 'They made it abundantly clear last night they won't come and they won't even meet you beforehand.'

'So what are you saying?'

'What if we scaled back the wedding? We have the church and I have the dress and you've got your suit. I've been lying here all night thinking about wanting to be your wife. That's what matters to me. So what if we got married just the two of us? Then we don't have to worry about anyone else.'

Jake frowns. 'What about your parents? Won't they disown you? Or disinherit you if you defy them?'

I make a face. 'Right now, I don't care if they do. But I know them. They're digging their heels in. Once we're married, they'll come around. It was the same when I wanted to study law. They said they wouldn't come to my graduation or help with the university costs. But once the decision was made and I was studying, they accepted it. And they told William he couldn't move to Dubai. Now they fly out there more than they come to London.

'It's like they need it to happen to accept it. I know they'll fall in love with you the moment they meet you. We could still have a big party with cake and friends and family, but maybe later in the summer once... everything has settled down.'

Everything – an all-encompassing word. The other reason why scaling the wedding back feels like a good idea. I draw in a shaky breath and wait for Jake's reply.

He runs a hand through his hair. It's messy from sleep, sticking up where his fingers have ruffled it. Another time I'd have laughed and teased and pushed it back into place, but I stay quiet, giving him his time. I'm changing plans at the last minute and I don't want to throw him again. Or force him. The last time I did that, it was to push Jake into a weekend away to France, and look where that got us.

I want him to want this. To see it's for the best.

'You know, all I want is to be your husband,' he says at last. He reaches for me, brushing a strand of my hair away from my face. 'I don't care how or where or when it happens.'

I sigh, relief a blustery autumn wind.

'But,' he continues, 'I also don't want you to have any regrets. I would hate for us to do what you're suggesting and then a year down the line, twenty years down the line, you wish we'd waited or done things differently.'

I shake my head and feel the first smile touch my lips. Of course Jake would say these exact words. 'I actually think it'll be romantic just the two of us.'

I can see him recalibrating as he nods 'Same day. Same church. Just us,' he says. 'OK. Let's do it.'

'Really?' I ask.

He squeezes my hand. 'Yes. You're right. This is better. Until we know who is behind the recordings and messages and what they want from us and why, it would be better to keep a low profile. It would be easy to hide in a church full of people.'

My breath catches in my lungs. 'You think Neve would come to our wedding?'

His Adam's apple bobs as he swallows. 'I think this way – a small wedding – just us, we'll be able to control it.'

We lie in silence for a long moment. His words pound into me. The thought of Neve turning up uninvited on our wedding day sends icy fear trailing across my skin. *'Until we know who is behind the recordings and messages and what they want from us and why...'* Jake's words spin in my thoughts.

A second later, he shuffles across the gap between us, scooping me into his arms. I sink into his touch as his hands roam my body. The distraction is a comfort blanket over my worries and I give way to it, needing this time where all I think about is Jake and our bodies entwined. Soon I'll have to leave the apartment and head to the office, and there will be no escaping the fears of what's lurking in the shadows and the icy claws to the question Jake didn't ask just now. The one I'm trying not to think about. It's not just who is doing this or why. It's what they'll do next.

7 DAYS UNTIL THE WEDDING

TWENTY

HANNAH

It's Saturday – a week exactly until our wedding – when Neve steps out of the shadows of the narrow cut-through and into my path.

Terror grips me. I try to yell. But the sound dies in my throat. And it wouldn't matter anyway, I realise, eyes darting around me, taking in the empty courtyard. The sun has already dipped below the building. I'm completely alone in the dusky evening light.

I'm rooted to the spot. My legs, already tired from the run I've just finished, are jelly, refusing to move. Thoughts bombard my mind, charging then crashing against each other as my stomach knots.

This is the woman I found in my apartment, standing among the mess of my rifled-through life. This is the woman who Jake thinks he saw in France. His ex who became so obsessed with and possessive of him during their relationship that it nearly destroyed his life. A woman he travelled halfway around the world to escape from. And now she's back. Now she's here, standing before me with a knowing smile.

Where the hell is Jake?

My chest heaves with the gasp of my breath. I can feel my heart pounding against my ribcage, so hard it feels like something will break inside me.

But this is what we wanted, wasn't it? This was Jake's plan yesterday when he'd met me from work to walk me home like he's done every night since that shadowy figure in the cut-through.

'We need to do something, Han,' he said, taking my hand and throwing a glance over his shoulder.

'We are,' I replied. 'We're waiting for the private investigator you found to get back to us with information on the number sending us those messages.' I shivered, remembering the flurry of threats that landed on Jake's phone this week from that same number.

The French police are appealing for information on your dead friend. Shall I call them and tell them what you did?

Have you figured out what I want yet?

Ready for more?

And last night's.

Do you think walking your pretty fiancée home every night means I can't get to her?

'It's taking too long,' Jake said. 'The threats are getting worse. We can't sit around and wait to see what they'll do next. I've been thinking about it all day, and I think we should set a trap to draw them out. We know they're still watching after last night's message—'

I shook my head, finding my own gaze searching the

commuters and busy streets of Farringdon, trying to sense if I felt eyes watching me. 'What kind of trap?'

'What if we make them think you're alone? You could go for a run tomorrow.' His words came fast, like it was all mapped out in his head. 'Then they might try something again, but I'll actually be there and we can see who's behind this.'

'You want to use me as bait?' I cried.

'It wouldn't be like that. I'll be following you. I'll stay a minute behind you at all times. We'll plan out the route before you go. I won't let anything happen to you, Han. I swear it.'

Jake kept talking. Explaining every last detail. All the ways he'd make sure I'm safe, and finally I agreed. He was right. We had to do something. And so at 4 p.m. we pulled on our running kits and Jake kissed me goodbye; promised me one more time he'd be there to protect me.

I ran slowly at first. Allowing my muscles a few minutes to warm up. Then faster as the adrenaline of what we were doing spurred me on. The late afternoon sun was warm on my skin as I cut through the city and down to the Strand and across Waterloo Bridge to the South Bank, weaving around tourists and buskers. Taking in the music of the carousel and the feeling of life carrying on. One mile then two then three. Crossing back to the north of the city at Tower Bridge and coming back on myself, just like we'd planned.

And now stupidly I'm alone with his crazy, off-the-rails ex in this dusky evening, and I realise how foolish the plan was. Like poking a hornets' nest and waiting to see what happens instead of running as far and as fast as our legs will carry us.

'Hello, Hannah,' Neve says with all the ease of greeting a neighbour or a colleague. Her Ohio accent is stronger than Jake's. His has softened in the years he's lived in England. Only when he's tired or stressed or horny does the accent strengthen.

My reply is automatic. Thirty years of politeness drummed into me, outweighing the cold fear flooding my body. 'Hi.' I bite off the word and carry on walking into the open of the courtyard. Goosebumps rage across my skin as Neve follows. Maybe it's the sweat cooling as I catch my breath and the sun dipping below the roof of the apartment building, casting the courtyard in shadow. Or maybe it's Neve herself making me shiver.

My eyes dart around the courtyard and I wonder again where Jake is. He said he'd never be more than a minute behind me, but that minute has come and gone. He should be here by now.

My gaze moves back to Neve. Even though I've seen her once before, standing confident and righteous in the middle of my apartment, she's still a surprise. She's taller than me – nearly Jake's height. Intimidating and knowing it.

She has ice-blonde hair cut into a sleek bob that sits above her shoulders, shaping the sharp features of her face. Intense dark eyes, accentuated with thick eyeliner. A small nose ending in a point and lips painted bright red. She's wearing black ripped jeans and a faded black Meatloaf T-shirt.

In the heart-stopping moments I found her standing in my apartment, I hadn't appreciated how striking she is. It's not a classic beauty, but there is something about her I'm sure draws a second glance.

I look around the empty courtyard. Lights have switched on in the windows of the apartments rising up around us. I can hear distant laughter. A few windows are open. If I screamed, would anyone come?

My gaze returns to Neve. There's a wild detachment in her eyes that sends a bolt of ice through my body. A feeling worms in the pit of my stomach. A sense this woman will be my undoing. A feeling that she has the power to destroy us.

'What do you want?' I ask her. I mean the question to sound fierce, but a tremor betrays my fear.

Neve smiles, flashing perfect white teeth. 'To talk to you.'

I hesitate, unsure if I should engage with this woman who

has already caused so much chaos in my life. But my curiosity gets the better of me. 'Talk about what?'

Neve looks at me with those penetrating eyes. 'Can we go somewhere? Grab a drink?'

Again, it's as though we're friends. It's unsettling.

I shake my head. 'No, we can't. If you've got something to say, say it now. Otherwise leave me alone.'

She makes a face, brows rising, lips pinching. It's a look that says she thinks I'm the crazy one.

'You broke into my apartment,' I say through clenched teeth. 'We're not friends. I'm not going for a drink with you.'

'Like I told the police,' she says with a loud sigh, 'the door to your apartment was already open. I went in to check everything was OK and found it trashed. I was there, like, twenty seconds before you showed up and started screaming at me.'

I close my eyes. I don't even remember shouting at her that day. A heavy exhaustion presses down on the top of my head. It's been a week of scaling back our wedding plans, shrinking it down until all that's left is the church service and our vows. We saw the vicar this morning. He looked at us with pity in his eyes as we explained our changes, but he said he'd find two church volunteers to attend as witnesses.

Now, when I imagine Jake in his new grey suit, clean shaven, hair neatly styled, standing at the top of the aisle, the pews are no longer filled with my family and our friends, but empty. I imagine myself stepping into the church in my dress and the way his face will light up. It feels right.

We've lost money on the deposits for the hotel ballroom and the band and the DJ, but I don't care. Jake convinced me to keep the cake. 'We'll eat a layer and freeze the rest for the party,' he said.

Today, we contacted the last of the guests, crossing them from the same list we'd made as the RSVPs had arrived last month. For our wedding meal, we've booked a table for two at a

Chinese in Mayfair that serves the best hoisin duck I've ever tasted. It felt good to have everything organised for next week. To be in control.

It's why Jake suggested this plan. A way to take matters into our own hands and find out who's watching us while we wait for the private investigator he found to contact us. An ex-detective called Gary who Jake described as, 'A bit of an asshole but seems to know what he's talking about and promised to get back to me in a couple of days.'

'Let's say I believe you,' I say in a tone that makes it clear I don't. 'Why did you come to my apartment then?' I ask.

'Like I said – to talk to you,' she replies.

Her words throw me. I have a strange sense of the world shifting around me. It reminds me of the theatre. Standing on stage while the background moves to the next scene.

'There are things you don't know.'

TWENTY-ONE

HANNAH

'You came to see me?' Surprise rings in my voice. She's lying, I tell myself. She's obsessed with Jake. This is about them, not me.

'Of course. I want to help you.' Then Neve offers a small smile, and in that gesture something changes in the air or maybe inside me. She no longer seems the dangerous woman I thought she was when she was standing in my apartment. The monster I've painted her to be this week.

I'm still wearing my running kit, and I cross my arms for warmth as a cold breeze brushes my skin. The lampposts in the courtyard blink and then switch on, casting pools of yellow light around us, pushing back the shadows.

'Come on, Neve,' I say. 'You can't seriously expect me to believe you came all the way to England to talk to me?'

She laughs. A head back, loud cackle. 'Oh my God, you think highly of yourself, don't you? I'm in England because of my job. I work for Walmart corporate. Didn't Jake tell you? They own some of your stores. And while I'm here, I tracked down Jake, and when I saw he had a girlfriend, I thought I'd do a solid for the sisterhood and give you a heads up about what you were letting yourself in for.'

My heart continues to thump in my chest, knocking against my ribs. I don't want to ask the question that comes, but I have to. 'What do you mean?'

Neve moves closer, but I find I'm no longer shrinking away from her. 'Jake is lying to you.' The words come out in a rush as though she's been wanting to say them for the longest time. 'He—'

Before Neve can say more, the sound of footsteps pound on the pavement and Jake bursts through the cut-through and into the courtyard, closing the gap between us as fear contorts his features.

Relief floods my body at the sight of him.

'Hannah!' His breath comes in heaving gasps. A second later, he steps between me and Neve as though she's holding a weapon and he's trying to protect me.

'I told you to leave her alone,' he hisses at Neve. His hand grabs mine, holding it tight as he moves away from her, pulling me with him.

The smile drops from Neve's face like a mask, leaving a stony glare in its place. The shift in her is as unnerving as it is instant. A moment ago, she was acting like my friend, and now she looks ready to kill us both. I can't believe I allowed her to suck me into whatever story she was about to spin. Thank God Jake arrived when he did. I can't trust this woman, I remind myself.

'Hey, I'm just talking here,' Neve replies, voice laced with venom. 'I thought your little girlfriend needed to know a few things about you.'

When she looks at Jake, it isn't love or obsession I see; it's hate. I remember what Jake told me about Neve's behaviour in Westlake. How she'd told his clients lies about him and called his parents in the middle of the night. Whatever anger drove her to those actions six years ago hasn't gone away. My heart feels like it stutters as I wonder again what this woman is capable of.

Tension radiates from Jake. He throws a glance towards me. 'Don't listen to her, Hannah,' he hisses. 'Whatever she's told you, it isn't true.'

Neve rolls her eyes and gives me a pointed look. 'Of course he's going to say that. He doesn't want you to know the truth. Let me guess – he's told you I'm crazy, right?'

'Of course I have,' he fires back. 'Or have you forgotten what you did to me?' His voice cracks with desperation.

'What I did to you?' She laughs.

He takes another step towards the apartment building. I stay close to his side, but there's something I have to ask. It builds inside me and is out before I can think it through. 'Did you follow us to France? Was it you at the farmhouse? Are you sending us those messages? Because if you are—'

Another peal of laughter cuts my threat short.

'Not guilty,' she replies as though the questions are ludicrous. I can't tell if she's lying.

Frustration is nails scratching my insides. We set this trap to see who was behind the threats and now Neve is standing before us just as wild and crazy as Jake warned me she was. Why isn't he saying anything?

'Let's go inside, Han,' Jake whispers, snaking an arm around my waist, moving me along.

Another eyeroll from Neve. 'Yes, Han. Follow your boyfriend inside.'

Jake sighs, shaking his head. 'Neve, please leave us alone. I can't help you anymore. I'm marrying Hannah.'

I let him guide us towards the building.

'Do you trust him?' Neve calls after us.

I turn and her eyes are still blazing.

In the next moment, it seems as though a deafening silence hangs in the air. Strange and uncomfortable. Jake's step falters. I can feel his heart racing where his chest is pressed close to my body.

'Of course I do,' I reply. 'We're getting married.'

She purses her lips. 'Then you're a fool.'

'Don't listen to anything she says,' he whispers, yanking open the glass entrance doors. 'She's completely crazy.' He turns to face me.

'It's OK,' I say, squeezing his hand. 'I know.'

Relief floods Jake's face, but as we step inside, I can't stop myself looking back. Neve is still there, still that wildness in her eyes. For a moment there, before Jake arrived, I'd felt myself sucked in by her. Like maybe she really was there to talk to me. Like she had something to tell me about Jake. My cheeks heat with my own stupidity. And yet in the eerie glow from the streetlights, it isn't anger or hate I see in Neve's expression anymore. It's exasperation.

Just as the glass doors are closing behind us, Neve hurls a final damning remark at us. 'You have no idea who you're dealing with.'

Jake slams the door closed behind us, and we hit the stairs two at a time. I swear neither of us draw in breath until we're inside my apartment with the door locked.

TWENTY-TWO

JAKE

A desperate, urgent anger rages in Jake. It's a fight to control the heave of each breath and the desire to lash out at something – the wall, the door, himself. Not Hannah though. Never Hannah. He glances at her as he pulls out his key and opens the door to the apartment. Her hair windswept from her run. Her face pale with the shock of Neve's appearance. Heat rushes through him.

He'd convinced himself using Hannah to draw out the person behind this nightmare was the only option. He was so focused on making a plan, following it through, doing something – anything – that he lost sight of what's important. He put Hannah in danger today. If anything had happened to her, he'd never have forgiven himself.

And something could've happened. Claude was murdered, and whoever did it has their sights set on them. This isn't a game. They could be next to die. How could he have lost sight of that? His fists curl into two tight balls, nails digging into the palms of his hands as he grits his teeth. This is all his fault.

The moment they're in the apartment, he's flying around, closing the door, turning the lock and stepping towards

Hannah. He can't catch his breath, but he has to make sure she's unharmed.

'Are you OK?' The next question chases after the first before he can stop it. 'What did she say to you?'

'I'm fine.' Hannah sighs. 'She didn't really say anything. Only that she had something to tell me about you.'

'What was it?' he asks, voice loud above the sudden thudding of his pulse in his ears. He needs to calm down. They're safe. Neve can't get to Hannah or him right now.

Hannah crouches to the floor to untie her trainers. 'I don't know. You arrived before she could tell me.' She stands, her eyes locking with his. 'Any idea what she was going to say?' she asks. There's a suspicion in her gaze he doesn't like. Can't stand to see. Two minutes with Neve and Hannah's already questioning him.

Jake shakes his head. 'Nothing. There's nothing to tell, I swear. This is exactly what she does. She's manipulative, Hannah. She comes across as super friendly and cool, sucking you in, making you think she's your friend. Then she'll tell you I'm a terrible person. How I broke up with her and ruined her life. It's exactly what she did six years ago. She turned all my friends against me, ruined my business. Even my family were barely speaking to me at the end.'

Memories from his past flood his mind causing a cold dread to shoot down his spine. He squeezes his eyes shut, trying to block out the images, then forces them open again, shooting Hannah a pleading look. 'You can't trust anything that woman says. Neve is just trying to hurt us.'

There's a beat of time – a moment – when she looks at him, eyes searching his face as though waiting for more. Then it passes and Hannah is nodding as she hugs her arms to her body. 'At least we know it's Neve.'

He frowns, unsure what she means.

'The recordings, Jake. The messages. Claude murdered in

France,' she hisses, her voice dropping to a whisper. 'We set the trap and she showed up. She can say she's got nothing to do with this all she wants, but this proves she's behind it all, doesn't it?'

Her words hit him. He's been so wrapped up in wanting to get Hannah away from Neve, he hadn't put the two things together. A dread is squirming inside him, a wriggling snake-like thing. Despite everything that happened in Westlake, he hadn't really thought she was capable of this level of spite. Capable of murder.

'Will she send those recordings to the police?' Hannah asks.

How does he answer that? He kicks off his trainers and moves into the apartment, dropping onto the sofa. The anger is passing, but in its wake is a jittery, too-much-caffeine feeling.

He's barely slept since France. When he does sleep, the nightmares dig their claws in, leaving him just as exhausted as hours spent staring into the darkness. In every nightmare, he's back at the point when his anger blinds him and his fists clench and he's lashing out, fist pounding into the fleshy skin of a face.

It's the same nightmare he's had for years. Always waking to heavy breathing and his fists balled so tight his fingers ache. Only meeting Hannah put a stop to them. Something about her lifted his emotions, or maybe the physicality of sleeping beside her acted like a ward. He doesn't know how to make the nightmares stop again, but the wedding – their perfect day – he has to believe that's the answer.

'Jake?' Hannah pushes, moving to stand by the sofa, staring down at him.

'It feels like she's just toying with us right now. She hasn't asked for anything. I don't know what she'll do. I need time to think. Maybe there's a way we can get something on her...' His voice trails off, head spinning. 'I just... I'm scared, Hannah. I hate admitting that to you because I want to be the person you can turn to – to lean on – but Neve scares me. What she's capable of scares me.'

He closes his eyes again, and a moment later Hannah is beside him on the sofa, her hand slipping into his. 'I'm scared too.'

'I know,' he says. 'I'm sorry.'

'Where were you?'

He opens his eyes and finds Hannah is staring at him with a fear that cuts into his soul.

She bites her lip. 'You promised you'd be no more than a minute behind me, but I was in that courtyard with Neve for way longer than a minute.'

There's an accusation in her gaze again, and he finds his hand is tightening around hers, desperate to reassure her.

'Gary called me while I was running. I stopped to take it. I'm so sorry. I knew we were close to home and I wanted to know if he'd found anything.'

'What did he say?' Hannah asks.

His stomach sinks as he recalls the investigator's words. 'The number is from a pre-paid cell phone. There's no way to trace who owns it. Gary said if the number calls me, he can triangulate the location of the cell so we'd know where they are.'

Jake can still hear Gary's voice in his head and the irritating way the man clears his throat before every reply.

Frustration tightens across Hannah's jaw. She waves her hand towards the window and the sky now the colour of a deep bruise. 'We know where she is. She's outside our building right now.' She shakes her head. 'I get that we need to do something, Jake, but are we any better off now than we were before we found this private investigator?

'I was terrified in the courtyard when I saw Neve,' she continues. 'I thought your plan to use me running alone to draw out the person behind this was crazy, but now we know it's her. Neve was in France. You said yourself you saw her in the village. She must have followed us and was at the farmhouse when Claude came by. She would've seen what happened in the square and saw an opportunity to frame us for his murder. It all makes sense. Who else would do this to us? And if she's prepared to kill someone to hurt you, what else is she prepared to do? Are we next, Jake? Am I? Is she going to try to kill me?'

His reply when it comes is strangled. 'I don't know. Based on what she did last time, I don't think she'll stop until everything is burned to the ground. It seems pretty clear she wants to ruin our lives.' He swallows. 'I'm so sorry, Han. I've dragged you into this nightmare. You don't deserve any of this. I keep thinking about how I left Westlake. I really thought running away was my only option.'

'You can't blame yourself for Neve's actions,' she says. 'We all make mistakes. Especially when a relationship is ending. None of this is your fault. It sounds like she didn't give you much choice back then either.'

Jake nods. He thinks of Neve's piercing gaze, full of bitterness and accusation. If he'd arrived even a minute later… The thought causes a rush of panic clattering through his body. It's sickeningly familiar. His control over his life is slipping. It's Westlake all over again.

And Manchester all over again too…

He told Hannah he moved to London to be closer to the tech clients using his software. But it was more than that. Gary's words from the call earlier charge into his thoughts. *'This person threatening you – is it connected to the work I did in Manchester?'*

The question had stopped him dead. When he first suggested the idea of a private investigator to Hannah, he could tell she was horrified. And so he pretended to search for one, never telling her he had a contact he'd used before. Besides, he could hardly tell her he had a private investigator in his contacts without explaining why he'd needed one in the first place.

He'd been in Manchester four years when it all went wrong. His fresh start souring just like things had done in Westlake.

He'd needed the help of a private investigator and to start over once again. This time in London.

Gary's question had hit with the force of a bullet. He can't believe he hasn't asked that question himself. Hannah might be convinced Neve is behind this nightmare, but for the first time Jake wonders if his ex is the only part of his past he should be worrying about.

TWENTY-THREE
JAKE

Could what happened in Manchester be catching up with him? The question circles his thoughts – a tornado, a frenzy. When Hannah's cell lights up with a call from her parents, he takes the opportunity to grab a shower and five minutes alone.

By the time he emerges in a clean pair of shorts and a T-shirt, his head is still spinning, but Hannah has finished her call.

'Everything OK?' he asks.

She looks up from the sofa, startled. 'It's the same bullshit about them wanting me to cancel the wedding. I'm currently messaging with Mum now too,' she says with a sigh. 'I just can't think about this stuff with everything else going on.'

'Do you want a drink?' he asks, padding barefoot to the kitchen. She shakes her head as he grabs a beer from the fridge. He pops the top and takes a long slug. Then another. The cold beer eases the chaos in his mind. He drops onto the stool at the counter and tries to pull his thoughts into some kind of order.

Claude. France. Neve. The break-in. The threats. The recordings. And now another part of his past he doesn't want to think about is elbowing its way into his mind. When he'd escaped Westlake and fled to Manchester, he'd been a mess.

Neve had almost destroyed him. He was a shell of himself. Feeling utterly lost and doubting every decision. It took him months to find his confidence again and start attending the business networking events inside the impressive dome of Manchester Library.

Eventually, he found his feet in a new business venture, partnering with another tech guy who shared Jake's passion for developing software. The business Jake is about to sell to Novexia International allows its users to manipulate their business data and create reports that can show them highly specific weaknesses in their business. When used correctly, it has the potential to save companies millions.

Jake knew it could be big. So did his business partner, Tom. When Tom tried to steal the business from under him, Jake came so close to losing everything. It's the same desperate fear he feels now but so much worse. Before, it was just a business. And thanks to some dirt Gary found on Tom, Jake was able to keep his software and start again in London.

But now he has Hannah – the love of his life. It's their whole lives in the hands of someone hell-bent on destroying them, or worse – killing them. How much more is coming for them? How much worse is it going to get? Jake never told Hannah about what happened in Manchester. It wasn't his fault, but that doesn't mean he's not embarrassed. He made bad decisions and paid for it. He doesn't want Hannah to see that side of him. It was easier to explain the move as purely a business decision to be closer to the clients who use his software.

He's made mistakes in his past. There have been times he's let his temper get the better of him, but he's not that person anymore. And he's struggling to believe anyone would go so far as to kill an innocent man to frame them for murder. It's insane. He can't believe Tom or even Neve would do this.

He's been so swept up in the threats that he hasn't had a chance to draw breath and see the bigger picture. Even now, he can't keep hold of the thought that something about this isn't right. All he knows is that whatever happens next, he'll do anything to protect his future with Hannah.

Jake looks down at his beer bottle, surprised to find it already empty. The fuzz of the alcohol has done its job, and even though he knows he should be keeping a clear head, he finds himself reaching for a second, popping the lid and taking another long slug before he can talk himself out of it.

The moment his phone buzzes from the counter, he knows the alcohol was a mistake. Hannah leaps up from the sofa, eyes wide and uncertain. Fear darts through his veins, clearing his head.

'Is it a message? Is it Neve?' she asks.

'No. It's a call.' He shows the screen to Hannah, and she gasps.

'Plus three-three is a French number,' she says.

He frowns. 'Who in France would know...?' The answer comes before he finishes the question. His blood turns to ice. 'That police officer. Allard.' He remembers the moment he gave the officer his number in the kitchen. Why didn't he give him a fake?

Fuck!

'Are you going to answer?' Hannah whispers.

Jake stares at his phone screen, imagining the sound of ringing in Allard's ear. Fear is pummelling his body. There's no way he can answer and muster the easy confidence of a man who's done nothing wrong.

'Let's see if he leaves a message,' Jake says, surprised at the certainty in his voice. 'We don't want to be put on the spot if he's going to ask us a question.'

Hannah nods and they fall silent, waiting for the call to cut to Jake's voicemail. He can feel his pulse pounding through his body. He thinks of that grainy video of them with the rolled-up rug outside the farmhouse. And this call coming now on a

Saturday evening an hour after Neve tried to confront Hannah.

Has Allard been sent the recordings?

Jake's barely breathing by the time the call ends. They stand together, frozen, eyes locked on the screen. Somewhere outside there's the distant peal of a police siren. A reminder of everything at stake.

Cold sweat breaks out on his body. Another minute passes before the voicemail notification appears. He steals himself and presses play, tapping the loudspeaker. A second later, the strong, unmistakable French accent of the police officer fills his ear. 'Good afternoon. This is Stéphane Allard, French police. I have some questions for you relating to the disappearance of Monsieur Dubas. Please call me on this number as soon as possible.'

The voicemail ends, and in the silence that follows, Hannah makes a noise in her throat. A strangled, 'No!' as he fights the urge to double over.

'What questions could Allard have?' he says, words coming as fast as his racing heart. 'What could he have found?'

'The recordings,' Hannah says with the same panicked tone.

Jake's mind races. 'It won't be that. Think about it. It wouldn't be a polite phone call. It would be the police at our door. Sirens and handcuffs. Jail.'

But something has triggered this. Then Jake remembers – the call from Hannah's mother last week. Jake was so scared Hannah was going to cancel the wedding, he barely registered her comment. *'My parents have given the police access to look inside the house.'*

He remembers leaving the opulent French house on that Monday morning. Eyes scanning every flagstone, every crack, every nook and cranny. He was so certain they cleaned everything; destroyed everything. But that certainty feels thin and flimsy in his thoughts. What if they missed something?

What if they hid Claude's body, let a murderer go free and were sucked into this nightmare of threats and fear, only for the police to find something anyway and it all be over? A sharp lump of emotion lodges in his thoughts.

Hannah drops onto the stool beside him, and from the expression on her face, it's obvious she's having the same thoughts. The need to do something grips him again. He can't let his control slip any further. He unlocks his phone and opens up a message to Gary. The PI couldn't help with the cell number Jake gave him, but maybe there's more he can do.

'Are you calling Allard?' Hannah asks.

He shakes his head and taps send on a message. 'I don't think we should. Not yet anyway. I've just asked Gary to find out what he can about the police investigation into Claude's disappearance. If Allard has something, I want to know what it is before I speak to him.'

Her eyes are still wide with fear, but she nods slowly. 'How long will Gary take?'

'I don't know. A couple of days. I've told him it's urgent.'

Hannah sighs. 'I don't think I can take much more of this,' she says, and Jake draws her in his arms and kisses the top of her head.

'You smell clean,' she whispers. 'I need a shower.'

She's halfway across the living room when he calls to her. 'Han?'

She turns. 'Yeah.'

'We'll get through this.'

'How can you be so sure?' she asks.

'Because I love you, and I'll do anything to protect you and make this right.'

She nods. 'We can do it together. Right now though, I need a shower and then food.'

'Thai?' he asks.

'Are you only saying that because you know I'm supposed to cook tonight?' she asks, smiling for the first time.

He makes a silly face. 'It's just... food poisoning a week before our wedding probably isn't a good idea.'

She huffs a laugh. 'Hey, my cooking isn't that bad. But Thai sounds great. Don't forget—'

'Extra chilli in the noodles,' he says before she can. 'I know.'

The exchange feels so normal, it hurts to realise how far from themselves they've drifted this week.

She smiles again. 'Maybe we should stop using cooking dinner as our punishment for losing bets.'

'Well,' he says, shooting her a mischievous smile, enjoying the relief from thinking about the threats, enjoying the buzz of the alcohol in his body, 'if that's the case, then I have a confession to make.'

'What?' she asks.

'I don't know how to tell you this, but the thing is... I always win our bets.'

'No you don't,' Hannah protests.

He nods. 'I do, actually. I just pretend to lose because I feel bad for you, and let's be honest, when the prize is you cooking dinner, I'm better off hiding around the corner and playing the loser.'

Hannah laughs. 'I can't believe this. Are you seriously telling me that for our entire relationship, you've always won our bets?'

He pauses to think. 'There was one time at the store when I couldn't find the ground ginger and you only had to pick up lettuce.'

'What about the maze in Hampton Court Palace?' Hannah says. 'I definitely reached the middle first.'

He shakes his head. 'Nope. I was there at least ten minutes before you.'

'Unbelievable.' She laughs again. 'I'm going to take my loser ass for a shower then.'

She starts to back away but stops. Freezes. Her mouth opens like something else has just occurred to her, but then she shakes her head and disappears around the corner.

His own thoughts stop.

He thinks back to that Saturday afternoon and the hike. The realisation turns his stomach. He's just told Hannah that he always wins the bets. Will she make the connection to France? Will she realise that when she was walking up the driveway, he wasn't coming from the lane like she thought – like he told her? He was coming from the gardens of the farmhouse.

He was first back that day.

He meant what he said to Hannah just now. He'll do anything to protect their perfect life. He's already done so much to get here.

TWENTY-FOUR

HANNAH

In the bathroom I peel off my running vest and shorts. My skin prickles with cold, and my leg muscles ache where I didn't stretch after the run. I twist the temperature dial in the shower as far as it will go.

The voice message on Jake's phone is still swirling in my thoughts.

'This is Stéphane Allard, French police.'

He's asking Jake to call him. There are questions about what happened in France, and Jake thinks the private investigator can help. An unease spreads through me. Our wedding is a week away. It feels like nothing at all, and yet the closer we get, the further away it feels. I don't know what will happen between now and then, or if we'll even make it to next Saturday.

As I step under the hot spray of water, it's the altercation with Neve that comes racing back into my thoughts.

'Let me guess – he's told you I'm crazy, right?'

'Jake is lying to you.'

We set the trap. I was the bait. Whoever was watching us would think I was alone and might step out of the shadows. That was Jake's plan and it worked. I thought Jake would ask

Neve about France. I thought he'd demand to know why she's sending us these threats and what she wants from us, but when he raced into the courtyard and to my side, all I saw in him was fear. It makes sense. If someone nearly ruined my life, wouldn't I be desperate to get as far away from them as possible?

'*I want to help you.*' There was no malice in Neve's voice. She seemed sincere.

As he pulled me into the building, I told Jake I trusted him. I thought I did.

I do!

Except... I can't shake the feeling that I'm missing something. A niggling doubt crawls beneath my skin. Neve has planted a seed in my thoughts. A thorny weed.

What hasn't Jake told me? What don't I know about the man I share my life with, my body, my bed? Whatever it is, I have seven days to find out. The thought leaves me feeling unanchored. Drifting. Unsure what to believe.

I'm exhausted and raw as I finish in the shower and scoop my wet hair into a bun. I find myself reaching for my mascara and tinted moisturiser as though needing some armour. Jake has seen me without make-up many times and always says he prefers my face without it, but I feel more myself with a dab or a flick of something, like I'm less vulnerable.

I pull on a pair of denim shorts and a black T-shirt and walk through the apartment to find Jake in the kitchen. He's slouched against the counter with a half-drunk bottle of beer in one hand and his phone in the other.

He lifts his head and uncertainty dances in his eyes. Maybe he's waiting for tears and outrage. His plan today put me in danger and we both know it. Maybe he's expecting me to demand to know more about Neve. I'm too exhausted and broken to do either. When I take in the mess of Jake's brown hair where he's raked his hands through it, and the circles under his eyes, I realise how stressed he is. How tired and beaten down he looks. It's usually Jake focusing on the future, but right now it's what I want too.

I offer a half-smile – an olive branch – because the air around us is charged as though we've fought, but we didn't. Not really.

'Hey,' I say.

The relief in Jake is instant. His shoulders sag as though he was holding his breath, waiting to see how I'd react, and finally he can exhale.

'Hey yourself,' he replies, tilting the beer towards me. 'The Thai's here. I put it in the oven while you were in the shower.'

'You should've shouted. I didn't mean to take so long.'

He offers a small smile. 'And disrupt your shower? Never. I know how much you like long showers.'

Jake places the take-out containers on the counter and we eat side by side. We keep things light over dinner, talking about the latest message on the Quiz WhatsApp group from Tabitha announcing her pregnancy by posting a photo of the scan and the caption: *New quiz member coming this Christmas!*

I tell Jake a story about Tabitha at our halls in Cambridge and the time she was so late home, she missed the curfew and ended up shimmying up a drainpipe to her bedroom, only to find the window locked. She was stuck for an hour while someone called the fire brigade. It makes us both laugh.

After dinner, I let Jake scoop me into his arms and carry me to the bedroom. We tug off each other's clothes, and Jake lays me down and covers me with kisses until we both can't stand it anymore and it turns into more.

Only afterwards, Jake snoring softly from the beer he's drunk, do the niggling doubts return. But this time I don't think it's about what Neve said to me. I retrace the evening and think about Jake's playful confession about our bets. It's cute really that he wanted me to win sometimes, and I really do hate cooking.

And that's when I realise. My thoughts leap back to the farmhouse in France and suddenly my eyes fly open. I gasp then fall silent, holding my breath until I hear Jake's next sleeping exhale.

We made a bet on our hike from the lake. 'Fastest one back?' I said.

Then Jake's delighted surprise. 'You seriously think you can beat me?'

I had no intention of racing that day. The truth is, I'd needed to collect my thoughts and process the fight in the square, but Jake had been so worried about my reaction to his flaring temper, I couldn't tell him that. I remember being surprised I'd won. Jake's path to the road was more direct than my wanderings through the vineyards, and I'd been in no rush.

I recall the moment Jake jogged up behind me in the driveway. I heard him coming and I turned, and even though I hadn't registered it at the time, I'm almost certain that he came into the driveway from the wrong direction, as though he'd been looping back on himself from the garden, skirting the edge of the property behind the bushes to reach the road again.

'*I always win... hiding around the corner and playing the loser.*'

Always?

Every time?

The thoughts land with sickening clarity. Jake reached the farmhouse before me. How long did he wait for? I think again of my slow, rambling pace. Ten minutes? Fifteen? Twenty? What was he doing in that time?

I've never thought about how long the body had been lying on the rug when we stepped into that hallway. But I remember wiping away those shoe prints with the fluffy white pool towels and how the blood moved across the flagstones, not yet dry despite the heat of the day. If Jake was there earlier, did he see something? Did he do something? I shut down the dark rabbit hole my mind is trying to drag me into, but it's too late.

Neve's warning returns. *'You have no idea who you're dealing with.'* I thought she was talking about herself. Warning us of what was to come. But if Neve was really there to tell me something about Jake, then maybe that comment wasn't about her. Maybe it was about him.

Since the break-in, the panic and terror has been a constant thing. But it's always been for Neve. For something unknown. For shadows and threats and what's coming for us. A sensation is already tiptoeing through my body, as quiet as a mouse. Turn and you'll miss it. For the first time, I wonder if the real danger is sleeping beside me. Am I safe with Jake?

5 DAYS UNTIL THE WEDDING

TWENTY-FIVE

HANNAH

I'm yanked from an uneasy sleep by a noise. An electronic chime. In the fog of exhaustion, it takes me a moment to realise it's the doorbell. It comes again, jarring in the stillness of the night. Instantly, the fear is a hand around my throat.

Jake's voice is urgent. Alert. 'Hannah?'

'I heard it,' I whisper as the silence now rings in my ears. I blink in the darkness until my vision clears and I see the time on the small bedside clock – 3 a.m. I can't have slept for more than an hour. Another two and I'll be dragging myself out of bed and getting ready for another week at the office.

Jake snatches his phone from the bedside table and taps the screen.

'The police?' I say, unsure if it's a statement or a question.

In the glow from Jake's phone, his face is drawn, terror etched into his features. 'Could be Allard,' he whispers back, and I'm certain we're both thinking of the call Jake didn't answer on Saturday night or the second one that came yesterday. That clipped tone urging him to return the call.

Jake opens the doorbell app and taps the image recorded by the camera. It's not the police but a shadowy figure dressed head to toe in black. Two seconds of footage. A rush of blurred movement and then all goes black.

'They've covered the camera,' Jake hisses.

His words twist in my stomach like a knife. 'Is it Neve?'

'I can't see,' Jake says, replaying the video and peering at the screen.

I find my eyes shifting from Jake's phone to his face, searching his expression. I don't know what for. A sign he's lying to me? I bite the inside of my mouth as frustration hits. I can't shake Neve's warning. That feeling he's keeping something from me.

Jake slides out of bed and pulls on the clothes he was wearing yesterday.

'What are you doing?' I ask.

'Going to check,' he replies like it's a delivery man and not a murderer standing on our doorstep.

'Are they still out there?' I ask. They? Do I mean Neve or someone else? I want to ask Jake if we're next. If we're about to be murdered with a kitchen knife like Claude was, but he disappears from the bedroom before I have the chance. And even though my legs don't want to hold me, I force myself up and tiptoe after him, shivering in my camisole and shorts.

Jake is by the front door. He presses a finger to his lips, urging me not to speak as he listens for movement or noise. Seconds pass in slow, agonising beats until finally he shoots me a look I can't read and opens the door.

My breath snags in my throat, but the hall outside my apartment is empty. There's a package sitting on the doormat. Brown paper, nondescript but somehow still terrifying. Jake scoops it up, and he's about to shut the door when his head pokes out again and he's grabbing something else.

A second later, he slams the door shut, locking it fast before holding out a piece of card. 'This was stuck on the camera.'

I step forward to take it and gasp. It's a postcard. The image is a rolling vineyard with an old chateau in the distance. Printed on the front are the words Languedoc-Roussillon. On the back in block capitals are the words, FORGET SOMETHING?

Jake steps to the kitchen and rips open the package so the contents drops onto the counter with a clatter of metal. A gargled cry escapes Jake's throat. He steps back, hand covering his mouth. I don't breathe as I inch forward and my eyes catch on the Le Creuset carving knife with the solid wood handle. The same knife I used to slice the watermelon in France. The same knife I last saw lying beside Claude's body.

Beside it is something else too. A white bloodied handkerchief lying on the counter. The initials CD are still visible in the corner of the material, embroidered in elegant script.

'Claude's,' I choke.

Jake nods and drops his hand from his mouth. 'Is that the knife?'

'I think so.'

'You didn't... What did we do with it?' he asks.

Is he accusing me of something? I frown and shake my head. 'I moved it before I rolled up the rug. Then we left to take his body to the lake. I thought you'd taken it.'

'I thought it was still in the rug with the body,' he whispers back, face paling. He opens his mouth to say more, but whatever words are forming, they're stolen by the sharp buzz of a message landing on his phone. I rush to his side and read the words.

I have plenty more evidence! You'll never get away with it.

Jake fires back a reply, fingers surprisingly steady.

What do you want?

The next message chills me to my core.

You'll find out soon.

We stand, frozen, staring at the screen. My heart continues to race as Jake backs away from the counter, tugging me with him and pulling me to the sofa. We sit down, and I wrap my arms around myself.

'What do we do with that stuff?' I ask, voice trembling. My gaze snaps to the door as though they're still out there. I shiver, feeling somehow watched.

'I'll wrap them in separate bags and drop them in a couple of large bins at different locations in the city,' he replies.

It's the logical thing to do. The safest. And yet my thoughts falter on how quickly the idea came to him. Suddenly, I'm back at the farmhouse, walking up the drive, Jake jogging to catch up. I remember the sheen of perspiration on his face. The way he seemed to be still catching his breath. I'd put it down to the rush of our bet and the heat, but was it something more than that?

Jake rubs his hands over his face before turning towards me. 'I'll call Gary later and see if he's found anything about the investigation into Claude. We won't be able to keep ignoring Allard for much longer.'

I close my eyes, fighting back a sudden wave of emotion. The need to cry and scream. I feel Jake's hand slip into mine. 'Hannah?'

'I'm scared,' I whisper. Scared for everything happening to us. Scared that the man I'm supposed to be marrying in five days isn't who I think he is. Jake pulls me into his muscular arms, steady and warm. I lean against him, searching for the comfort I need. But all I feel is the hollow loneliness of my past sweeping through me like a damp, wintry mist.

Because I've been in love before. Wild, mad, thought-it-was-forever love. My family said we were too young, but we didn't care and we didn't listen. Before I can stop them, the memories come flooding in. I see his face in my mind. I see the dark hair and darker eyes – two pools into a soul I swore matched my own.

We were together for ten years. An entire decade of my life consumed by him. I clench my jaw, allowing two lines of tears to fall down my face. Seventeen months on and I still don't understand how such a perfect, all-consuming, intense love ended so badly. Then I hear his laughter in my head. That dancing, knowing sound.

I bolt upright, opening my eyes. Needing to see my reality. Needing Jake. Meeting him changed my life. He'll never know how dark my past is, how the emptiness nearly ate me alive before we met. Maybe I don't know everything about Jake. Maybe he's keeping something back, but I'm doing the same, aren't I? Jake has no idea about the past relationship I swore would kill me.

He kisses the top of my head. 'We'll figure this out, Han.' But his words ring hollow as I glance to the kitchen and the dark-red blood on the handkerchief; the knife from France that disappeared while we were out at the lake that night.

'How?' I ask as I wipe away the tears from my cheeks.

'They said we'll find out what this is about soon. We just need to be ready.' His answer is calm, but beneath the surface I sense his fear.

'Be ready for what?'

'Whatever comes next,' he says, the words hanging over us like a guillotine blade.

4 DAYS UNTIL THE WEDDING

TWENTY-SIX

JAKE

Jake drops onto the sofa, hands trembling with exhaustion as he reads then rereads the email from someone in the finance team at Novexia International. The contract has been signed. The deal is done. The money has been sent.

He can't believe it. The final presentation was yesterday. After being jolted awake at 3 a.m., he'd been tired and jittery, drinking too much coffee. Talking too fast. Rambling his answers as the final questions were fired at him. But whatever he did, it was enough to get the deal over the line. They've asked him to take on a consulting role in the firm for when they roll out the software to sell to other companies. They can ask him to dance naked around the office every Friday and in his current state of mind he'd agree.

For years, he's believed he could make something of his life. He could be a success. Never wavering even when he took the hits in Westlake with Neve and then Manchester with his ex-business partner, Tom, Jake still clung to the certainty that he could be someone.

Here is the proof.

In twenty-four hours, the money will hit his account and

he'll be a millionaire. It changes everything. As soon as they're married, he'll tell Hannah about the sale and suggest they run. Find a little island somewhere in the Caribbean or even Bali. Make it their home not just their honeymoon destination. He's heard there's a good digital nomad community there.

It's not perfect. It means Hannah will have to leave her career and family behind, but considering how her parents treat her, he's not sure how much it matters. He's no longer certain they'll have their wedding party in the gardens of the estate in Bath where Hannah grew up. He's no longer certain of anything except how much Hannah means to him.

A door bangs from somewhere in the building and he jumps, heart lurching in his chest. The events of the last few weeks pummel his thoughts. Ever since that moment in the square when they met Claude, nothing has gone right for them. The knife and the bloody handkerchief he'd dropped in two different bins miles apart yesterday are still gnawing at him.

He told Hannah they have to hold their nerve and wait. Wait to see what this person wants. Wait to see what Gary comes back with about Claude. The investigator has promised to call this week, already explaining how difficult it is to find information from a remote area of France. Allard has called twice now. It feels like they're in a pressure cooker, running out of time.

He's certain it wouldn't be so bad if he could think straight. If he wasn't so tired. Sleep has become an elusive thing for both of them. When he does sleep, the nightmares still haunt him. He has vivid dreams of standing over Claude's body, wanting to save him and knowing it's too late. In the dream, when he looks down, it's him wearing those bloodied shoes, him with the knife in his hand. He wants to run away, but someone is always standing there, blocking his path. He can't see who it is. Sometimes he thinks it's Neve. Sometimes it's Tom. Sometimes it's Hannah. Whoever it is, he can never get away from them. He tries. Clenching his fists, lashing out, but the hits never land no matter how much he fights.

He wakes every morning exhausted and anxious, certain he can't take much more. He wonders about telling Hannah tonight about the money. Packing their bags and fleeing in the dead of night. Forget the wedding and waiting to see what comes next. He knows it could work, and yet still he hesitates. He's rushed into decisions in the past. Trusted the wrong people. Like Neve and then Tom. Both times it's blown up in his face. Both times he's found himself pushed into a corner, desperate and angry, making bad decisions he can't take back.

He refuses to be that person anymore. Better to wait until after they're married. Husband and wife. However stupid it might be, whatever the risks are in waiting, the wedding means something to him. It's only four more days.

The thought reminds him about the call from the vicar at St Pancras Old Church this morning, requesting they drop their birth certificates to him before Saturday. *'You wouldn't believe how many brides and grooms forget to bring them on the day. This way, it's one less thing to worry about.'*

He fires a quick message to Hannah asking where he can find her certificate. Her reply is instant.

Try the sideboard. I'll message you when I'm almost done for the day. It won't be late tonight xx

Twenty minutes later, Jake is kneeling beside the open sideboard in the living room. The entire unit is empty, the contents piled around him in a mess of papers, books, wedding magazines and tangled charging cables. He's found Hannah's birth certificate exactly where she said it would be. The paper in his hands is thick and expensive, with swirling calligraphy and official boxes filled with Hannah's parents' names and her date of birth and the location – the Royal Hospital in Bath.

Hannah Jane Fitzroy.

He tucks the certificate in the folder beside his own and places it on the coffee table, ready to drop it into the church tomorrow.

It's as he's packing everything back into the sideboard that he sees the greeting card tucked inside a wedding magazine. It's an engagement card with a huge red heart being held by a cartoon bunny. Inside, in Hannah's familiar handwriting, it says: *To my fiancé, I can't wait to marry you!!* It's signed with three kisses.

Hannah must have forgotten to give it to him. Maybe it got lost and she wrote another one – the card he now keeps in his bedside table. The words he remembers.

> *To Jake, I love you so much! Thank you for making me the happiest woman alive! Love Hannah xxx*

The explanation running through his head makes sense, and yet he can't tear his eyes away from the front of the card. It's not just that it's dog-eared and looks older than it should, it's that damn bunny. There's something so un-Hannah like about it. He can never imagine her choosing this card.

Is it...? The question starts to form. He wants to shut it down, but it's too late. Is it possible Hannah was engaged before? Married? He wants to say no. She would've told him, wouldn't she? But this card – the style, the age of it, the wording. It doesn't feel like it was ever for him.

Her words from the other night play in his thoughts. *'We all make mistakes. Especially when a relationship is ending.'* There was a rawness to her voice he'd put down to the confrontation in the courtyard with Neve. Now he wonders if it was something else. But why hasn't she told him?

Jake rubs at his face. He's so tired, he doesn't know what to think or what to do with this information. All he knows is he can't lose Hannah. If there are things from her past she's hiding then there must be a reason. Maybe if they weren't living in this constant nightmare, the threat of the recordings of them in France reaching the police, the knowledge that someone was there that day and knows what they did, maybe he'd ask her.

But Hannah is struggling too, and he already feels bad enough that he's dragged her into this hellish mess. He can't push her right now. But that doesn't mean there's not another way to find out the information. He thinks of the money about to hit his account. The mistakes he's made in the past trusting the wrong people. He's certain he can trust Hannah, and yet before he can stop himself, he reaches for his phone.

A moment later, Gary is saying, 'Hello,' in his ear. 'I'm still looking into your Claude fella. It's a common name in France so it's taking a bit of time.'

Jake grits his teeth. It's not what he wanted to hear. 'If there's anything you can do to speed it up—'

'Yeah, I get it. I'll do my best,' Gary replies, and Jake ignores the agitation in his voice.

'That's actually not why I'm calling. There's something else I need.' A deep well of loathing opens inside him for what he's doing, but he has to know.

Gary makes a noise in his throat. Jake remembers the sound from a few years back when the PI had helped him with the mess in Manchester. It annoyed him then too. 'I'm all ears.'

'It's about Hannah Fitzroy,' Jake says. 'You did a background search on her last year.' He still hates himself for the time eleven months ago when, a week into his relationship with Hannah, he'd called Gary and asked him to look into her. He'd only been in London for six months when he'd met her. He was still picking himself up from what happened with Tom, struggling to trust and fearing he'd get it wrong again.

'I remember,' Gary says after clearing his throat.

'Can you take another look? Dig a bit deeper.'

'Is there something specific you're looking for?'

Jake scrunches his eyes shut. He's already regretting calling Gary. 'You did education and career and parents. I just wondered if you can dig up anything more personal. Past relationships, that kind of thing.' He swallows back the rising hatred for what he's doing. He tells himself this is to help Hannah too. If he knows more about her past, he can be a better husband to her.

'Anything else?' Gary asks.

Jake cringes. He wants to explain to Gary how important it is for him to trust Hannah after being burned so many times before. When he first met her that day on the bike ride, she'd seemed so perfect. Beautiful and smart and funny. He just had to be certain he could trust her.

Stupid of him. Hannah is the most open person he's ever met. Gary had come back to him two weeks later, when Jake was already falling hard. The file was slim. Hannah didn't have social media profiles. He guessed it was partly because she valued her privacy and partly because she worked in corporate law. There wasn't much to go on. Her education at a boarding school in Suffolk, followed by a law degree from Cambridge. Mentions of her parents and her brother who lived in Dubai. Everything Gary found fitted with what Hannah had told him. But now Jake wonders if they missed something. He tells Gary none of this. It's a transaction for the investigator.

'Yes,' Jake says. 'We're getting married on Saturday. So if you can let me know what you find before then.'

'It doesn't give me much time,' Gary replies with a puff of air through his lips. Jake has never met Gary in person but imagines him to be overweight and bald. A man that always smells of body odour and whatever food he's just consumed. 'It'll cost extra for overtime.'

'That's fine,' Jake replies. From tomorrow, money will no longer be an issue. 'Whatever you can do. Thanks,' he adds before they say their goodbyes.

He ends the call, feeling sick to his stomach with what he's asked Gary, almost calling him back and telling him to forget it. But then he stares down at the engagement card in his hands and the worry squirms in his stomach again. He tucks the card back in the sideboard and shoves his worries to the back of his mind. It'll be nothing. A mistake she didn't want to tell him about. And the least of their worries right now.

Four days until the wedding. His heart starts to pound in his chest. The need to do more takes hold. His thoughts pull back to the doorbell camera and that postcard stuck to the lens. He takes a breath, swallows down the terror threatening to take over and picks up his phone again. He can't put it off any longer. He knows exactly who he has to talk to. There are things from his own past he has to make sure Hannah never discovers.

3 DAYS UNTIL THE WEDDING

TWENTY-SEVEN

HANNAH

By Wednesday I feel like a shell of the woman I was three weeks ago. I've lost weight, and beneath the layer of make-up, my skin is ashen. Dark smudges rest beneath my eyes. I can barely concentrate at work, barely sit still at my desk. Every noise makes me jerk.

I've begun to hate how open plan the office is. Even the kitchen area has low counters and is visible anywhere on the floor. The HR manager told me on my first day that it demonstrates transparency to the clients, but I heard one of the secretaries claim it was to enforce productivity. *'We can't even have five minutes in the kitchen with a coffee without our bosses logging it on our time sheets. There's nowhere to hide.'*

The secretary had a point. Every hour of the day needs to be allocated to a client. It's relentless, and the joy I once found in this work has slowly diminished over the last six months. Sometimes I think about leaving. The freedom of endless days to myself. Every morning it's been an effort not to call in sick. But the alternative is long days pacing the apartment. Feeling trapped. Talking to Jake. Raking over every last detail of what's happening to us.

I still catch myself searching his features, questions about the day at the farmhouse on the tip of my tongue. Last night, I pulled away from him in bed for the first time, not wanting the intimacy that's driven so much of our relationship. I blamed tiredness, and Jake said he understood, but I could tell he was hurt.

I'm finding myself wishing Jake hadn't arrived in the courtyard on Saturday so suddenly. If only Neve hadn't been interrupted. Sometimes I find myself convinced it would've been a whole lot of nothing. Just causing trouble, like Jake warned me. Other times, I feel shaky with the feeling I'm missing something.

After the wedding, I tell myself. Things will be different then. It's the same words I've repeated a dozen times this week. Three more days. It's all I can think about as I make my way through the offices. A confident stride. My laptop and a notebook in my arms. Blowing out a long, stressful sigh. I look like I'm on a mission. Too busy to be disturbed. It's a look I've cultivated in the last few weeks.

The secretary I overheard complaining about being watched was wrong. There is somewhere to hide. On the floor above the open-plan offices is a reference and storage room. Shelf after shelf lined with legal journals and every reference book imaginable. As well as boxes and files of contracts we keep in case we ever need to refer back to them.

There's one desk, one lamp and an uncomfortable wooden chair that looks like a relic from a different time. I drop my laptop and files onto the desk with no intention of opening them, grateful most people who work at the law firm seem to have forgotten this place even exists.

When I need a moment – when my thoughts are scattered and I want to kick off my heels, sink to the floor and just exist unseen – this place has become my sanctuary. But even the silent peace can't stop my mind from reeling. I'm terrified for what's coming next, my thoughts zigzagging from the threats to Neve to Jake and whether I trust him.

There are no answers to be found, but I stay on the floor, back against the wall, heels kicked off, and my legs stretched out on the scratchy carpet tiles. Time passes. No one comes to search for a document or for me.

There's the nagging sense that I should be doing something more, but my mind is whirring and unwilling. I reach for my phone and numbly scroll through my emails, barely registering the work my colleagues are discussing.

Suddenly, a new email lands in my inbox. A link to what looks like a local French news site. I remember setting up the news alert on the way home from France for any posts mentioning Claude Dubas or the Languedoc region.

An icy chill floods my body as the site loads. I think I gasp as I scroll down the page, feeling sick and untethered. I don't breathe as I tap Jake's name on my call list, feeling like this is the beginning of the end. No way back.

The line rings endlessly; each unanswered tone sends a dart of panic through my body. Jake always answers. Always. His phone is practically an extension of his hand. I end the call and immediately redial, willing him to answer as I shove my feet into my heels and hurry down the stairs, not bothering to wait for the elevator. My heels click rapidly against the polished floor as I rush out of the building.

The street is teaming with the first wave of commuters making their way home. The thought of squeezing myself into a full Tube carriage feels too much to bear. Instead, I throw out my hand and hail a black cab.

As the taxi pulls into the traffic, I try Jake's phone again, my stomach twisting tighter with each unanswered ring. I check the Find My app and it shows him in the apartment. So why isn't he answering?

My phone is still gripped in my hand when a notification

from the doorbell camera lands on my lock screen. I open the app, my heart skipping a beat. Standing outside the door to my apartment is Neve. She's there right now! Then it's like she senses me watching because she looks into the camera and winks as she smiles down the lens.

I'm not surprised she's back. You don't go to the lengths she's gone to and simply give up. The questions I've tried to ignore this week come hurtling back. What does she want? What was she going to tell me? A frantic energy surges through me. When I think about the church and Jake waiting for me, I no longer see empty pews but Neve sitting in the front row, ready to derail us.

On the camera, the door is opening and the camera pans around to show Jake in his jeans and a white fitted T-shirt. I expect him to startle at the sight of Neve. To shout and rage, but instead he steps back, and a second later she's walking past him into my apartment, and the door is closing and the camera switches off.

Something curdles in the pit of my stomach. An image flashes before my eyes. Jake brushing away a strand of hair from a face that isn't mine. Kissing red lips. I shut the thought down. It won't be that, I tell myself, but still I will the taxi to hurry as it moves slowly through the traffic.

We hit the main road and get stuck behind a line of buses. I can see the cut-through just ahead and tell the driver to pull over. I tap my phone to pay and stride towards the apartment building. I'm barely looking as I step into the cut-through between the apartment buildings and collide with a man who seems to come out of nowhere. The force of his shoulder against mine shoves me back.

'Sorry,' I stammer, the apology automatic as I step aside, too focused on Neve to look up at the figure. He keeps moving anyway, head down and already disappearing around the corner towards the main road.

Then my heart starts to pound and my feet stop dead. These things happen in the same split second, but it's not until the next moment when my mind catches up that I register the heavy cologne that floods my senses with a thousand memories.

Tears prick my eyes at the force of it, and a noise escapes my mouth. It's just the aftershave, I tell myself, like I've done a hundred times before when I've caught the scent that rakes up memories of a past that makes me want to turn and run. Pack a bag and disappear all over again.

It's just the same cologne – I repeat the words over and over, trying to catch my breath, trying to ignore the rattling fear coursing through my veins.

By the time I reach the courtyard, I'm still breathless, but my legs feel steadier at least. There's a group sitting on the benches in the garden. They're all holding knitting needles, balls of wool on their laps. They look up as my heels tap the pathway.

Just as I reach the glass entrance door, Neve pushes through it, and I remember why I was rushing in the first place. Her head is dipped and she's already jogging down the steps in canvas pumps and a red maxi dress that matches her lipstick.

'Neve?' I call after her, and she spins round, startled.

There's a wildness in her eyes again, though it's not triumph I see but fear. Her arms are hugging her body, her shoulders hunched. She sees me then makes to turn away again as though I'm suddenly nothing to her.

Before I can think about what I'm doing, my hand is out, grabbing her arm. She yelps, shrinking back, nothing like the confident woman I saw on Saturday or standing in my apartment after the break-in.

'What's wrong?' I ask, dropping my hand.

'Ask your boyfriend.' The words are fired back but not fast enough to hide the quiver in her voice.

'I will, but right now I'm asking you.'

Her eyes dart to the doors of the apartment she's just come through. Is she worried Jake is going to appear? I'm certain if he checks my location on the app, he'll come flying down to pull me away, but he's not expecting to meet me outside my office for another hour at least. For a split second, I remember the news report from France and want to rush inside to Jake and tell him everything, but this is my chance to get answers from Neve. I have to know what she was going to tell me.

'I'm fine,' she says, seeming anything but. 'And before you go accusing me of stalking you, Jake invited me over. He wanted to talk.' Another darting look to the doors. 'And we have, so now I have to go.'

'Wait. What's going on, Neve? What did you want to tell me on Saturday?'

Something fierce flashes in her eyes. 'I wanted to help you! That's why I came. I wanted you to know that Jake isn't the charming man you think he is. He has a dark side. He twists the truth to suit him any time he wants. He destroyed my life and then he left when I was still trying to pick up the pieces. That's what I wanted to tell you. He'll take everything from you and then he'll disappear. It's what he does.

'I didn't break into your apartment. I didn't stalk you to France. I'm not crazy or any of the other things Jake has probably told you about me. I've been in England for work, but I'm flying back to Cleveland tomorrow. So whatever shit Jake has dragged you into, it isn't anything to do with me.'

'He hasn't—'

'Yeah right. Jake asked me about France, you know? And you did the other day too. It makes me wonder what happened on your romantic getaway.'

'Nothing happened,' I say too quickly.

Neve shoots another look to the doors and around the courtyard. Her eyes seem to linger on the cut-through a moment too long, and I throw a glance over my shoulder, remembering the figure who came out of the shadows and that scent in the air as we collided. But when I look, there's no one there.

'If it involves Jake,' Neve continues, 'then no doubt he brought the trouble with him. He does that a lot. Good luck, Hannah. You're going to need it. When this' – she waves her hands in the air – 'all goes wrong, give me a call.'

The certainty she uses feels sharp – a knife slicing through the last of my confidence. Neve walks away then. I call after her, wanting to know more. How did Jake destroy her life in Westlake? Is this just Neve's interpretation of the break-up? Or did something else happen that Jake isn't telling me? Before I can find my voice, she's jogging across the courtyard and disappearing into the cut-through. I let her go this time, turning to the building and heading up the stairs to my loft apartment.

As I put the key in the door, I take a deep breath, trying to steady myself as Jake leaps from the sofa, eyes wide with guilt. What have you done? I wonder, the suspicion hot in my blood.

'Jake isn't the charming man you think he is. He has a dark side.'

'He'll take everything from you and then he'll disappear.'

TWENTY-EIGHT

HANNAH

'Hey,' Jake says with a smile. The guilt disappears from his face so fast I find myself questioning if it was even there.

'You're home,' he continues. 'Why didn't you tell me you were leaving work? I'd have come and met you.'

'You didn't answer your phone,' I reply, and there it is again, the sheepish look darting across his face.

Suspicion prickles beneath my skin, but I say nothing as I slip out of my heels and scoop my hair into a ponytail. I want to give Jake the chance to explain why he invited Neve to our apartment without telling me. This is the woman tormenting us day and night, threatening to ruin our lives. A stalker. A murderer. Except, even as the thought runs through my head, I realise I don't believe it. Neve might be many things, but the woman I saw just now isn't capable of murder.

'Is everything OK?' he asks with a searching gaze.

The anxious fear I felt at the office hits my stomach again. Nothing is OK. It hasn't been for a long time, and I'm not sure it ever will be again. I have to tell Jake about the alert on my phone, but Neve's words and the fear I saw in her is pressing into my thoughts. If I tell Jake what's happening in France, it will become the all-consuming thing it is, and Neve and whatever happened here will be shoved aside and forgotten. I don't want that to happen.

For days now, I've had the sense Jake has been keeping something back from me. Our wedding is in three days. Now is my chance to get answers.

'The merger was finally sent for signatures,' I reply. 'I couldn't face starting something new. What have you done today?'

He nods to the open laptop on the table. 'Tidying up a few things for a new client.'

I stay silent and wait for more, but it doesn't come. I'm reminded how little Jake talks about his business. I've always thought he prefers to forget about it when he's with me, the same way I do, but as the silence stretches out, the lack of detail feels secretive. What isn't he telling me?

I step into the kitchen and grab a glass of water. My hands tremble, reminding me of the moment in the farmhouse kitchen with Jake, being questioned on Claude's disappearance. I don't know if this feeling pounding through me is for the scent of cologne I caught in the cut-through and the memories it's unleashed, or seeing Neve, or this moment and how much I hate confrontation and raised voices and anger and where it goes after that.

It's why Jake is so easy to be with. The temper I saw from him in the village square in France is not the Jake I know. His instinct is always to step back and regroup; make a plan. It's reassuring, but it also means nothing is ever said in the heat of the moment. No words flung at each other. I wonder now if it's kept us from sharing more of ourselves.

I bite the inside of my lip and lift my gaze to Jake, watching his expression as I speak. 'I saw Neve on the doorbell camera.'

For a second, he doesn't react. Then the grimace comes and he rubs at the stubble on one side of his face as though in pain. 'I wanted to talk to her about everything that's going on and see what she wants. I should've let you know. I'm sorry. I didn't want to upset you, but it was stupid.'

Stupid to do it or stupid to forget about the doorbell camera and the fact I'd find out, I wonder but swallow the question and ask another instead. 'And you invited her here?' Anger laces my words. 'To my apartment after she broke in, when you could've met anywhere in London?'

He cringes and scrunches his eyes shut. 'I didn't think. I'm sorry, Hannah. I wanted to talk to her privately so she couldn't make a scene. She used to do that a lot – pick a fight in a restaurant or on the street, then start yelling her head off about what a dick I was.'

The words ring true. I think of how friendly Neve was with me on Saturday but how quickly she shifted to something when Jake appeared.

Jake continues, eyes pleading. 'I only arranged it today. I was going to tell you tonight.' It feels like a lie, and we both know it.

'So what did she say? I'm assuming she didn't confess to murdering Claude and framing us for it?'

He shakes his head. 'That's the thing – the more I've thought about it this week, the more I've struggled with the idea that Neve is behind this, and I wanted to talk to her to test my theory out.'

His reply is reasonable and measured, and it takes me a moment to realise he hasn't answered my question. I want to know what he said to Neve. I want to know what she said back, but that's not where he's taking this conversation. Frustration courses through me. I slam my glass onto the counter, cutting him off. 'So why not tell me this? Why keep it a secret? You should've told me you were meeting her, Jake. How can I trust you after this?'

The word 'trust' seems to hang in the air between us. A

bomb about to detonate. I thought I could trust Jake, but Neve's words are still spinning in my thoughts, and there's Jake's confession too. How he always wins the bets we make with each other. Unwittingly telling me he was back at the farmhouse before me. It occurs to me in the loaded silence how it was Jake's suggestion to hide the body. He convinced me it was the only way. He was so certain the police wouldn't believe us. Is it because he knew something I didn't? Is it possible he...? I cut the thought dead. I remind myself of the threats and the shadowy figure in the cut-through. The person we saw on the doorbell camera too. How can that be Jake? It can't! Neve's got under my skin.

I'm about to apologise, to pull back my words and close the gap between us, but then there's a shift in the air – a crackling tension – and Jake is spinning away from me and striding across the apartment. I think he's grabbing his shoes to storm out, and it's on the tip of my tongue to tell him to stay, but then he's crouching down by the open sideboard and pulling something out.

A second later, he's up again and whirling round, stepping towards me. 'Yes, Hannah, you're right, OK?' Every word he speaks is short, bitten off. 'I didn't tell you about inviting Neve over. It was stupid. I didn't want to worry you, OK? But don't tell me you've not kept things from me.'

My pulse pounds in my ears. Thoughts of the cologne I smelled in the cut-through fill my head. He can't know about my past. Can he? 'I've been nothing but honest with you,' I say, but my voice falters.

'Really?' He's at my side in seconds, thrusting something towards me. 'If that's the case, then what's this?'

My gaze drops to the card Jake is waving in front of me. I take in the bunny on the front and the world stops. It feels like my heart is cracking open.

'Where did you find that?' I whisper, my voice caught in my

throat as I stare at the engagement card. The soppy smile of the cute cartoon animal seems to be mocking me. I remember how happy I was when I wrote that card. I should've thrown it away years ago, but a stupid, sentimental part of me wanted to keep it.

'In the sideboard,' he replies, waving a hand towards the piece of furniture like it's to blame and not him. 'I found it when I was looking for your birth certificate.'

The break-in, I think. The mess. Papers everywhere. All the chaos pushing the one thing that could undo us into the open. The anger that was humming through my body only seconds ago evaporates, leaving me hollow. I feel the breath knocked out of me as tears prick my eyes, and I push past Jake and sink down onto the sofa before my legs give way.

Jake follows me into the living room. His next words are sharp – needles piercing my skin. 'Why didn't you tell me you were engaged before?'

'Because I was young and stupid,' I say quietly. 'And then you proposed so fast and I didn't want you to think that I said yes to every man who asked me. I didn't want you to think that this didn't mean everything to me.' A sob heaves through me. My gaze keeps pulling to that card in Jake's hand. It's a fight not to snatch it from him, hold it tight, keep it safe.

I scrunch my eyes shut and cover my face and let the hurt of another lifetime consume me. And there's the question again – the one that catches me by surprise sometimes when I'm in the shower or on a run or doing a million other things and suddenly it's there. How could such a wild, all-consuming love have gone so wrong?

Jake is quiet. I feel the shift of the sofa as he sits down beside me, close so our legs are touching. He tugs one of my hands gently from my face and then the other and closes them inside his.

'It's OK,' he says, his tone soothing.

I shake my head, freeing more tears to roll down my cheeks. 'It's not.'

'It will be though,' he replies. 'I wish you'd told me, but I understand why you didn't. We fell in love so fast, didn't we? I think there are things we've both held back because we've skipped a few steps.'

My voice when I speak is thick with tears. 'I was stupidly young, and I didn't listen to my parents or my friends when they told me so. We got engaged and then we broke up, and it was awful.' A torrid, tearing pain yanks at my insides. My heart feels as though it's being crushed. Yes, we were stupidly young. Meeting at drama camp when I was seventeen and he was eighteen, but we were together for years before the engagement. And years more after that. We'd planned our wedding down to the colour of the macaron table favours. But if I share the truth with Jake, he'll ask me why we didn't get married, why it all fell apart, and I can't bring myself to go back there.

Pain cuts across my chest. Tears fall, hot down my face.

Jake lifts an arm up, pulling me into him. 'So that's why your parents are so against our wedding? Because they think you're making the same mistake again?'

I hesitate and think about what he's suggesting before I nod. 'Exactly that, but it's not the same, Jake. What we have is so different. Please,' I cry. 'Please don't read too much into this and pull away.'

'Pull away?' He offers a lopsided smile, and in that second, as his eyes catch mine, the fight between us is over. 'Hannah, I could never. There's nothing you could say that would stop me wanting to marry you on Saturday. For better, for worse, right?'

I lean against his chest and take in his words, letting them soothe the pain like ice to a burn.

Jake brushes a hand through my hair. 'I love you.'

'I love you too,' I whisper through the hurt. Then I pull myself up and wipe the tears from my face. 'With Neve—'

'I'm so sorry, Han,' Jake says quickly. 'You're right – I should've told you.'

I shake my head, not caring anymore. 'You don't think she's behind this now, do you?'

'No,' he replies with his usual certainty. 'When I asked her about France, she seemed genuinely surprised and denied leaving London.'

'She could be lying,' I reply, although I'm not certain either.

'I know. But here's the thing – who did we tell we were going to France?'

I frown, trying to think. 'I told my boss and HR. And my parents so they knew we were using the house.'

He nods. 'And I told a few clients. Hardly anyone knew we were going. It was all so last minute. We decided on the Thursday night and left on the Friday morning. Neve would've had to have not only found out we were going, but found transport and followed us all the way. Our ferry was fully booked too, remember? We got the last space. So how did she follow us?'

'She didn't,' I reply as I realise what Jake is saying. 'And there's no way she could've known the address of the house or the area of France we were heading to. Even if she'd flown or got the train or the next ferry, she wouldn't have found us. But then, how did anyone know we were there? Who else would do this?'

'What if we take Neve out of this completely?' he says. 'Someone broke into our apartment to look for something or trash the place. Someone killed Claude and framed us. They then hung around, probably to see the police arrest us. Then when we hid Claude's body, they decided to film us and torment us instead. Either way, someone is trying to destroy us. Or worse...'

'But who?' I cry. 'Who is doing this and why? Why us, Jake? That's what I can't get my head around. We're normal people. Nobodies.'

'Could it be... your parents?' Jake cringes like he hates that he's even suggesting it.

I gasp. 'No. Claude was one of their closest friends. They'd never have killed him or done any of this stuff. I know they've been harsh about the wedding, but they're my parents. They love me.' The emotion builds again, and my lip quivers.

Jake's gaze moves to the card still clutched in his hand, but I force myself not to look. 'What about the man you were engaged to before me?' he asks.

'No.' The single word is strangled. It can't be, I think, but still my mind races to the cut-through and that familiar scent and all the memories I keep locked away. So much love. So much hurt. Jake is waiting for me to explain my past, but it's still so raw.

A memory flies at me with the force of a fist. Those dark eyes so intense it was like they could read my soul. Bile burns the back of my throat as I hear the last words he ever spoke to me. *'Do you really think there's anywhere you can go where I won't find you?'*

TWENTY-NINE

JAKE

Jake holds Hannah close, wishing he could take away the hurt radiating from her body.

'Hannah,' he soothes, running a hand over her back.

She jolts, pulling away, eyes wide like she's just realised something. 'Jake, there's something else. The French police—'

Before she can continue, his phone hums on the coffee table. His screen lights up with a message and they both freeze.

An oily unease slips through his body. Before he can act, Hannah snatches up his phone and holds it between them as she taps in his passcode.

Five words cut into him with the ease of a sharp blade.

We're watching your every move.

We.

His mind races back. He can't be certain but he doesn't think any of the previous messages have used the plural before. What the hell is this?

Another message arrives.

He scans it just as fast, the dread growing inside him with every beat of his heart.

We have something else for you to watch. Don't try to run! We're tracking your movements.

A dozen expletives charge through his mind, but he takes a breath, trying to keep calm for Hannah. He has a sudden memory of being back in the farmhouse, sitting at the kitchen table while Claude's lifeless body lay on the rug just metres away. The struggle of trying to calm Hannah and decide what to do. The frenzied need to make a plan. The same hysteria bubbles again, but how can they make a plan when they don't know what the hell is going on or who is doing this.

'Another video.' Hannah's voice is barely a whisper. 'What now?'

No part of him wants to tap the white triangle of the new recording that's just been sent, and yet it calls to him, sucking the air out of his lungs, urging him to do it. What else could they have?

Hannah is quicker to react, and before he's ready, she's tapping the screen. As the video starts to play, Jake feels his mouth drop open. He thinks he swears, but the noise is drowned out by the roaring in his ears. It's them. Not the farmhouse in France. But here. This apartment. This living room. And it was filmed minutes ago as they argued – Hannah standing by the breakfast bar and him moving towards her with the engagement card in his hand. There's sound too. Their voices tinny and distant as they argue.

'Oh God,' Hannah cries, leaping up, scrambling towards the front door. 'Someone's here.'

'No. It has to be a hidden camera.' The thought isn't any less unsettling. He swallows, forcing himself to stand and, with his phone in one hand as the video replays, he steps across the room to the bookshelf. He stands on his tiptoes, fingers reaching to a place out of sight, tapping the bare wood until he finds something. A second later, he draws back and there's a small camera in his hands. Like the nanny cam he's seen on TV shows usually hidden in teddy bears or ornaments.

How long has it been there? What have they seen?

He tries to think, but there's so much to process. He closes the camera in his fist, blocking the lens from recording anything more.

Hannah moves tentatively towards him as though the object in his hand could hurt them. 'Do you think...?' Her eyes dart around the apartment. 'Are there more?'

A noise escapes his throat, and they both turn to the bedroom. 'Let's find out.' He steps to the kitchen and drops the camera into the sink, drowning it in water. Then together they search every corner and shelf and hiding place they can think of, finding nothing.

'They said we can't run,' Hannah says when they've finished their search. She sips from a glass of water that shakes in her hand. 'So what do they want?'

He buries his head in his hands for a moment. His pulse is thudding in his ears. Everything is happening at once. It's like he can't draw breath from one horror to the next. No time to think. To plan. To take action. 'I don't know. But this is bigger than we thought, Han.'

'What do you mean?' she asks.

'Think about it. The only time this camera could've been put here was the break-in before we went to France.'

Hannah's face is drawn and pale, but she nods. 'So the whole reason for the break-in was to plant this camera and watch us? Then whoever did this heard our travel plans and followed us to France. But why?' she asks. 'If they wanted to kill someone and frame us for murder, why do it in France? Why not do it here?'

Jake shakes his head. He doesn't have the answers, but Hannah is right. Nothing about this is making sense. 'What if they followed us to France, waiting for an opportunity to mess with us – to destroy us – and then they watched what happened with Claude in the square, and when they saw him at the farmhouse, they saw an opportunity?'

'That's a lot of ifs,' Hannah replies.

She's right. And they're no closer to understanding why and who. Nauseating dread spreads through his body.

We'll tell you what we want soon.

Again: *We.*

'This isn't one person,' he says, as much to himself as to Hannah. 'Look.' He shows her the message again, watches her eyes widen with the significance and the same fear drumming in his body.

'I just... I don't understand. Is it two people? Three? Four? Who are they? What do they want from us?'

'I don't know.' Jake taps his phone, watching the video again.

He hates how angry he looks as he turns to Hannah. He doesn't recognise the scowl on his face. Then his attention turns to her as he thrusts the engagement card towards her. He watches the devastation contort her features and how she falls to the sofa. He's never seen her look so sad.

Her reason for not telling him about her previous engagement makes sense. Their relationship moved so fast. Maybe they did skip over a few steps in the getting-to-know-each-other stage. But is that the only reason she didn't tell him?

As he rewatches the same moment twice more, a thought starts to worm through his mind. He remembers the words Claude spat at him in the village square. *'Hannah is a smart woman, but she's easily led.'*

Why would Claude say that? Did something happen to Hannah before they met? Something that has her parents and the likes of Claude worried she's about to make another mistake?

All this time, he's been so sure whoever is behind this is connected to his past. His mistakes. But what if... what if this isn't about his past? What if it's about Hannah's?

THIRTY

JAKE

The question has barely formed in Jake's mind when Hannah is gasping, rushing across the apartment for her bag. In the beat of time he's alone, he tries to turn the thought over, see how it fits with everything happening. Claude's murder. The threats. He was so certain this was about him, but maybe he's wrong.

A second later, Hannah is back in the kitchen, and there's no time to dwell on the niggling idea trying to take root in his mind.

'What is it?' he asks, taking in Hannah's expression. She looks like she's going to be sick. His own stomach roils. What could be worse than finding a hidden camera in their apartment?

She unlocks her phone, turning the screen to show him. 'I set an alert for any French news about Claude. This was shared on a local news site for the Languedoc.'

He peers at the screen. There's a photo of a smiling Claude, sitting in a café wearing a white linen shirt and a bemused smile. Seeing the man look so alive causes fear to clutch his chest. Bile burns the back of his throat as he thinks of France and Claude. He wishes he could take it all back. Why did he have to lose his temper and lash out at Claude?

Jake closes his eyes. He swears he can feel the heat of Hannah's suspicions burning into him. Why did they split up on the hike? Why did he race to be first back? The enormity of what they did crashes through him as he forces himself to scroll down to read the article. Except it's all in French. Frustration grips him. 'What does it say?'

Hannah turns the screen back towards her. 'It says there's growing concern for local man, Claude Dubas. How long he's been missing for and then stuff about where he was last seen. There's a suggestion he may have fallen and died. Local police and residents are organising a search on Saturday of Le Lac Blanc and the surrounding area. They're waiting for a dog unit to be brought in from Montpellier to join them.'

Jake swears under his breath. The feeling of being out of control beats down on him. He's barely had a second to think since Neve left the apartment. For a moment there, he'd thought he'd fixed something. Making sure she understood once and for all there was nothing left for her. But it's all gone to shit!

With dogs picking up the scent of decay, they'll find Claude's body in minutes. He thinks of the Persian rug from the farmhouse. It will take the police no time to discover the rug belongs to the Fitzroy family.

'I don't know what to do,' Hannah says, her lower lip quivering. 'As soon as they find his body, we're done for.'

He nods. Everything they did can't be for nothing. The nightmare of the last two weeks can't be for nothing. His worries about Hannah's past disappear. Right now, it doesn't matter if this is about him or Hannah. It doesn't even matter who is behind it and what they have planned next – the danger they're in. All that matters is Claude's body being discovered. One step at a time, he thinks. And whatever that step is, he knows even with the niggling doubts in his mind that he wants to take it with Hannah.

'What if we left?' he says.

Hannah's eyes widen. 'You mean run?'

'Yes,' he replies, thinking of the money now in his accounts. 'We could start a new life anywhere in the world.' The words come out in a rush. This wasn't how he wanted to suggest his plan.

Her eyes glaze with tears, but he can see she's considering it. 'We'd be running for the rest of our lives,' she says. 'We'd be fugitives. For what? We didn't kill anyone. And if we run, whoever is threatening us has said they'll send the video to the police.'

'Does it matter if they do?' he cries. 'If the police are going to find Claude's body wrapped in the rug from your farmhouse, then the recordings aren't going to make any difference.'

Hannah nods as she scrunches her eyes shut. 'To leave our whole lives behind though – my career, my family—'

'All that matters is that we're free and we're together,' he pushes, the idea taking hold again. It's on the tip of his tongue to tell her about the sale of his business and his wealth.

Hannah bites her bottom lip, arms hugging her body. 'If running is our only option, then I get that, but if there's even a chance that there's another way out of this, we have to try, don't we?'

'But is there?' he asks.

He hates the look of desperation and failure pulling at her features. 'I didn't think this far ahead,' she says. 'I only thought about how no one goes to the lake because of the curse. I didn't think about what would happen when Claude never came back. I'm sorry.'

He briefly wonders if there's some truth to the old story about the witch casting a spell on the land. They went to the lake and look what happened. He doesn't believe in curses.

Plan, act, plan again. That's how he lives his life. That's how they'll get out of this.

He takes her hand. 'It's not your fault. We did what we thought was best at the time. That's all we can ever do.' His voice is hollow, and he isn't sure he believes it. If they'd taken more time in the farmhouse that night to think, would they have found a better plan? But they were both panicking, and he could sense Hannah freaking out. He'd needed a way forward before she latched on to the idea of calling the police. He couldn't let that happen.

'Jake?' Hannah cries. 'What are we going to do?'

He swallows, mouth dry. He needs a glass of water. 'I don't know yet. Let me think.' He steps away. Even the few metres gap between them is a relief. The need to be strong for Hannah is all that's holding him up. If it wasn't for her, his bags would've been packed already. He'd be gone. He's been here before. Standing on a precipice, knowing he's going to have to jump. One way or the other. It comes down to which direction to throw himself in. He hasn't always got it right. An image flashes in his thoughts: warm blood on his hands, seeping between his fingers, and that breathless, blinding anger.

This is his pattern. Make mistakes and run away. He can't keep doing it. And Hannah's right – throwing their lives away and starting again, even together, has to be the very last option.

In the kitchen, he pours himself a glass of water and sinks down on the stool at the breakfast bar. A moment later, Hannah sits beside him, pushing a shaking hand through her hair. When she speaks again, her voice is ragged. 'If only we'd thought of hiding Claude's body somewhere else. If we could go back now and undo it all...' She trails off then starts again. 'If they find his body, Jake, our DNA will be all over it.'

'I know,' he says with more sharpness than he means. Then, 'Sorry. I'm thinking. Give me a minute.'

She falls silent, hurt radiating from her alongside the fear and panic thick in the air, but it's useless to keep raking over what could happen. A minute passes like that. He sips at his water and thinks. He thinks of the location of Claude's body and the search. He twists it around and around in his head until he keeps finding himself at the same place.

'You were right,' he says eventually. 'We have to go back.'

'What?' She shakes her head. 'I meant go back in time, rewind it all.'

He nods. 'I know, but what if we actually go back? The search is organised for Saturday, right? It's three days away.' He pauses. Neither of them mentions that Saturday is also their wedding day. 'We can drive back to the lake. We can move his body and take it somewhere else. Dump it in the sea or bury it in the middle of nowhere. Somewhere it'll never be found. It's the only way to keep this from coming out. We have to move the body. Then even if the dogs find the scent, there'll be nothing for the police to go on.'

Tears fall down Hannah's face, and she wipes them away with a swipe of her hand. 'I get what you're saying, and maybe it's the only way out of this, but we can't leave. We're being watched, remember? They said they're tracking our movements. Whoever is messaging us has told us not to run. If they see us leaving, they'll think that's exactly what we're doing, and then they'll send the videos to the police anyway. We have to carry on as normal.'

The unanswered questions scream in his thoughts. The 'who is doing this?' fear he can't escape day or night, but for once, that question is the least of his worries.

'You're right,' he says. 'They'll be expecting you to leave for the office like normal tomorrow, but I work in the apartment most of the time. It's not unusual for me to be here all day. If I can get away unseen, they'll have no idea I've gone. And just to be sure, I'll send a few emails tonight cancelling meetings and saying I've got food poisoning. We don't know how they're keeping tabs on us, but we'll make it look like I'm ill in bed.'

'But they're tracking us? That's what they said.'

He nods. 'It can only be on our phones. I'm sure I'd have noticed someone following me. There could be malware on them.'

'Can you remove it?' she asks.

'Not without alerting them,' he replies. 'I'll leave my phone in the apartment and pick up a cheap unregistered one so we can stay in contact.'

Hannah bites her lip. 'What do I do?'

'You carry on like nothing is wrong. Like we're getting married in three days.'

'Are we?' she asks.

The pressure builds inside. He has a sudden urge to scream at her that he doesn't have the answers. He swallows; gets hold of himself. 'Yes,' he replies, praying it's true. 'I'll be back in time. We'll wait until the early hours of the morning tomorrow, and I'll take the car and drive back to the ferry and then to France. I can be there by the afternoon. I'll move Claude's body to the car and drive it somewhere else far away and bury it. I'll be back before they realise I'm gone.'

Hannah is quiet for a long moment, and then she nods. 'I'll pack a bag for you.' She stands and strides away in the direction of the bedroom.

Jake slouches against the counter. They have a plan at least. All he needs to do is stick to it. They can still be OK. He desperately hopes it's true.

He won't allow himself to think about the state of Claude's body. The decomposition from two weeks of summer heat, even in the cool of the cave. The sickening dread roils in his stomach. He can do this. He'll hide Claude's body and make it back in time for their wedding, and it will all work out.

He knows he's skipping over the threats and the recordings

and torment, but right now he'll only focus on this one thing he can control. The police are searching the lake for Claude's body. He has to hope whoever is behind this isn't watching the lake as well as them. He has to get there before the search. Whatever happens next, he will protect them. He can't lose Hannah. This is the certainty that pushes him on.

They're in this together. For better, for worse.

1 DAY UNTIL THE WEDDING

THIRTY-ONE

JAKE

Dawn is a whisper on the horizon – a single candle flame in the pitch-black. Jake opens the car door and stretches. The air smells of wild garlic and a dewy woodland freshness. After a night spent sweating in a hot car, it's a welcome relief to be standing in the fresh air. He rubs the exhaustion from his eyes and tries to clear his thoughts. Today is Friday. One day until their wedding. One day until the dog unit arrives and police search this area and find Claude's body.

He's lost so much time. The journey took him longer than expected. After finding the hidden camera on Wednesday and seeing the news about the search, he'd left London in that strange dead time between night and morning, the engine of Hannah's small Audi sounding megaphone loud at 3.40 a.m. as he'd driven out of the parking garage and then to the south-east coast and the ferry port. It was only when he arrived at Dover that he realised he should've booked ahead. The first two ferries leaving for France were fully booked. He only made it on the third at lunchtime because one vehicle hadn't checked in. At least it gave him time to stop in a hardware store for supplies and buy a cheap unregistered phone, messaging Hannah so she has his number.

By the time the ferry docked at Calais yesterday, it was already mid-afternoon. Jake drove fast, the motorways mercifully clear as the landscape shifted from warehouses to open fields of green and clusters of houses spreading into towns, then to the rolling vineyards and chateaus, each one grander than the last with turrets and towers rising above the distant fields, reminding him of the image on the postcard someone stuck to the doorbell camera.

Someone. But not Neve. The new certainty brought no relief. Only more questions. About his past and Hannah's too, although all he has there is questions. He'll need to talk to her properly when he gets back. Hours driving with nothing to do but think. The same questions they've been asking each other for weeks spun in his thoughts. Who? Why? What next?

The more he thought about it, the more he felt certain this could be about something Hannah hasn't told him about. Her own crazy ex? Her family? It's a relief to think his own past hasn't caught up with him because if it wasn't Neve, then that only left what happened in Manchester and Tom, his ex-business partner. Tom might've been a great software designer, but he lacked planning skills, and even though Jake hadn't figured out how this nightmare started, how it fitted together or what was going to happen next, he knew it required a level of complexity beyond Tom's capabilities, especially considering how they left things in that alleyway.

No. Not Neve. Not Tom. But then he remembered the threat.

We're watching your every move.

Not one person. But two? Three?

By the time Jake approached the outskirts of the abandoned quarry, it was late and he was wrung out from the questions pummelling his mind. As his headlights cut through the pitch-black darkness, he knew he couldn't venture beyond the treeline in the dark. He remembered the sheer drop of the cliffs either side of the bumpy, steep path. Even with the torch in his bag, he wasn't sure he'd be able to navigate his way to the ledge and the cave, not to mention moving Claude's body in the dark. With the equipment he bought in the hardware store and the plan in his head, he thinks he can move it alone, but he needs light to do it.

And if he tripped, if he fell, if he needed help, how would he ever explain what he was doing here. So he waited the night out in his car. Tried to sleep but felt too wired, starting at the sound of every bird or animal call as his mind spun, until finally dawn broke.

In the minutes he's spent stretching, the candle flame of light has grown. The light around him has moved from black to grey. Still the questions come. Is he doing the right thing? If he's caught with Claude's body... He cuts the thought dead. There is no easy way out of this. Only risks.

The first rays of sun illuminate the white cliffs in a soft golden glow. Le Lac Blanc, Hannah called it. The white lake. No doubt named after the almost white limestone cliffs reflecting on the water's edge, giving an eerie paleness to the water, adding to the strange beauty of this supposedly cursed land.

As the darkness is pushed into shadows, Jake can make out the trees rising around the water below. He slings his backpack over his shoulder and starts to walk. Pine needles crunch under his boots, sounding too loud in the silence. The foliage has grown wilder in the weeks since he was last here – the pathways more overgrown, the trees and bushes thicker and richer in colour. It takes him a long time to find the path Hannah led him down – first on their hike, holding hands, laughing. The second time by torchlight, the wheelbarrow threatening to tip with the weight of the rug and Claude's body hidden within it.

It's the same weight he'll need to carry up this ravine and to his car soon. This time without a wheelbarrow. He thought of going to the farmhouse to get it, but the path is steep, and pushing it up the rocky path isn't the same as guiding it down. Besides, he wasn't sure if the house was empty, and he had no desire to run into any more of Julia and Marcus's friends. So instead he plans to use the supplies he picked up from the hardware store near the port yesterday morning – the heavy-duty plastic sheets and rope. He has a vague plan to create a harness and pull the body up behind him.

He's nearing the bottom of the path when a sudden noise stops him in his tracks. A scream. A shout. A cry. Someone is here. He freezes, dropping down on the path, pushing into the thick bristly foliage, barely registering the branches and thorns scratching his body. For a sickening moment, he wonders if the search has been moved to today. He'll be arrested on the spot and hauled away for life in prison.

He stays still. Hidden. Trying to slow the heaving gasp of his breath as the trees close in, trapping him. The noise comes again. The same crying scream. But this time Jake hears it properly. It's not a human cry but a bird's squawk. Adrenaline tremors through his body, leaving him light-headed, but he scrambles to his feet and forces himself to push forward.

He senses the lake before he sees it. The stillness ahead of him, the occasional soft splash of a fish or an insect breaking the surface. He remembers the turning to the right at the water's edge and the barely there path into the treeline. But before he can reach it, the stones beneath his feet give way and he's sliding feet first, ass hitting the ground with a spine-jolting thud. He registers the splash before he feels the cold wetness seep through his left foot as it hits the water.

He hisses an expletive as he waits for the pain of a broken bone, but he's OK. The worst is a sharp cut on his hand from where he reached out to stop his fall and a thorn dug into his palm. He's jolted, bruised and shocked, but not badly hurt.

Jake lets the thought settle before drawing himself up on weak legs. He wishes he'd brought some water in the backpack. But there's no way he's going back to the car now he's this close.

It takes him another twenty minutes to find the ledge, wishing Hannah was there to guide him for every one of those minutes. Twice he turned into the trees at the wrong point. But he finds the ledge eventually, and deep down he's glad Hannah isn't here. It isn't just the need to maintain the routine for whoever is watching the apartment. It's to spare her this next awful part of moving a decaying corpse. It'll be easier without her. He won't have to be strong for her, which is good because he's pretty sure he's going to be heaving his guts up and balling like a baby very soon.

The sun has risen over the cliff edge, throwing its light over the lake and into the trees as he pulls himself onto the ledge, hips and knees scraping the hard stone.

He swallows, the emotion rushing up to greet him. How has his life come to this? Of all the bad decisions he's made, of all the awful things he's done, this has to be one of the worst.

Jake rails against the voice in his head telling him to stop, to go back, to run, and instead he lowers himself to the ground and pushes forward into the cave. With the sunlight behind him, the cave is dark, and it takes his eyes a moment to adjust. Then he's crying out, pushing back, coming up too fast too soon, banging his head, desperate to get away.

What the hell?

This isn't happening.

It isn't possible.

But as Jake forces himself to look again, he sees only an empty cave. No sign of the body he and Hannah put here two weeks ago. No bulging rug. No dead Claude.

THIRTY-TWO

JAKE

Jake stares for a long time into the emptiness of the dark cave. He pulls the torch from his backpack and shines it over every inch of the rough stone walls just in case there's a turning or ridge he's forgotten. Any second, his torch light will find what his eyes couldn't see the first time – the bumpy rug and Claude's dead body. But it doesn't. No matter how much he stares, the cave is empty. His head spins with the knowledge. He remembers pushing and shoving and rolling that rug to the very back of the darkness to the exact spot where the torch is now shining.

What the hell?

He shimmies out of the low cave, scuffling his body along the ground like a retreating worm, before his head is clear from the low ceiling and he sits up and blinks in the bright sunlight now pushing over the top of the cliffs. His first thought is that he's in the wrong place. The wrong path. The wrong ledge. The wrong cave. Except he isn't. He remembers this ledge. He remembers staring at the lake below, his legs dangling over the edge beside Hannah's as they'd joked about marrying here.

But if this is where he and Hannah hid Claude's dead body two weeks ago, then where is it now? A trembling starts to work its way through his body. He's so tired from the journey and the sleepless night in the car waiting for this moment. He can't think.

Should he be relieved? There's nothing for him to lug up the ravine and into the boot of Hannah's car and drive away with, hunting for a place he can bury the body while praying he isn't seen or stopped by the police. Or terrified of what the hell is going on? Where is Claude's body? Who took it? And why?

He doesn't have answers. He tries to think, but he's so tired. Who would move a dead body?

He wonders if Claude is still decaying somewhere nearby and will be found in the search tomorrow.

He sits for a long time on the ledge, every thought hitting a dead end. Nothing makes sense. He thinks again that he's missing something. There's nothing here for him to do, and yet he can't pull himself away. Can't leave. Instead, he calls Hannah. With the time difference, he's an hour ahead, but he doubts she'll be asleep anyway. It rings and rings, cutting to voicemail. He wonders if she's in the shower or still asleep. He fires off a message from the cheap phone he bought yesterday.

Call me!!! x

Minutes pass, enough for his ass to ache from sitting on the hard rock. When there's still no reply from Hannah, the worry begins to gnaw at him. He checks the time again. Every weekday since he's known Hannah, the alarm on her phone has chimed at exactly 5.40 a.m. She's got out of bed. Showered. Dressed for work. Make-up and hair, and left the house with a protein smoothie in her bag to drink on the way.

Which means she should've seen his missed call and message by now. The worry expands. Claws and sharp teeth.

He wishes he had his phone and could check where she is on the app. He feels anxious without it, keeps reaching for it.

He wants to call Gary too. Has he found anything about the police investigation into Claude's disappearance that Jake doesn't already know? It occurs to Jake that Gary should've been the one to tell him about the police search, not Hannah. He wonders if the investigator is even doing anything.

The sun burns the back of his neck as he climbs back to the car. It's only been two weeks since he was here, but the temperature has risen. The exhaustion feels like a heavy winter blanket. Itchy and hot. The air in the car is no better as he glances a final time at the lake and starts the journey back to Hannah.

An hour later, the adrenaline has seeped away, leaving only exhaustion. All he wants is to be home with Hannah. To make sure she's OK.

Thoughts and questions tumble in his mind. His past and present colliding. Westlake. Manchester. Neve and Tom. He should never have left Hannah. In the fog of tiredness, the white lines on the road seem to lift upwards as though guiding Jake from the road and into the sky. He could fly home then. He imagines a pilot taking control and Jake sitting back and closing his eyes. They're so heavy, and the car is so hot.

In a far-off part of his mind, Jake wonders if he'll crash and die. He remembers the warm blood oozing onto his hands and wonders if death is what he deserves. If everything that's happening is what he deserves.

After all, he's a bad man.

He's a murderer.

THIRTY-THREE

HANNAH

My phone rings at lunchtime. It's been gripped in my hand for the last hour as the walls of my apartment have inched closer, but still I start at the noise and the unknown number displayed on the screen.

Is it Jake? I missed his call while I was in the shower this morning and he's not answered mine since. I have no idea what's happening. I don't know where he is or what he's doing or even if he's OK. All day I've been unravelling. The first thing I did when I turned off my alarm was email my boss to tell her I was taking a personal day. I told her it was the stress of the wedding tomorrow. I'm sure she understands. I should've booked the day off anyway, but I've always preferred to keep busy, and I thought I'd be nervous today. Restless. I am, but it's got nothing to do with the wedding and everything to do with Jake travelling to France early yesterday morning.

Please be OK! I need him to come home – and soon. The last couple of weeks have been some of the hardest in my life. We've both been pushed to our breaking point. It's no wonder things have felt strained. No wonder I've allowed doubts and suspicion to creep into my thoughts. But Jake was kind and understanding when I told him about my previous engagement. I know he loves me. He's driven hundreds of miles to move a decaying corpse just to give us half a chance of getting out of this nightmare. It makes me all the more certain we should go ahead with the wedding tomorrow. Jake is my everything, and I'm his.

All of yesterday and last night, Jake's words have raced through my mind. *'We could start a new life anywhere in the world.'* Each time I've stepped into my bedroom today, my gaze has been drawn to the small suitcase already packed in the corner of my bedroom, ready for tonight. When we changed our wedding plans, I almost cancelled the room booking for myself at the Great Northern Hotel by King's Cross station, the same hotel we'd booked for the reception and party we're no longer having. But Jake and I talked about waking together on Saturday morning and both agreed it won't feel as special to get ready side by side.

Tonight, I'm supposed to say goodbye to Jake. Tomorrow, we'll meet in the church. The plans are all in place, and yet, with Jake in France, it feels impossible.

When I looked at that little suitcase in my bedroom today, all I could think about was Jake's suggestion to run. Part of me yearns for it. To dump the contents of the suitcase on the bed and repack it with a few of my belongings. But we've come so far, done so much to get here. Running would be throwing it all away.

In my hand, my phone continues to hum. I stare again at the number. What if it isn't Jake? What if this is about the recordings and the threats? I heave in a breath and catch the whiff of cleaning products in the air from last night when I'd blasted music and scrubbed the apartment just for something to do. But now the scents catch me off guard, throwing me back to the hallway of the farmhouse and the reek of bleach from Jake's cleaning after we'd cleared up the blood. So much blood.

I shiver, and the memories consume me until I'm being pulled apart like wool spooling from an unfinished jumper.

The phone shakes in my hand. It's still ringing. I can't answer in this state. I lift my gaze, staring around the apartment, looking for something to anchor me in this present. It's the mirror that grabs my attention. The woman staring back isn't me. Her brown hair has fallen over her face; her blue eyes are wide and skittish. I touch my hair, smoothing down a strand. The woman in the mirror does the same.

I take another breath and it feels as though the air reaches my lungs this time, and I swipe at the call on my phone before I miss it and lift it to my ear. 'Jake?' I say, desperation carrying in his name.

'I'm afraid not.' The reply is only three words, but it's enough to open a chasm inside me. Before I can think or breathe or do anything, I'm being dragged back to a past that is still too raw to think about.

A decade of memories come flooding back without warning. His face – those dark eyes, only a shade lighter than his black hair, his smile – broad and cheeky, always melting me. The touch of his hand on mine. We were so madly, deeply, stupidly in love, or at least I thought we were. He made me feel alive and seen in a way no one had ever done before. All those nights we lay in each other's arms talking and laughing and planning our future together – the wedding and the happy ever after our families always thought we were too young for. But we grew up together in that relationship. We were in each other's lives for nearly ten years, and eventually our families saw that we weren't too young. We'd just found our soulmate early.

But then everything changed. Like a storm cloud creeping over the sun. He changed. Suddenly, I wasn't the most important thing in this life. Everything I said and everything I did was wrong. Our last argument hits me like a gut punch. The tears running down my face that night feel so real I touch my cheek, surprised to find it dry. How broken I'd felt. How I knew it had to end. That I'd die if I stayed. My threat to leave him. Not the first time, but I'd really meant it. And that reply I still hear whispering in my nightmares.

'Do you really think there's anywhere you can go where I won't find you?'

It's been seventeen months since I packed in a hurry, the moment he'd left for the bar. Throwing clothes into bags, scooping my toiletries on top. I still feel the urgency and heartbreak like it was yesterday. But he didn't follow. He didn't find me. In those long, empty days that followed, all I had was the loneliness threatening to eat me whole.

Only when I met Jake did I start to think I could heal. When he told me in France what happened with Neve, I understood more than most how dark relationships can turn at the end. Jake wasn't the only one who'd run away from something. Someone. But how could I have told him that without opening the door to a past that is still too raw to voice? Even now, the deep gravel of that voice – those three words – is enough to rip me open once more.

'Hello, Hannah,' he says. 'It's been a while, hasn't it?'

I can't conceal the tremor in my voice. 'Hello.' I want to ask what he wants, but I think I know.

'It's time to talk about what happened in France, don't you think?'

The world stops. My head is suddenly filled with images from the farmhouse. The body on the rug. All that blood. What Jake and I did. The trap that was set for us. For two weeks, we've been tormented by videos and threats. For weeks, we've asked each other who is behind it. Who would go to such lengths to destroy us? Maybe I was wrong not to tell Jake about my past. Because here is the answer.

'Let me explain exactly how this is going to go,' he says before I can find the words to reply.

The name comes unbidden into my thoughts. The wild, crazy, all-consuming love of my life. There is little point stopping it anymore.

Tom.

THIRTY-FOUR
JAKE

A noise slams into the side of Jake's brain, jolting him from an uneasy sleep. A groggy confusion covers him like a fog. His neck screams in pain as he moves, sits up, blinks in the bright sunlight pushing in through the windscreen. Noises come at him. Wheels on tarmac, engines, the whoosh of traffic speeding by. A truck passes close, jogging the small Audi. His throat is sandpaper dry, and he reaches for the bottle of water on the passenger seat, gulping back the hot liquid.

He peers out of the window to the endless motorway, the tall pines growing in straight lines beside distant lanes and rich green fields. He remembers he's in France. He was driving back to Calais and the ferry and London and Hannah. The thought of her makes him sit up and scramble for his phone. That's what woke him – the ringing of it. The sound of the cheap phone unfamiliar but enough to pull him from his exhausted sleep. He grabs at it, relief washing over him at the sight of Hannah's number. When she hadn't answered this morning, he'd thought... It doesn't matter now.

'Hey,' he says, rubbing the sleep from his face. His voice is a croak, and he wonders how long he's been asleep. The clock on the dash reads 1 p.m. which makes it 2 p.m. in France. The realisation clenches his insides. He only meant to take a quick nap so he wouldn't crash, but it's been hours, and he's still a long way from the port and a ferry home.

'Jake?' Hannah's voice cracks.

'Hannah, why haven't you been answering? We have to talk. Claude's body was gone.'

'What do you mean? You've... you've hidden it somewhere else?'

He shakes his head even though she can't see. 'No. I mean I went to the cave this morning and it was empty. Someone's already moved it.'

There's a silence before Hannah speaks again. 'I don't understand. How—' She stops and starts again. 'It doesn't matter now.'

'Of course it matters.'

'No,' she cries. 'Listen to me, Jake. He just called.' Hannah's voice is wrong. Too high. Too thick. Hearing her worry slices into him. 'The man who's sending the recordings and the threats. The one who killed—' Her words break off in a sob.

He forces a calm into his voice he doesn't feel. 'Tell me everything,' he says, and he can imagine her wiping her tears and nodding.

'He called my phone about thirty minutes ago and started giving me all these instructions. He told me to open my laptop and go into the settings—'

'Aren't you at work?' he cuts in. His pulse is galloping through him. He's desperate to start the car and push on, get home to her, but he needs to concentrate.

'No,' she replies. 'I... couldn't focus. I took a personal day. Does it matter now? I had to type in some kind of access code, and then the next thing I knew he had control of my screen somehow. He was moving the cursor, and he told me to stay on the line and watch.'

The realisation is sharp. He thinks he makes a noise in his throat. Remote user access. Jake knows it well. Back in Manchester, it was how he and Tom shared their software developments when they weren't together, until Jake found the secure platform they uploaded the software to for them both to access.

He'd told himself Tom wasn't behind this. Couldn't be. The man didn't have the planning skills. And there was the thing at the bar that night when Jake lost his temper. After Gary found the details on Tom. After Jake made sure the business was his.

It was impossible. But then the 'we' in the messages snags in his thoughts. This is Tom. This is the ex-business partner Jake hasn't seen since he left Manchester six months before he met Hannah. He knows it. He's sure of it.

Ice shoots through his body as beads of sweat form on his brow. He licks his lips. They're dry and cracked.

It all comes rushing back to him. Meeting Tom at the networking event after he'd been in England a while. Seeing the potential in combining their skills. The niche software Tom had developed alongside Jake's charm and skills as a salesman. He'd thought they'd be unstoppable.

It had all gone so well at first. Jake had helped Tom develop some of the user interface and started putting meetings in place with businesses. But Tom got greedy and impatient. He couldn't see Jake's value and wanted to work alone again. All Jake's work would've been for nothing. What was he supposed to do? Sit down and take it? He couldn't let his new life crumble so easily like it did in Westlake.

Jake knows he went too far. He's not proud of what he did – downloading the software from the platform they'd shared then deleting it, cutting Tom's access – stealing what had first been Tom's. Then when Tom kicked off and threatened legal action, Jake hired Gary and found some information on Tom which made it impossible for him to get his software back from Jake.

Then the night at the bar happened. Jake thinks he might be sick. Tom pushed his buttons that night. Jake still remembers the way his fists clenched. That warm blood oozing through his fingers. Why did that bouncer have to step in? The firm hand on his shoulder. Jake spinning round, fury scorching through his body, ready to take on the world. He never meant to hurt anyone. Never meant for anyone to die. But Jake killed a man that night, and then he ran, leaving Tom with the dead bouncer and a whole world of trouble.

Jake went too far. Made mistakes. But Tom has to be in prison, doesn't he? He left Tom to take the fall for the bouncer's death. Even if he'd been charged with manslaughter, Tom wouldn't be out of prison yet. Jake's mind races. He stayed away from the news when he came to London, wanting his fresh start. Couldn't bear to look. A stupid error. Maybe Tom wriggled out of the charge somehow. But then, where has he been all this time? Why is he doing this now? It's been well over a year. It has to be connected to the business sale. The timing is too perfect.

Hannah's voice drags him back to the car. 'He... went to this place... I don't know what it was – maybe a website,' she continues. 'The screen was completely black apart from a line of little icons of all the recordings we've been sent. And then the cursor clicked on another video and it was... it was someone actually killing Claude.'

'What?' Jake's question is strangled. His heart is racing so hard it feels like it will trip over itself and tumble to a stop.

Hannah heaves in a shuddering breath. 'The phone must've been set on the window ledge in the hall and caught everything. Claude coming through the door and being stabbed. I saw him die...' Her words trail into gulping sobs.

'You saw who did this?' The words come rushed and urgent. She sobs. 'Yes. His name's Tom—'

'Oh God, Hannah. I'm so sorry. What did he tell you?'

'What do you mean?' she asks.

'Tom is my ex-business partner. We worked together in Manchester, but we fell out. I never thought he was behind this. I never thought he'd go so far.' He closes his eyes for a beat.

'Tom is your ex-business partner?' Hannah asks, her voice sounding distant.

He lifts the phone from his ear, checking the signal. It's only a cheap phone. The last thing he needs is for the damn thing to cut out.

'Yes. Look. It's too much to explain now, but this is all my fault, Hannah. I'm so sorry. I swear, I'll tell you everything when I'm back. I'm driving now. I'll be back late tonight. We can talk properly then—'

'He wants money, Jake,' Hannah blurts. 'He said if we pay in the next two hours, he'll send us the video of Claude being murdered as protection. He won't go to the police, and neither will we. And if we don't send him the money, he'll delete the video of Claude being murdered – the only one that proves it wasn't us – and send the others to the police instead.' Her words end in another sob.

Jake's mind races. There's evidence he didn't kill Claude. He knows he didn't do it. Of course he knows it. He made it back to the farmhouse first the day of the hike and wandered the gardens for a while, waiting for Hannah. He could've gone inside, but he'd been picturing the victorious smile on Hannah's face at winning their bet. He feels sick thinking about what was happening inside the farmhouse in those same moments.

His nightmares have blurred Claude's death with the bouncer in the alley outside the bar on his last night in Manchester. He didn't kill Claude, but his temper has cost him, and now his past has caught up with him in the worst possible way. But suddenly there's a way out, and for the first time in his life, it isn't running away.

'How much does he want?' Jake asks, thinking of the money sitting in his business account right now.

'Half a million pounds. And we have just over an hour left to pay.'

'Fuck!' he hisses.

Hannah's words come quicker, her voice rising with the same panic he feels. 'I said we didn't have it, but he said I was lying. He said he knew we did. Then he told me to write down a bank account to send the money to, and then he closed the page and left my laptop and hung up. I can access maybe a hundred thousand right now, but everything else is tied in the trust fund. It'll take days to get it.' She draws in a breath. 'I'm scared, Jake.'

'It's OK—' he starts, even though it isn't. Somewhere in the back of his mind he registers the words *trust fund*. Hannah's never mentioned it before. It doesn't matter now.

'This is my fault.' She sobs again. 'There's something I need to tell you tonight...' Her words trail off as the emotions take over.

Her pain spreads through him as his own. How can she think it's her fault?

Hannah is saying something, but it takes him a moment to hear it. '...to run, Jake. Don't come back to England. Turn around and go to Spain, and... I don't know... go somewhere far away where you can be lost.'

'Han—'

'I'll pack a bag and I'll come find you. You'll need to swap the car.'

'Just a second,' he tries again, but she's still talking, making urgent plans.

'Can you get to a cash point?' she asks. 'The police will be monitoring everything the second Tom sends them the videos, so do it soon then throw away your bank cards.' Her words come out in a rush of panic.

'Hannah!' he shouts, and this time she hears him. Falls silent. All along, he'd planned to tell her about the sale of the business and his wealth on their wedding night. But if he doesn't tell her the truth now, there won't be a wedding.

'I can pay them,' he says.

'What?' Her voice rings with confusion.

'I've got the money. Novexia – the client I've been working with. They didn't just want to licence my software. They wanted to buy it. The deal went through last week. I can pay, Hannah.' Despite the panic and fear and this awful moment, a zing of something still travels through his body. He's rich. He's successful. It's everything he's worked for.

'Why didn't you tell me?' she gasps.

He swallows, searching for the right answer. 'I wanted it to be a surprise on our wedding night. I wanted to show you that I could give you the lifestyle you deserve. And now I can get us out of this, once and for all.'

It suddenly makes sense. The torture of the last few weeks. And now the request for money. Tom wanted to punish Jake for what he did, and he wants his cut of the sale. Jake draws in a shaky breath. For the first time in days, he feels like there's a light at the end of the tunnel. All he has to do is get to it.

'Where are you?' Hannah says. 'Are you nearly home? There's not much time.'

The relief is sucked away in an instant. He stares out the window again at the endless highway. He is nowhere near the port. If he left right this second, it would be hours before he's home. All his business accounts – his banking app – it's on his phone. His phone is in the apartment in London, more than four hundred miles and a ferry crossing away. There's no way he can make it back in time.

THIRTY-FIVE
JAKE

Jake doubts the piece-of-junk phone he bought before getting the ferry is capable of supporting the apps he'd need to download. But it doesn't matter anyway. Setting them up, getting access; he'd need his passwords and codes, and they're in the apartment too. For a moment, he thinks of calling the customer service department at the bank, sending the transfer the old-fashioned way, but the wait on the call centres is crazy. When he called last week to upgrade his business account, he'd waited forty-five minutes to speak to another human. He can't risk running out of time.

But it doesn't matter. He can't make the transfer, but Hannah can.

'Hannah?' he says.

'Yeah?'

'You'll need to do the transfer from my banking app on my phone. I can talk you through it.'

Jake stays on the phone with Hannah, talking her through each step. The knots that form in his stomach are spiked. Tom's asking for half what he was paid by Novexia for the software.

Despite everything, it's a kick in the balls to give it away so freely, but at least he's not asking for the full amount. Jake wonders why he isn't. It can only be that Tom doesn't know the details of the deal or how much Novexia are paying. Whatever the reason, giving half the money will be worth it to be done with this nightmare. Besides, the money doesn't matter now. Hannah has her own wealth. A trust fund, no less. They'll be married tomorrow and can share everything. It will be OK, he tells himself as he waits in the silence for Hannah to speak.

'I've done it,' she says. 'God, I'm shaking all over. I wish you were here.'

'Me too. I'll be back this evening. I promise.'

'Thank you,' she whispers. 'For paying—'

'Don't thank me,' he replies. 'We're in this together. The important thing is that it's done and—'

Hannah's gasp cuts him short. 'The video of Tom murdering Claude has just been emailed. I've got the proof we didn't kill him.'

Jake squeezes his eyes shut and fights the desire to cry. It's over. The constant fear of being arrested lifts from him like bricks dropping from his shoulders. 'I love you,' he says in an exhale of relief.

They say their goodbyes, and Jake starts the engine as the urgency to be home with Hannah thrums through him.

It's late by the time he parks in the underground car park, the tiredness of the journey lifting as he races to the loft two steps at a time.

'Hannah?' he calls as he rushes through the door.

There's no answer. Jake's pulse starts to race. He strides to the bedroom, his breath catching at the sight of the empty bed, still neatly made.

But then there's a noise behind him and he's spinning towards it, and Hannah is sitting up on the sofa, her eyes heavy with sleep.

'I couldn't go to bed without you,' she says, stretching as she stands. The fear disappears in a puff, and he's running at her, scooping her into his arms and kissing her, searching and desperate, so grateful she's here. She's OK. She waited up for him. She loves him. He's surprised when a relieved sob catches in his throat.

'I've missed you,' he says in a husky whisper.

'I love you,' she says. 'I love you so much.'

'I love you too.' He draws back to look into her eyes. 'It's over.'

She grimaces but nods. 'I've filed the recording of Tom killing Claude on the cloud of my laptop just in case we ever need it.'

'Should I—' He's torn. Wanting to see for himself, but the images in his mind are already so vivid.

She gives a fierce shake of her head. 'You don't need to. I've seen it. I've got it.'

He nods. 'I've been so worried about you.'

'I'm fine. I promise.' She smiles, and he can see she's OK. They're OK.

They kiss again, and it's tentative at first, then harder. His hands find the skin beneath her top and roam across her body. Desire stirs in him, hot and urgent, and at first she's arching into his touch, but as his fingers tease the edge of the waistband of her jeans, she draws away, steps back.

He arches his brow in question, and she laughs.

'We're getting married tomorrow,' she says, swatting his arm. 'You'll have to wait.'

A grin stretches across his face. The first easy smile he's felt since the first day of the getaway in France.

'I'd wait forever and a day for you.'

The cheesy line makes her laugh, and it's the best sound he's ever heard in his life.

Her gaze shifts to the door, and he looks to her suitcase and the large white dress box, stacked neatly on top.

'I don't want to leave you,' she says. 'I don't want to stay in a hotel tonight.'

He's torn too. The need to keep her close is fierce. 'I don't want you to go either,' he says. 'But... this is one tradition we should keep, Hannah Fitzroy, don't you think? I want to be waiting in that church for you to take my breath away. I want to remember the moment I see you in your wedding dress for the rest of my life.'

She steps forward and holds him tight; kisses him a final time. 'Is it really over?' she asks.

He nods. What else can he do? 'Yes. I really think it is. We've now got evidence that Tom killed Claude. If the police try to arrest us or if anything else happens, we'll be able to use it.' He motions to the sofa. 'I need to tell you about Tom and explain. I made some mistakes in Manchester, Han. This was about revenge for him. I'm just so sorry he dragged you into it.' His voice wobbles. He won't tell her about the bar that night, but she deserves the rest. She deserves an explanation.

Hannah shakes her head. 'It's OK. I... I wasn't honest with you about my ex either.' She pauses and looks like she might say more but seems to change her mind. 'We both have a lot to talk about. But we also have the rest of our lives. Let's just be happy it's over tonight, OK? Let's focus on getting married. And then I think I should take some time off and we should go on our honeymoon straight away. Get a break from everything.'

He feels his face light up. 'I love the sound of that. Now let's get you out of here because I need a hot shower and some sleep before tomorrow.'

Hannah smiles, slipping on her shoes. He carries her suitcase and the box with her dress in it down the stairs for her, making sure she's safely in a taxi for the short journey to the hotel. Only when he's alone in the apartment with the door locked does he go to the fridge and gulp down a large glass of Hannah's Sancerre. Alcohol is probably not the best idea the night before his wedding, especially after the last thirty-six hours, but he needs something to dull the sharp edges of what's happened. He pours a second glass and only then does he grab his phone and sink onto the sofa.

There are no messages or missed calls from Neve or Gary, thank God. Nothing the PI can say matters anymore. Hannah has told him all he needs to know about her ex, and now she knows the truth about him selling his business and his wealth. Claude's body is gone, and even though Jake wishes he knew where, wishes he could be sure the police will never find it and come for them, they have the evidence it wasn't them who killed him. It's over.

His fingers tremble a little as he logs into the banking app. Half a million pounds is so much money. The loading roulette wheel fills the screen. He reminds himself that Tom deserved the money. The software was his to start with. Jake stole it.

The banking app loads, and it stings to see half the money gone. He checks the transfer Hannah made. It's to a company called Olden Holdings. He googles them, but there's nothing, and what would he do if he found something – a name? An address?

Tom has his videos, and they have the only one that matters – the evidence they didn't murder Claude. The evidence that Tom did. This is what they paid for. Not just the destruction of the videos incriminating them but for the video incriminating Tom. They've manoeuvred their pieces into a dual checkmate. Neither can destroy the other without destroying themselves. Clever, he thinks. Just the kind of thing Tom would think of.

He pushes the thought aside and finishes the wine. Then he takes a long shower and slips beneath the covers. The bed feels empty without Hannah beside him. Tomorrow they'll be married and they can focus on their future. Their bright, amazing future.

And yet, as Jake closes his eyes to the exhaustion, his heart continues to pound against his ribcage, and he has the nagging sense that he's forgotten something.

THE WEDDING DAY

THIRTY-SIX

HANNAH

The hotel room at the old station hotel is elegant. The furniture a deep red-brown, smooth to the touch and polished to a shine. Delicate lace curtains frame the tall windows, letting in soft rays of sunlight. It's old-fashioned but not tired. The carpet beneath my bare feet is soft and feels new. There's a fresh bouquet of roses on the table, scenting the air with sweetness.

The window overlooks the older section of King's Cross station. A throwback to the Victorian era and grand steam engines. I can hear the faint beep of train doors opening and closing. The soft rattle of the engines pulling in and out of the platforms. It's all wasted on me.

Snakes slither and coil in my stomach – nerves I didn't expect to feel. Finally, my wedding to Jake is here. Days and weeks and months I've looked ahead to this day and imagined Jake standing in the sunlit church waiting for me. It's all I've wanted, but nothing feels like I thought it would as I stare at my reflection in the mirror. I'm scared and lonely and sad, and it isn't how I wanted to feel today.

Less than a ten-minute walk away, Jake will be pulling on his suit in our apartment, fastening his tie. He rarely wears one, and on the few occasions he has, I've straightened it for him. I wonder if he'll remember to do it before he leaves for the church. How is he feeling? Is he excited? Nervous? Is today everything he wanted it to be? I wish I knew what he was thinking. He looked so tired last night. I hope he slept better than I did.

I knew I wouldn't sleep on the night before the wedding, but I thought I would be looking ahead, too much excitement buzzing in my veins. But instead, I lay awake churning over the events of yesterday. That awful moment I answered my phone and heard that husky, familiar voice.

Then my shaking hands as I'd called Jake. I'd tried to tell him Tom was my ex, but Jake cut me off, confessing his own connection to Tom. It was the last thing I expected him to say, and his words threw me. I couldn't find my voice to explain my own part in this. It was cowardly to let Jake think this is all on him, but I'll tell him everything later. Every dark, terrible detail.

Jake thinks this is over. I wish I could believe it, but deep down I know it's just the beginning. All those videos and threats we've had. Everything we did at the farmhouse. Does Jake really think money is enough to make it go away? This has been about revenge, not money. But we've made it. Our wedding day is here. I've been counting down the days for weeks.

I dab gloss to my lips and stare again at my reflection, trying to calm the nervous juddering of my pulse. My make-up is subtle. I don't want to look like someone else today. My skin looks smooth and dewy, with just a bit of rosy blush on my cheeks. My eyes are lined with a soft brown pencil, and my eyelashes have been brushed with mascara. I've tied my hair back in a simple twist. Despite the late start to spring, summer has come in a hurry, and the day is set to be hot. I want my hair away from my neck and face.

I pick up my phone and check the tracking app. Jake's icon shows him moving along the road outside the apartment. He's left for the church already. Of course he'll want to be there early. I need to get dressed. I glance to the ornate Victorian wardrobe where my wedding dress hangs. It's ivory white, clinging to my body all the way to the floor where it drops in a pool of rippling silk. I felt like a 1920s film star the moment I slipped it on. The straps are delicate lace, but the neckline is modern, dropping into a low V shape at my breastbone.

My fingers hover over my phone. I almost message Jake just to check one final time that he's OK. That he still loves me. A last piece of reassurance before I leave too. But I trust him to be at the church waiting for me.

There's a knock at the door. I think of the room service I ordered that's taken an age to come. A breakfast of fruit and yoghurt and a single glass of champagne. None of which I can stomach. The snakes twist inside me again.

I tighten the cord of my bathrobe and open the door without checking the peephole. The next seconds come in a rush. I reel back, mouth dropping open at the sight of the man standing before me. I want to turn and run, to slam the door and lock it, but instead I freeze, not breathing, not moving, as he barrels past me into my hotel room, pushing the door shut behind him without a word. Then he's turning towards me, and all I can think is how this is the trouble I knew was coming for us.

THIRTY-SEVEN
JAKE

Jake woke this morning from a deep sleep feeling refreshed, the fear and uncertainty of the last couple of weeks gone and the nightmares of anger and clenched fists and blood with it.

As soon as he was showered and dressed in his suit, hair styled, shoes shined, he started to think of all the things that could still stop him from reaching the church and marrying the woman of his dreams. A car accident. A mugging. A pregnant woman in need of assistance. A child with a lost dog.

It was a relief to have these nothing worries again after the constant life-or-death fears, but he left early anyway – striding quickly, smiling to himself in the morning sunlight and arriving at the church before the doors were unlocked.

He was only there ten minutes before the vicar pulled open the heavy ornate wood doors and ushered him inside. Jake likes the vicar. He's a slight man in his seventies who runs marathons on his days off. When he speaks, his voice commands attention – part of the job description, Jake thinks.

The church is cool. The light from the stained-glass windows casts a rainbow of colour across the empty pews. The perfect filter. The perfect day. Dust particles float lazily in the slivers of light, creating an ethereal atmosphere. The musky scent in the air reminds him of old books and history. Outside, he hears children yelling with joy at games of tag and soccer. A ball thuds rhythmically against a wall followed by the frustrated shout of a resident telling the kids to shut up. Jake wonders briefly if they should've kept the organist after all. It felt too much for just the two of them, but he hadn't thought about the noises of the outside world drifting in.

'Ready?' the vicar asks, appearing from a hidden backroom and fastening his long cloak.

A grin spreads across Jake's face. 'I think so.' He knows so.

The vicar gestures to the space on the raised platform in front of the pews, and Jake takes his spot. Not even the lingering sense that he's forgotten something is enough to bother him as a calm settles. Across the dais, two women in their sixties wearing blue floral dresses fuss around a flower display. Jake flashes a smile, thanking them for being here to witness their marriage.

And then there's nothing left to do but wait for Hannah. She'll be on her way, pulling up in a taxi any moment. The thought fills him with an indescribable energy.

From beside him, the vicar clears his throat, and Jake's gaze moves to the clock on the wall above the door. It's exactly 10 a.m. Any second, Hannah will appear in the open doorway. He can't wait to see her in her wedding dress.

There's a low hum from his jacket pocket – his phone is ringing. He shoots the vicar an apologetic smile and looks at the screen in case it's Hannah. Instead, it's Gary's name he sees. Jake rejects the call. Whatever the PI has to tell him, it can wait until Monday. But a minute later, his phone rings a second time. He's not giving up.

'Sorry,' Jake says to the vicar. 'I'd better just tell them I'm trying to get married here.' The comment makes the vicar smile, and quickly Jake takes a step away and accepts the call.

'Gary, it's not a great time. I'm about to get married.' Even as a whisper, his voice echoes in the empty church.

His eyes are drawn to the clock once more. Hannah is only a few minutes late. He imagines her in a taxi stuck behind a slow-moving bus or a cyclist, wishing she'd walked the ten minutes from the hotel. And yet the first fluttering of nerves dance across his chest. *She'll be here*, he tells himself. *She's on her way.*

'I know, mate,' Gary says. 'But I thought you'd want to hear this.'

'What is it?' Jake asks, curiosity getting the better of him.

Gary makes the noise in his throat and it's all Jake can do not to hang up. 'A few things,' he says. 'Firstly, the French man you asked me to look into – Claude Dubas.'

Jake closes his eyes for a second as the calm beauty of the church is overtaken by images of the dead body on the rug. Then the empty cave. The recordings. The demand for money. He doesn't want to think about this now.

'What about him?' he forces himself to ask as his gaze drags back to the clock. It's probably fast.

Then Gary speaks and Jake feels the world shift beneath his feet. 'He doesn't exist.'

THIRTY-EIGHT
JAKE

'What?' The single word is loud, echoing across the empty pews. Beside the flower arrangement, the two church ladies exchange a look, and he can feel the eyes of the vicar burning into his back as he turns away from them and lowers his voice. 'What do you mean Claude doesn't exist? I met the man.' Jake did more than meet him. He knocked him on his ass in the middle of the village square, and later he mopped up the man's blood. Whatever Gary thinks he knows, he's wrong.

'Whoever you met doesn't go by the name of Claude Dubas. I ran every search possible,' Gary explains. 'I looked at all the properties surrounding the address you gave me in the Languedoc. I looked at church records in the area. I joined local Facebook groups. I called the café in the village you mentioned. Thank God for Google Translate. And I'm telling you, there's no Claude Dubas living anywhere in the region.'

Frustration hammers into him. Gary is wasting his time and his money. He wishes he'd never answered his phone. He doesn't need this right now. He glances to the clock again. Hannah is five minutes late. It's not like her.

But Jake can't let this go. Gary is wrong. 'What about the

police search?' he says. 'I saw an article about his disappearance on a local news site.' Not to mention the call from Claude's wife and sitting in the kitchen of the farmhouse with Allard, lying to the police officer about what they did. Then dodging his calls for the past week. Not to mention Claude is a close family friend of the Fitzroys. Practically an uncle to Hannah.

Of course Claude exists. Jake helped hide his dead body, for fuck's sake.

'Forget it,' he says to Gary. 'The man I'm thinking of must go by a different name.' That would make sense. Maybe it's a French thing. Maybe his middle name is Claude. Or it's his dad's name. How the hell should he know? It doesn't matter now anyway.

'Jake?' Gary barks into his ear. 'Are you there? There's something else—'

But from beside Jake, the vicar is clearing his throat, and Jake can't hear any more. As he ends the call without saying goodbye, his gaze flicks to the doorway, breath hitching at the thought of Hannah waiting for him to catch that first glimpse of her in her dress. But the doorway is empty and the minutes keep passing. Where is she?

He feels sick. His shirt too tight. His tie strangling. Hannah isn't the type to be late. Especially not today, after everything they've been through at the hands of Tom and his sick game of revenge on Jake for stealing his software and how he left him that night in the alley outside the bar with the dead bouncer.

His heart is battering in his chest as he opens the app and finds Hannah's location. Not at the hotel. Not on her way here. But at their apartment. Why would she be there? He taps her name and waits for her to answer, but her phone cuts to voicemail. He doesn't try again. Maybe she's forgotten something and had to detour back to the apartment. Maybe she's already on her way again. But she would've called. She would never leave him standing here like this. Waiting.

It's this final realisation that jolts Jake into action. An electrical charge hits every cell in his body at once. Something is very wrong. He might not know what it is. Might not understand yet, but that doesn't mean it's not happening.

Jake moves then. Striding then running then sprinting. If the vicar calls after him for an explanation, he doesn't hear.

He runs like he's being chased. Like a hand is about to reach out and grab him. He runs like he did that night in the alley after the fight with Tom and then the bouncer.

He never meant for things to get physical. Tom called him from the bar one Friday night after their partnership had fallen apart. He already sounded halfway to drunk when he asked Jake to meet him.

'You know the software is mine,' Tom said when Jake arrived to find Tom sat waiting for him with two pints. 'And you don't have the skills to develop it.'

Jake shrugged, looking around the busy bar. Girls in their late teens dressed in minuscule tops and skirts with leering boys wearing too much aftershave. Christmas music blasted from the speakers. 'You're too much of a perfectionist, Tom. That's always been your problem. The software is great. I'll find businesses who want to licence it. It just takes time, that's all. Something we'd have had if you'd trusted me.'

'Let me back in,' Tom said. 'Partners again.' It was impossible to miss the pleading in his voice. The desperation.

Jake wanted to do it. He wanted to believe it could be how it was. Tom was right – Jake knew nothing about the ins and outs of software development. That's why they'd made the perfect team. But the trust between them was gone. Jake could see it in the way Tom looked at him. Jake had stolen from him, and there was no way to forgive and move on.

'Sorry,' Jake replied, meaning it. 'I didn't want it to end like this between us, but it's over. Walk away.'

He left the bar then, unable to sit there for another minute.

Seeing how pathetic Tom looked caused a rock of guilt to form in his stomach. But Tom followed, staggering a little from the alcohol. The street was busy with groups of drunk party-goers, oblivious to the chill in the air as they yelled and laughed. No one looked up when Jake moved through the crowd and turned onto a quiet side street. No one noticed when Tom's hand grabbed his shoulder, pulling him into the alley behind the bar that stank of rotting garbage and vomit.

'What the hell?' Jake shouted as Tom shoved him once then twice.

'You can't do this to me,' he yelled, spittle flying into Jake's face.

'It's already done,' Jake said and shrugged. And perhaps it was that shrug, like it didn't matter, like it was over, that caused Tom to shove him again. Jake wasn't ready for it, and he staggered back, knocking against the brick wall. Pain shot through him, igniting an anger so bright he couldn't see anything else.

'I'm going to the police,' Tom screamed then, hurt and anger contorting his face. 'Let's see what they think about what you've done.'

Before Jake could stop himself, his fists were up and swinging hard, and he was that boy again, ready to fight the world. He wasn't about to lose this new business. Tom's threat of legal action was dead thanks to the information Gary found on him, but Jake didn't know what the police would say and had no intention of letting it get that far.

His fist smashed into Tom's face again and then again, only stopping when the bouncer from the bar stepped into the alley and, in his fury, Jake couldn't stop himself from whipping round and hitting him too. Over and over, until the blood of the man's nose oozed through his clenched fists, warm and sticky, and he fell to the ground. Jake ran then, not daring to look back at the two men on the ground.

He didn't stop running until he reached London and

checked the news sites; felt the bottom drop out of his world. ONE DEAD AND ONE BADLY INJURED IN BAR FIGHT. He remembers the pounding of his fist into the bouncer's face and the way he fell back. That crack of the back of his head on the concrete. He'd killed him. He was a murderer. And he'd left Tom to take the blame.

A car horn blasts as Jake races across a road without stopping. His breath comes in shorter gasps as much from the memories as the exertion. But he doesn't slow down as he weaves around pedestrians and pushchairs, ignoring the tuts and the yells and thinking only of getting to Hannah.

He's gasping for breath as he reaches the apartment. His feet are shredded from running in his new wedding shoes, and his shirt is sticking to his skin, but he doesn't care. Doesn't stop. He takes the stairs two then three at a time and bursts through the apartment door, yelling Hannah's name, and she's right there on the sofa like she's been waiting for him.

'Hannah,' he gasps again.

She turns and he takes in the sleek way she's twisted her hair and the make-up. All that's missing is the dress, he thinks, as he takes in her jeans and white T-shirt. Fear grabs his throat. Has she got cold feet? The question is chased away by a single thought – he can fix it.

'Hey,' she replies with a weak smile, bottom lip trembling.

Jake wipes his face and tries to catch his breath as he closes the gap between them.

'Thank God you're OK.' He searches her face for the answer to the question he doesn't want to ask. *Why didn't you come to the church?*

Hannah opens her mouth like she's going to speak, but no words come. He sits beside her and takes her hand.

'It's OK,' he says, wondering if he might cry too. 'I still love you.'

She shakes her head. 'You don't understand,' she whispers.

'Then tell me,' he pleads, and a pain cuts across his chest as he perches on the edge of the sofa beside her. He can't be this close to getting everything he wants and lose now.

'I...' The word dies in her mouth at the sound of movement from the kitchen.

Jake was so focused on Hannah that he didn't notice the French police officer – Allard – standing by the counter, watching them.

A noise escapes Jake's throat. All the calls he never returned. Of course it would escalate. Allard has come to London to talk in person. This is why Hannah didn't come to the church. He wonders if she's showed him the video she was sent after paying Tom. The proof that while they might have lied, they might be in some trouble here, they're not murderers.

But then another man moves to stand beside Allard, and Jake's thoughts spin violently as he tries to make sense of what he's seeing and can't.

Claude is dead. They hid his body.

Claude doesn't exist.

Claude is standing in their apartment beside Allard. Very much alive.

THIRTY-NINE

HANNAH

My pulse thumps through my body as Jake takes in the two men in the kitchen. The first is shorter, older, with a shock of thick white hair. He's wearing the same black shirt and scowl he greeted me with when he stepped into my hotel room this morning and it hit me that today wouldn't be the end of the nightmare but the beginning.

The second man is taller, the same height as Jake, but a slim build with a narrow face and a sharp nose. He's dressed casually in jeans and a navy T-shirt.

I watch the confusion pull at Jake's features. Despite how fast he must've run here from the church, he looks good in his suit. As handsome as I imagined. The realisation makes me think of my wedding dress, still hanging on the wardrobe door of the ornate Victorian wardrobe in the hotel. I wonder if I'll ever see it again or if the cleaning team will find it. Will they assume I got cold feet or that I was jilted? Neither are true, but that's a word I'm not sure I know the meaning of anymore.

Jake's eyes find mine briefly before he's staring back to the men as though he's torn over who to talk to, what to think, what to do. I wish I could explain, but my ears are ringing with the pounding of blood rushing through my veins, and fear has stolen my voice. I feel frozen and powerless. It's my fault we're all here. People don't move on from the kind of love Tom and I shared. It's been seventeen months since I last saw him the night he left for the bar and I packed my bags to leave under the lights of the Christmas tree. It feels like no time has passed at all.

Jake stands, moving out from the sofa, positioning himself between the men and me as though sensing the danger in the air, like an electrical storm about to hit.

'Who the hell are you?' he asks, voice loud, but I think I catch an undercurrent of trepidation. Has his confusion given way to fear? It will soon – once he realises. Once he knows what I know.

The taller man cocks an eyebrow in amusement. He doesn't answer Jake but says, 'I'll stand by the door.' The French accent is gone, but there is still that air of authority we sensed in the farmhouse when he introduced himself as Stéphane Allard. It wasn't just the uniform or the accent – it was him that sucked us in.

In a burst of long strides, he's by the door, blocking the only exit from this apartment. The air shifts, the tension growing – so thick I can almost see it rippling around us. I'm not the only one. Jake's posture is rigid, eyes narrowed.

It's the older man who answers Jake. 'I'm Robert Green. This is my son, Robert Junior.' He gestures across the apartment. 'Everyone calls him Bobby.'

Another noise escapes Jake's throat. I can see him wrestling with his temper and his need to be in control.

'I don't care what people call him. I want to know what the hell you're doing here.' He throws me a searching glance, and all I can do is stare back at this man who is everything to me. The force of my feelings for Jake rise up, threatening to take over.

Jake turns to Robert. 'This is our wedding day.' Suddenly, his phone is in his hand and he's holding it out like a weapon.

'Explain yourself right now or I'm calling the police and having you done for trespassing.'

I bury my face in my hands. In the shock of being alone in the church, in his frantic run to get here, in the confusion of finding these men in our apartment, it hasn't dawned on Jake yet how much I've been keeping from him. I force myself to look up as Robert speaks. 'I'm Tom's father.'

It's impossible to miss the colour draining from Jake's face; the bob of his Adam's apple. He shoots a nervous glance to Bobby, still blocking the door. I wonder if Jake is noticing the subtle resemblance to his brother. Bobby is taller than Tom and his hair lighter, but there's a similarity in the way he walks, moving his entire body just like Tom. They wear the same cologne too, but Jake probably doesn't know that.

The expression on Bobby's face is pure hate. It slices through me – a physical pain I want to wince away from.

'Right.' Jake slips his phone into his jacket. He rubs both hands over his jaw. 'So this is revenge?' Jake asks, hands falling to his sides. He looks like he's going to drop back to the sofa, but he remains on his feet. 'Because of what I did to Tom. I knew he couldn't have pulled this off on his own. So this entire thing has been' – he waves his hands in the air in that way he does when he can't find the words – 'what... a sick game to mess with my head and ruin my relationship with Hannah?'

I bite the inside of my lip. Jake still thinks this is his fault. I have to tell him the truth. I sit forward, about to stand too. 'Jake, I—'

His eyes when they land on mine are anxious. His hand touches my shoulder. Gentle but firm, keeping me in my seat. 'Stay there, Han. I'll handle this. I'm so sorry you've been dragged into this mess, but it's between me and these men here.'

'Dragged me into what?' I ask, swallowing the hard lump of emotion building in my throat, but I have to ask. I need to understand how much Jake knows.

Jake grits his teeth, his jaw tight, and I watch indecision play out.

Frustration nips at me. He wouldn't lie now, would he?

'Jake,' I hiss. 'Tell me what's going on. Please.' And the thing is, I know the answer. I know what he did to Tom. I know why he thinks these men are here for him. But I have to hear him say it.

He nods and drops his gaze like he can't look at me. 'This is what I was going to tell you last night. And I need you to know, I'm not proud of this, but before I moved to London, when I was in Manchester, I started working with Tom on a piece of software he'd developed. He was looking for investment and support, and so we became partners. He did the technical stuff, and I did more of the usability side and tried to get us investors and find businesses who wanted to licence the software.

'And then... Tom changed his mind,' Jake continues. 'He was getting impatient, and he couldn't see how much I'd done for us. He said he didn't want to work with me anymore. Just came out with it out of the blue one day.'

Bobby huffs from his position by the door. 'So you stole his work.' Anger is humming from his body, causing a prickling fear to creep over me. It's a reminder that I have no idea how this is going to play out or if we're all going to walk out of this apartment alive. 'Don't bother trying to deny it.'

Jake shoots me a pleading look I can't decipher then nods at Bobby. 'You're right. I took his software. I stole it,' he corrects, his voice cracking. 'I knew how special it was. How much it was worth if we could just get going with it. He'd put it on an online platform we could both access, and I downloaded it and deleted the platform, cutting off his access. It was wrong, but you have to understand that I was upset too. I'd spent months of my life promoting and supporting Tom and helping him shape the software into what it was. I trusted him, and he repaid that trust by telling me he was walking away.'

'Keep going.' Robert's command is almost a growl. The tension in the air seems to press against my skin, like a weight pushing down on my body, keeping me in my seat.

Jake covers his mouth with his trembling hand for a moment before continuing. 'He was upset. He threatened to sue me if I didn't give him his work back, but I hired a private investigator and found he didn't have the money to even speak to a lawyer. There was nothing he could do.'

He looks at Robert before he continues. 'Believe me, I feel really bad about what I did. I know I took his dream and I destroyed his life. I'm really sorry. I guess he's got half the money now from the sale, and you've all ruined my wedding day and probably my relationship.' His tone shifts from apologetic to bitter as he continues. 'So whatever this sick game is you've played, I'm out. Well done. You fooled me.'

Jake spins towards me, crouching by my feet and gripping my hands in his. I sense Robert stiffen at the movement, but he lets this play out. The lump in my throat returns – a sharp rock blocking my airway.

'I'm so sorry, Hannah,' Jake says, his voice thick with the same emotion I feel. 'I'm sorry I wasn't honest with you about this at the start. I'm sorry for everything we've been through these last few weeks. I'm sorry I've ruined today, but if you give me another chance, I can make this right between us.'

He still doesn't get it. The fear in my body is shifting, stepping aside to allow the frustration to push forward.

'This isn't about you,' I whisper.

'I'm sorry, but it is. It's between me and Tom. I guess he's here somewhere?' Jake glances to Bobby then Robert, and his stupidity is enough to ignite something in me. I yank my hands away and stand so fast that he falls against the coffee table, looking up at me in wide-eyed confusion.

'Don't you get it,' I cry out as I heave in a wheezing breath.

Seventeen months of hurt and anger, and that damn rock in my throat won't leave. 'This isn't about you, Jake. It's about me.'

He frowns and pulls himself up. He looks like he's going to reach for me, and I stagger back, putting the sofa between us.

'Han, what are you talking about?'

The emotion builds. The strength of my feelings for Jake threaten to overwhelm me. Not love.

Never love.

But hate.

This man is everything to me. Not because I want him or love him or even like him. He is everything to me because in destroying him, I can get justice for what he did. I've thrown everything I've had into playing the woman in love, the woman Jake thought I was. And I'd do it all over again if it led us to this point.

The words, when they come, are thrown at him, bitter and harsh. 'Tom's dead. And it's your fault.'

FORTY

HANNAH

Jake stumbles back as if my words are a physical punch. 'What? Tom's dead? No, that can't be...' His eyes dart wildly around the room before settling on me again. His pupils widen, and it's as though something clicks into place in his thoughts.

'Tom is your ex,' he says. 'That was who the engagement card was for.'

Hurt slices through my chest, sharp and unyielding, thinking of that card and the love Tom and I shared.

Jake thinks for a moment, his eyes narrowing on me. 'This isn't just about your past, is it? You're part of this,' Jake says, and I nod.

Finally, he understands. This isn't about him. It's about me. This is all me. His mouth gapes, his shoulders sag and he drops to the sofa as though his legs won't hold him anymore.

'I didn't know he was dead.' He hunches forward, dropping his head into his hands before rubbing his face. It's an effort not to scream at him. Does he realise how pathetic he looks when he does that? A stupid, lost little boy.

I move so I'm standing opposite. I have to see his face and his reaction as this plays out, but I'm careful to keep the coffee table between us. Robert takes a step closer; cautious. Not trusting.

When Jake lifts his face, he looks suddenly older, as though the realisation of Tom's death has aged him. He opens his mouth. Then closes it. I imagine he's wondering where to start. Before he can find the words, his phone buzzes in his hand, and he looks at the screen before swiping to accept the call.

'Gary,' he says by way of hello as he shoots me another questioning look and puts the call on speaker. From across the room, Bobby exhales an expletive. That hate for Jake is like heat from a fireball.

A memory from my old rental home flashes through my mind. A few weeks before Tom died. Standing in our cramped kitchen, old cupboards and cracked tiles. Damp creeping up the walls but still our home. It's where we were happy for so long. Tom and I both chasing our dreams. His to develop software to help small businesses manage their finances. My dream wasn't law. Never anything as stuffy. I wanted to act. Ever since I plucked up the courage to attend the drama club run by Tom's father in my teens.

'He can't do that,' I cried as Tom explained what Jake had done. 'You could sue him. Get your software back.'

'With what money?' he shot back with such defeat my heart cracked. 'Jake's used up all our savings already on his networking.'

I grabbed his arm, wanting him to listen, wanting him to fight for his dreams. 'So lie. Tell him you'll sue him, even if we can't afford it.'

'I did,' he replies. 'But Jake hired a private investigator to look into me. He knows I don't have the money for legal fees. There's nothing I can do.'

The memory isn't the kind that rips open my chest and pulls out my heart, but even now it still stings.

'Everything all right, mate?' Gary asks, voice tinny on the speaker.

'Yeah,' Jake replies. 'You had something else you wanted to tell me. It's about Hannah, right?'

Gary clears his throat, and I realise Jake was asking the investigator for more than just what he'd told me. I shouldn't be surprised.

'What is it?' Impatience rings in Jake's tone. He raises an eyebrow at me. A look I know well. It's the look he gets when he thinks he's going to win. He thinks Gary is going to give him leverage like he did with Tom. He thinks Gary has something on me he can use. I almost smile at his naivety.

'So,' Gary says, 'Hannah Fitzroy is the daughter of Julia and Marcus Fitzroy, who live outside Bath in Somerset. The entire family are absolutely minted. I'm talking trust funds and properties all over the world kind of rich. Hannah has one brother, William, who lives in Dubai. The entire family hates each other from what I can gather. They hardly speak. She's a corporate lawyer at Jenkins, Wyatt & Ross—'

'You told me all of this last summer,' Jake says, and I wonder if it's for my benefit. He wants me to know he did his research. I expected nothing less. Hoped he would, in fact.

'Did you find anything new?' Jake asks.

'I did, and get this: Hannah Fitzroy accepted a transfer to New York in the spring of last year. I put a call into the US office and spoke to her just to be sure. It's the same Hannah Fitzroy. She hasn't been back to the UK since. So whoever you're marrying, mate, it's not her.'

'Got it,' Jake says and hangs up, his jaw tightening with the anger he tries so hard to control but still slips through the cracks sometimes.

My lips twitch with a smile. All the fear leaves my body in a rush of relief. I've been terrified for hours and days and weeks that we wouldn't pull this off. That Jake would see through the story we'd built around him.

I have a flash of sitting at the farmhouse table, Bobby in the French police uniform sat opposite and Jake by the sink. I remember feeling utterly terrified that what we were doing was completely insane. I couldn't see how Jake would buy our story in that moment, but he did. That's the beauty of panic for someone like Jake. He hates being out of control, and when it happens, he can't think straight; he can't see what's right in front of him. All we had to do was keep adding the stakes and the fear. Keep his head spinning.

I smile properly then for the first time since Jake rushed through the door. I've been counting down the days to my wedding for so long. This is going to be fun.

When I next look at Jake, his face is tight with the rawness of emotion. He looks like he's been slapped in the face. Like he might cry. 'So you're not Hannah Fitzroy,' he says, half question, half not.

'My name is Jessica Lamb.' It feels foreign to say my real name aloud. I've been Hannah Fitzroy for a year now. Setting up my fake life ready for the day I'd meet Jake and be the perfect girlfriend to him. It's been the role of a lifetime. It's consumed me. Wholly and completely. At times, it's even felt real. The ultimate method acting. But I've never forgotten the plan and why we're doing this.

Another question forms on Jake's lips. I know what he wants to ask. How? When? Why? And I want to explain it all. Every little detail of this grand deception we've played. I want to watch the realisation dawn that all this time Jake was making his plans and his moves, thinking he knew the rules when he didn't even know the game.

'I'd been watching you for a few months before we got together,' I say, relishing the look of surprise on Jake's face.

'When?' he asks.

'Early spring last year. A few months after Tom died, when you'd moved to London.' I push aside the hollow emptiness thinking of that time after Tom's funeral when I was so lonely. So adrift in a dark ocean of grief.

'I watched you ignore some beautiful women and practically throw yourself at others. Then I realised – you were looking for someone with money. I knew you'd never fall in love with me as I was – an out-of-work actor with nothing to my name. And so I created a character who was wealthy. I knew you'd check on me and so it had to be someone real. I didn't study law at Cambridge but stayed close to home, studying drama at Manchester. During my university summers, I'd taken the most random jobs. One of them was working as a PA for Julia Fitzroy. Full board and good pay in a rambling old house in Bath.

'I got to know Hannah pretty well. She even got me the job as a contracts proofreader at her law firm in London when I needed you to think I was a lawyer.'

There's more I could say. Like how I had to make it real. Every detail thought of. The job at Jenkins, Wyatt & Ross wasn't hard, but it was dull and monotonous. And yet I'm surprised how much I enjoyed it at first. It was a distraction from my grief and anger, but it was also time away from Jake. I didn't need to work such long hours, but I could hardly play the overworked lawyer if I was nine-to-five. Besides, the more I was there, the less time I had to spend with Jake. The job wasn't the hardest part. That was convincing a man I hate with every cell in my body to love me. And that I loved him.

The law firm was important. It couldn't be faked. Sharing the Find My app created a trust for Jake. It showed him I had nothing to hide. It was also handy to keep an eye on his whereabouts. But the work got boring fast, and I spent longer and longer each day hiding in that file room, going over the final details of this plan we made that seemed half crazy and half genius. From the perfect meet-cute at the London to Brighton bike ride when Bobby made sure Jake crashed into me, to leaving Jake alone in that church waiting for a wedding that wouldn't happen.

It's taken months of planning. Every intricate detail. Even calls in the evenings, risky but we pulled it off by using the names of Julia and Marcus to make Jake think my parents were calling. An excuse to shrink down the wedding too. I didn't want anyone else with Jake in the church. Especially not the friends he thought I had – paid actors at our engagement party and the quiz nights we went to. I really have known some of the group since my teens, but from drama camps and auditions, not boarding school or Cambridge.

They were happy for the paid work. Bobby and Robert managed the quiz WhatsApp group, making sure Jake saw enough history and depth of my life never to question it.

'This is insane,' Jake says. 'You're all insane.'

I cross my arms, glaring at him. 'If that's the case, you drove us to it,' I say. 'I loved Tom. We were soulmates, and you took him from me.'

'How?' Jake barks. 'How the actual fuck did I drive you to faking a murder because I stole some software? It's insanity. We put his body in that cave, Han—' He stops himself from saying the name.

I shake my head, unable to stop the smile from spreading across my face. 'No, we didn't. Robert played dead, surrounded by pig blood on the rug – a fake by the way. Our budget wouldn't stretch to an antique Persian rug.'

I glance at Robert. His face is blank at the mention of money. When I first came to him and Bobby with the idea of deceiving Jake and getting revenge for what he did to Tom, I expected them to call me crazy like Jake is now. But a few weeks after the funeral, Tom's father and brother were grieving too. It felt like we all needed something to focus our pain on. I've known these men as long as I've known Tom. First as a drama student in Robert's drama club, then as a staff member running my own workshops as I waited for the big break that never came.

'I'll sell the house,' Robert said. 'It will give us the budget we need to pull this off.' And it did. It gave us enough to hire the farmhouse in France for the long weekend. It really had felt like home that place, something in the countryside reminding me of growing up in a rural village outside of Manchester. Adding framed photos of two young children in the dining room to make it seem like a family home and not a house for hire.

Then there was paying the rent on this loft for over a year. Plus a hundred little things all adding up. The expensive salon treatments, changing my naturally light blonde hair to brown to match Hannah Fitzroy and her mother's hair, not to mention the new wardrobe of clothes. The salary from the law firm helped, but it was hard at times to throw money around like I had the backing of a wealthy family, when really our money was getting tight. It was never about the money though. It was about this moment.

'Getting you to suggest hiding the body was hard,' I admit. 'I almost had to suggest it myself. It still would've worked, but I wanted it to be your idea. When I sent you off to get the cleaning supplies, Claude – or Robert, I should say – got up and we placed a weighted crash car dummy in his place. He hid in the next room while we did the rest.

'I know you're wondering why,' I continue. 'Why go to such extreme lengths of pretending we'd hidden a dead body. You see, it was about trust. We needed a situation where you'd be pushed to your limits and feel out of control, and it had to be high stakes. I needed you to think this amazing life we'd created for you would be ripped away at any second. It had to be all your dreams come true, so you wouldn't run away again.'

There are other reasons it had to be this way. The body in France. The threats. But we'll get to that.

The only thing that's been real is my fear. Fear Jake would learn the truth. And fear of Neve. She was the unexpected twist in our plan after Bobby trashed the apartment and made it look like we'd had a break-in so I could convince Jake to take the trip to France. He hid the camera too, but I could've done that myself. But then Neve showed up, and I didn't know if she was on Jake's side or not, but her presence in our plans felt like it could topple everything.

Jake shakes his head. 'Nothing you say is going to make me think this isn't next-level insane. All for some stupid software I stole.'

Fury flames beneath my skin. 'Tom's dead because of you.'

'How?' Jake throws back. 'How the hell am I to blame for a death I didn't even know about. The last time I saw Tom he was alive.' His Ohio accent is suddenly strong. I see the control starting to slip. Good.

It's Robert who replies, stepping forward and looming over Jake. 'Tom was proud. He didn't ask for my help and probably wouldn't have taken it even if I'd known he was in trouble and offered. It crushed him when you stole his work. He couldn't see a way forward.'

Robert continues, and I let the words wash over me, feeling the hurt rise up for those last awful months with Tom when our wild, amazing, everything love fell apart.

Tom thought all his dreams were over when Jake stole his work. It changed him. He wanted to postpone the wedding, cancel everything. I couldn't make him see that it was just one piece of software. He'd have other ideas. There would be other chances and other dreams, but he became moody, shutting himself away, going out at night alone and coming back steaming drunk. We fought constantly in those weeks, and more than once I threatened to leave.

'You're my soulmate,' he mumbled one night when he'd fallen into bed stinking of beer and whisky. 'I'll always find you. We're meant to be together.' And I laid beside him and cried myself to sleep because he was right. But I wasn't sure our love would be enough to save us.

'Again' – Jake's voice cuts Robert off; he accentuates the words as his own frustration starts to simmer – 'how is Tom going off the rails and killing himself my fault? I get that what I did was really shit, but I didn't—'

Bobby moves from the door with such speed Jake and I both jump. He grasps Jake's shoulder, growling the words. 'Tom didn't kill himself. He got in a fight outside a bar one night with a bouncer. That's how he died. And it's your fault because if you hadn't been the lowest form of human and stolen from him, he wouldn't have been out drinking, trying to find a way through what you'd done to him.'

The only sound in the silence that follows is Bobby's heavy breathing as he backs away. I wait for Jake to snap, but instead his eyes grow wide, his jaw slack.

'I... I had no idea he died like that,' Jake says.

For a moment, none of us know what to say or do. And so I push us forward, keeping to our plan. 'You took everything from Tom, and his death took everything from me. So we've done the same.'

'What do you mean?' Jake's eyes dart from me to Robert and back again.

I smile. My sweet, love you forever, Hannah smile. 'We've taken everything you care about. Me for starters. That perfect love of your life. The rich, beautiful girl with the family money who was going to set you up, make you rich for life.'

I take a breath, relishing the moment. 'And all your money from the sale of Tom's software, of course.'

Jake gasps. 'What?'

I'm happy to repeat myself. 'All you care about is your life and money, and so that's what we've taken from you. Your perfect life is gone. You're broke, Jake. I emptied out all of your accounts this morning. Every penny you got from selling Tom's software. Everything you've built. It's gone.'

It's why we needed him to go to France. Not only did it add a layer of confusion to what was happening, pushing Jake further out of his comfort zone, but we needed him there when I called to tell him about the threat and the deadline. Pushing and pushing until Jake felt backed into a corner. No way out but to trust me with his banking passcode and to tell me about the wealth from the sale of the business, as if I hadn't read his emails while he slept almost every night for months and knew all about the deal. We could've drained his accounts last night and disappeared, but I wanted him standing in that church. I wanted him to feel the hurt of losing someone.

From the sofa, Jake pales as he unlocks his phone and taps furiously at the screen. A glowing satisfaction fills my body as the realisation dawns on his face.

'You have nothing,' I say.

His mouth works like a fish out of water. Opening then closing. No sound comes. The roiling anger steals my breath as I stare at this man. He has been everything to me in finding a way to cope with my grief, a way to lash out and get the retribution Tom deserved.

I force myself to smile. It's done. I've taken from Jake like he took from Tom. And yet the victory doesn't feel like I hoped it would.

Something is missing.

FORTY-ONE

JAKE

Tom's dead. Killed in a fight outside a bar with a bouncer. Except that's not what happened. Jake killed Tom. These people have no idea, Jake realises. They blame him for the circumstances that led to Tom's death, but Jake did a lot more than that. He was there that night. He threw the punch that must have killed Tom.

A queasiness tumbles in his stomach. He hadn't known Tom was dead. Truly he hadn't. Or maybe he hadn't wanted to know. He bites the inside of his mouth, fighting back the emotions – the need to cry. His tie is strangling him again. He reaches for it, tugging it loose.

He's not a bad guy. He hasn't always been a good guy either, but he never meant to hurt Tom or the bouncer or anyone. He let his temper take over. A split second of stupidity.

He remembers reading the headline. ONE DEAD AND ONE BADLY INJURED IN BAR FIGHT.

The words had swum before his eyes. He'd doubled over. Puked his guts up on the street. He'd been so ashamed, so horrified that he'd closed down the website, refused to read on. He knew he'd regret that night for the rest of his life, but he'd told himself there was nothing he could do except move on, look forward.

But he'd always thought the bouncer was dead. Not Tom. He'd barely hit Tom before the bouncer had taken him by surprise. Jake had lashed out at the burly man with the eyebrow piercing over and over and over. But Tom must've fallen back from the single punch, too drunk to steady himself, and when Jake thinks back to the moment he turned to run, he can see Tom's body lying motionless on the ground, and the puddle in the darkness he thought at the time had been water but could've been blood.

The thought spins in his head with a hundred others, battling for attention, pounding in his skull. But only one screams through him. It's all over. Everything he's worked for, the life he thought he'd built with Hannah gone. The money gone.

His chest cramps, like a weight is pressing down on him, lungs unable to draw in a breath. Every penny gone. There has to be something he can do. Jake squeezes his eyes shut, fighting the nausea churning inside him. Hannah isn't Hannah. Claude isn't dead. It was all a scam, and he fell for it every step of the way.

He has nothing.

He stares at Hannah or Jessica, whoever this woman is. Really stares at the person he thought he'd spend the rest of his life with. Everything he's done these past weeks has been for them. To protect them. But it was just a sick game of revenge from a bunch of out-of-work actors wanting to make him pay. He can't believe he's fallen for it. So completely. Not for a single second did he suspect. And yet he sees now the tiny tells, the holes in this life he thought was real. He wanted it so badly he turned a blind eye. Like Allard's calls and the threats. Just enough to keep the panic pushing down on him but never really escalating. Never actually going to the police.

Think, he tells himself. He needs a plan.

There's a noise behind him – the latch on the door clicking. Bobby is standing by the open door. 'We're done here,' he says.

Robert nods.

The nausea builds. Done. They're done? They think they can take everything away from him and be done? Anger thrums in his body. He can't wrap his head around it. Everything he's done, every worry, every sleepless night has been a game to them.

A tension tightens across his shoulders and then his jaw. He feels the familiar curling of it in his fingers, but he won't lose control this time. Instead, he says nothing. He waits for their next move. He isn't sure who's in charge here, but he doesn't like the fury radiating from Bobby. He needs to be ready. Are they letting him walk out of this alive?

Robert throws a glance to Hannah – Jessica, he corrects himself, but the name doesn't stick in his thoughts. She was Tom's fiancée. He remembers the cheesy grin that used to spread over Tom's face when he talked about her. His unwavering belief that he'd found his soulmate at the age of eighteen and nothing would ever come between them.

He gets it. This woman standing before him might've been playing a part, but he really saw something special in her. He really believed they could've had their happy ever after.

She really had meant everything to him.

'I'll be right behind you,' Jessica says to Robert.

The older man hesitates, but there's something in Jessica's expression that seems to make him think better of protesting, and a moment later the door shuts and it's just the two of them, alone in this apartment with the sun streaming in through the windows. It really would've been the perfect day to get married. It's another reminder of everything he's lost.

'It's over,' Jessica says as she steps forward, reaching for a small sports bag by the sofa he hadn't noticed was there. 'I know you're scrambling right now, Jake. You're looking for your next move. Telling yourself you need a plan. But it's over.'

He hates that this stranger thinks she knows every last thing about him. Heat burns in Jake's body. In a split second, he's on his feet, flying forward, shoving Jessica down onto the sofa, standing over her, fists clenched at his side. Her eyes flash with an anger he's never seen in her before.

He smiles. Maybe they're not so different after all.

Jessica thinks she knows him.

Thinks.

Doesn't know.

Because Jessica has made one miscalculation. This was never about love for him either.

FORTY-TWO
JAKE

Jake's fists are tight at his side, but it's not the out-of-control anger this time but a controlled fury for this woman and all her scheming. She stole his money. But worse than that, she ripped away his future. The money from the business sale was good. Proof to Hannah and her family that he was capable. But it was a drop in the ocean to the kind of wealth and lifestyle they had. The lifestyle he planned to be part of just as soon as he and Hannah were married.

Hannah was the one.

The one person who could give him the life he'd always dreamed of. A life of wealth and prestige. It was never about love for him. It was about keeping Hannah happy because she was going to give him everything he wanted.

'Losing your temper again, Jake,' Jessica hisses, looking up at him with hate burning in her eyes. But she doesn't try to move from where she's sitting on the sofa. Him standing over her. They both know how little it would take him to hurt her.

She makes a show of sighing like she's bored. For the first time, he sees it for the act it is. 'You should know there's still a camera in this room, and I'm more than happy to tell the police about an assault charge.'

A pain shoots across his tightening jaw as another pulse of anger hits him. His voice when he speaks is a low growl. 'I think I'm done with your threats. I'm not going to hurt you. But you had your turn to talk, and now I'm taking mine.'

'There's nothing you can say that will make any difference.' She lifts her chin. 'I know everything.'

He cocks an eyebrow. 'Really? So you know I never loved you?'

She rolls her eyes. 'Of course you're saying that now.' But there's confusion playing on her face too. He clings to it.

'It's true. You were right when you said I was looking for a particular type of woman. I wanted someone with money to give me the lifestyle I wanted. When I found you, I thought I'd hit the jackpot. You were perfect, and I'd have done anything for you and the life you would give me. The doors you'd open with your family connections and your wealth. So yeah, you scammed me, but I was scamming you right back, Jessica Lamb. You think you took away my perfect life, but I was faking just as much as you.' A bravado carries in his voice, one he can almost believe. He remembers thinking Hannah was too good for him. Too good to be true. Now he knows why.

'I think it's pretty clear who's won,' she says, and he almost laughs at that competitive streak of hers. Not Hannah's but Jessica's.

'Here's something else you don't know,' he throws out, desperate suddenly to claw back some control. To crush Jessica as she's crushed him. 'Your precious Tom was weak. Weak willed, weak minded. Weak! He had no balls. Do you know he came crawling back to me, begging for us to be partners again when it was him that wanted to take the software for himself in the first place?'

'It was *his* work,' Jessica shouts. 'All you did was ask for money for your bogus expenses. Dinners out. Clothes. He trusted you, and you burned through his savings – our wedding savings – and what did you do for it? Nothing.'

'God, you sound just like Tom.' Jake pushes a hand through his hair, the frustration pulsing. Why does no one truly get him? Why is everyone so blind to the potential he sees in things?

'I was networking,' he continues. 'It takes time. And I think I've proven exactly what I'm capable of doing after actually selling the software this week. By the time Tom begged me to meet him that night, I knew he'd only drag me down.'

There's a pause, and in the silence, her eyes narrow. 'What night?'

He grits his teeth, realising his mistake. 'It doesn't matter.'

'What night?' she pushes again as her eyes widen and she carries on without giving him the chance to reply. 'You were there! At the bar the night Tom died.' She throws a hand to her face. 'Of course you were. How did I not realise? Tom had been struggling to cope after what you did. He'd been going out, drinking a lot, but he was never a fighter. Even drunk, he wouldn't have punched a bouncer for no reason. But you would've.'

A pressure squeezes Jake's neck. He reaches for his tie again. 'I don't know what you're talking about.'

'You do,' she cries. 'You were there.'

Jake's anger is simmering beneath the surface. He wants Jessica to shut up now, but she keeps talking. Repeating the words, going over it again. The night Tom died and his injuries.

'Did you smash the back of his head against a wall? Did you drag him into that alley to kill him because you knew he'd always cause trouble for you? That's it, isn't it? You're a murderer.'

The horror in her voice breaks something inside him. 'It wasn't like that,' he shouts, voice a strangled croak.

A silence draws out. Too late to walk away from this now.

And what difference does it make? They've already taken everything from him. He has nothing left. Rock bottom again.

'I tried to walk away that night. Tom was the one that came after me. He shoved me into the alley. He wouldn't let up. It was self-defence.'

Silent tears track two lines down Jessica's face.

Her words echo in his mind. *'You're a murderer.'*

It's true.

And in the quiet moment of the night, when he's honest with himself, Tom was just another con. Like Hannah. Like Neve and all those idiot investors in Westlake.

Jake has always had a knack with computers. Back in Westlake, he knew there was a market for refurbished office equipment. He could buy cheap from companies going bust and sell them on. His first purchase maxed out his credit card. It was a printing company closing down. He bought fifty computers cheap, selling them to a driving school for their pupils to use for their computer-based practice tests.

While he waited for other opportunities, he courted investors, promising low risk and high returns. People fell for his charm. Convincing people to believe in him was easy. But he got cocky. He took orders for computer systems he didn't have. Couldn't get hold of. He was out of his depth and overstretched. And so he took one final investment, this time from Neve, promising to triple her grammy's inheritance. A week later, he declared the business bankrupt.

He hadn't expected Neve to fight back. Going to every business he'd worked with and telling them what he'd done. Telling his family too, not that they were surprised. Neve really had gone crazy, stirring so much trouble, Jake knew his only way out was to start over. He used the inheritance from Neve that had never made it into the business and flew to England.

When she'd turned up in London, he'd been terrified of what she'd say to Hannah. In the end, he'd invited her over.

Told her he'd pay her back the money. He also told her that if he ever saw her again, he'd kill her. He hadn't meant it, of course, but he'd made sure she hadn't known that.

After Westlake, he moved to England with a new resolve to be smarter. He had to find those who wouldn't fight back like Neve had. Tom didn't have money, but he had something to sell. It was the next best thing. Jake meant what he said to Hannah. Tom had been weak. He knew the man would never have the balls to come after him. He was right, but he hadn't figured on his family getting Tom's revenge for him.

'You killed Tom,' Jessica whispers through the tears. 'You really killed him.' Then he sees the phone in her shaking hand, and he thinks of Bobby and Robert in the car. He might not have a penny to his name right now, but at least he can walk away.

He turns away from Jessica's pain and makes for the door. He has to get out of here before Bobby gets back. Then he's gone, bounding down the stairs, into the courtyard and down the cut-through. On the street. Running. No destination in mind. Just somewhere else. Anywhere else.

His confession pounds in his thoughts. He should've kept quiet. Let them think he had nothing to do with Tom's death. Let them think they'd got their revenge. They'd won.

He'll have to disappear. Change his last name even. He doesn't want to spend the rest of his life looking over his shoulder.

He's done bad things in his past. Terrible things. And now he's paid the price. A con man being conned. Fuck! Maybe one day he'll laugh about it. The irony. Maybe one day he'll look back and admire the planning and the long game it took for this con. But right now, it hurts. Right now, he's crushed.

He throws a glance over his shoulder before choosing a direction at random and finding himself heading towards Camden and Regent's Park. He tries to see the chessboard in his head and his next move, but it's broken, shattered into a hundred tiny pieces. It's the same feeling he had leaving Westlake. His life is over.

But he's started over before. He can do it again. He'll keep a low profile, look for the opportunities when they come. Eventually, he'll find his confidence again. After all, there will always be other women, other investors. Other cons.

SIX MONTHS LATER

FORTY-THREE
JAKE

The woman glides towards the exit of the delicatessen, her hands loaded with two full bags of expensive cheese and meats, sourdough, and pots of sundried tomatoes Jake has never understood the appeal of. He's just stepping through the door and grabs the handle, holding it wide for her to pass through. A flirtatious smile lights her face, pushing at the crow's feet around her eyes. She could pass for early forties, he thinks, although she's closer to fifty.

'You again?' she says.

He laughs. 'Hey, can't blame a man for wanting to stock up on his coffee before the weekend,' he replies, nodding to the row of glass jars behind the counter, each filled with overpriced coffee beans. He's been buying them at this time every Friday for a month, despite the fact he can't taste the difference between one or the other. He misses the diner coffee he drank by the truckload back in the States. Here, it's too strong and too bitter for his liking, but he buys a small paper bag each Friday anyway, careful to time his entrance just right.

'Same time same place next Friday then,' the woman says with a questioning tilt of her head.

A slow, practised smile stretches across his face. 'And maybe next Friday will be the day I suggest a drink at the wine bar next door and you say "yes".'

Surprise sparks in her eyes, and then her head of glossy black hair is swishing from side to side, but she's laughing. 'Maybe,' she says, and he can tell by the smile that she'll agree.

'Arabella,' she says then, lifting the two bags of shopping, as though if she wasn't holding them, she'd hold out her delicate hand with the pale white line on the ring finger where her wedding band used to sit.

'Jake,' he says. 'Nice to meet you, Arabella.'

He pulls the door back another inch and lets her pass. It took two weeks to get a smile, a third before she said hello and now a fourth to secure a date for next week. Slow and steady, that's his plan. No rushing in this time. No grand proposals. Arabella used to be married to a CEO of an investment firm in the city. In one of the biggest clichés of all time, the husband ran off with his secretary, twenty years his junior. No children, but Arabella did well out of the divorce, and from what he can tell from her socials, she's ready to move on and have some fun.

On the street, she huddles into her cashmere scarf against the bitter wind whipping past the Tudor buildings with their old beams and the rustic charm that draws in the expensive shops and those like Arabella with money to burn.

Five minutes later, Jake is walking away from the shopping area. He's always liked Windsor. The town is dominated by the royal castle and its stretching parkland. It's the quaint England he imagined when he moved from Westlake. But like all towns, it has its poorer areas, and after ten minutes of walking, he's passing under an old railway bridge, its underside covered in layers of graffiti, while every inch of the pavement beneath his feet is covered in pigeon shit from where they roost in the alcoves.

He quickens his pace. He's wearing the one decent coat he

owns – charcoal grey and expensive wool that he stole from the coat pegs of a wine bar two months ago. It wasn't rock bottom – that was on his first days after Jessica stole his money and tried to ruin his life with her games, when he picked purses out of the folds of pushchairs in the park. That was rock bottom.

It's been six months of stealing and blagging his way from one day to the next, barely scraping by. But he's met Arabella now, and his face is becoming known at the networking events. He's got a new company, selling full fibre broadband to the surrounding rural villages. Renting it from the company who installed the cables and adding a premium with a promise of exceptional customer service. It's small-time, but it was enough last month to move out of the single room he was renting in a run-down house in a shitty part of town. The apartment he's in now isn't much better. The walls are thin, and as he makes his way to the second floor, the thrashing beat of house music blares out from one of the other apartments.

He unlocks the door and walks down the narrow hall to the living room without turning on the lights. In the dark, he can pretend he's somewhere else. Somewhere like the loft in London. Is it strange that he misses that life and Hannah when it never existed?

With a sigh, he drops onto the lumpy sofa that came with the apartment. The fabric is beige and worn in places, stained in others in a way he doesn't want to think about. It's how he always starts his evenings. Sitting in the dark, thinking and planning. Outside the window, kids are kicking a ball against the cars. Any minute now, it'll set off an alarm and they'll scatter in peals of laughter.

The loathing for this place and this moment in time consumes him.

He has to give it to Jessica – she really fooled him. As the months have passed, his anger for what happened has morphed into a sense of relief. He lost everything, but it could've been worse. He's changed his surname, spent months looking over his shoulder, expecting them to come back for him. But no one has.

Jake still has his life. And he got away with killing Tom.

Most of the time, he can stay positive, look ahead to the opportunities he's finding in Windsor – like the beautiful, newly divorced Arabella, who he suspects would like to put two fingers up to her husband and his pregnant secretary with a good-looking younger man. But sometimes the constant grafting feels like it's eating away at his soul. All the plans, the thinking one, two, three steps ahead. He wonders if the day will ever come when he can just exist.

A car alarm sounds from the parking lot. A resident shouts from a window. Jake drops his head back onto the cushion, and it's then that something nags in his thoughts. He senses his muscles tighten a fraction, his pulse quickening. He opens his eyes; glances around the living room. His eyes have adjusted to the small gloom of light coming in from the streetlights outside. There's nothing out of the ordinary.

He moves to turn on the light. Stops. There's something damp and sticky on the sofa. On his hands. Instinctively, he reels back. Then two things happen at once. The first is the smell registering in his senses – the unmistakable tang of metal and rust. Of blood. The second is the pounding fist on his front door.

In a split second, he's on his feet. Mind racing. He slams his hand to the light switch and yelps as he takes in the white walls and cheap laminate flooring, which right now are covered in dark, sticky blood.

There's a curving flick of it against the wall and a huge puddle on the floor with a gap in the middle where it looks like a body was lying. Streak marks and footprints. It's the farmhouse in France all over again except without a body, thank God. He takes in other things too. A roll of bin bags, a discarded suitcase he's never seen before. A large knife he thinks came from his kitchen. Plus, sitting on the table in the corner, two phones side by side. Neither belong to him.

Panic seizes his body. His thoughts fly to Jessica, Robert and Bobby, and a 'what now?' dread consumes him.

The pounding at the door comes again followed by the yell of 'Police. We'd like to talk to you in connection with the disappearance of Jessica Lamb. Open the door please.'

Fuck!

It's the same game as France, except he's a step behind. No time to clean up. He can already see the trouble he's in as he takes a step. Not to the front door but to the sliding window and the balcony. For a moment, he wonders if he can jump. But it's just concrete below. No drainpipe to shimmy down. Best case scenario, he breaks both his legs. Worst case, he's dead. Either way, he won't escape.

There's only one option. He doesn't like it, but he yells, 'I'm coming,' as he heads down the hallway. There's a smear of blood on his hands and on the cuff of the coat he's yet to take off. Panic grabs him by the throat, squeezing the air from his lungs. He has no idea how he's going to get out of this, but he will, he tells himself. He always does.

FORTY-FOUR

JESSICA

I sit low in my car with a black bobble hat pulled over my cropped blonde hair and watch the doorway to Jake's apartment building. I watch the two police officers lead Jake out towards their waiting car. A hand touching the top of his head as he's guided into the back seat. He won't like that. Jake's expression is one of bafflement. He's always been good at stringing people along. He would've made a good actor.

More police units are arriving, lighting the dark evening in flashing blue lights. They'll be waiting for the forensic units to arrive and process the scene while the first car takes Jake to the police station. It's amazing the things you can learn from online tutorials now. Blood spatter patterns and how best to place a needle in your arm and bleed yourself. Unpleasant but necessary. Pig's blood wouldn't do this time.

Jake never cared about me. His revelation wasn't exactly a surprise. There are only two things Jake loves. Himself and money. Taking the money was easy in the end. We'd lined everything up for that moment he was driving through France, confused and frantic, his shiny new future in touching distance if only he'd trust me.

I thought it would be enough. Leaving him at rock bottom with nothing to his name, but even as I sat in that apartment and watched the realisation dawn on his face, it hadn't felt right. There was none of the closure or glee I'd hoped for. Then Jake's confession blindsided me. He wasn't just responsible for the events leading up to Tom's death. He'd actually killed him. The grief hit me with a rawness as sharp as the cold December day I first learned of Tom's death.

A part of me wanted to tell Robert and Bobby, but I could see they were ready to walk away. They'd found their closure. They were using their cut of the money to set up a drama school in Tom's name. He'd have liked that, I think. He never loved acting like the rest of us did, but he still lit up the stage.

They've said I can teach with them again, and for a while I thought I might. I thought a quiet life teaching drama on the outskirts of Manchester would be enough.

What we've done has been closure for them. Retribution. But even before I knew Jake killed Tom, it was about more for me. Jake took everything from Tom and from me. All we'd done in return was steal Jake's money and crush the dream life that hadn't existed in the first place.

It wasn't enough.

And so I started to plan a new game for Jake. He was easy to find. All I had to do was search online through the message boards of networking events across the country. I knew a name would appear on one eventually that would ring true. And it did. In Windsor. It made sense. He fell in love with the town when we visited for a weekend last year.

He was easy to find after that. When he moved to a small apartment last month, I rented a flat across the road and took a job in a café in a part of town I knew he would never frequent.

Then the following week, I ran into the local police station and breathlessly told them I thought someone was following me.

I gave them my real name. My real history. An out-of-work actor working in a café.

The desk sergeant was kind. They asked me about bad exes or work colleagues showing an interest. Anyone in my life I was wary of. I shook my head that time, but I went in again a week later and showed them messages on my phone from an unknown number. Flirty at first but turning aggressive when I hadn't replied. A file was started.

Over and over I went back. Everything I reported to the police, I tearfully told to my boss at the café too.

On my final trip to the police station yesterday, I told the officer I knew who the man was. I gave them Jake's name. I told them a story about Jake confronting me in the street outside my apartment. I told them I saw him watching my window from the apartment opposite. I even worked out which apartment it was and gave them the address. 'I... don't know where he works or where he goes in the daytime, but he's always there in the evenings watching me,' I said through the tears. 'Please... will you go to his apartment to talk to him? Tonight when he's back? Will you tell him to leave me alone? I'm terrified for what he might do. I'm scared for my life.'

They promised they would send a patrol car that evening. They thought it was to talk to Jake, but I made sure there was much more for them to find.

As soon as I was certain they believed me, I disappeared from the world. I didn't arrive for my shift at work. It was out of character. I'd already told my boss I was scared for my life. I'd given her the crime number from the police case and urged her to call if I ever failed to show for work. Another push to the police to visit Jake that night. I had to be doubly sure they would. I couldn't have him cleaning up another fake crime scene.

By this time, Jake had left for his meetings in Windsor and

the little rendezvous with the woman at the delicatessen afterwards. Plenty of time to set up the crime scene.

He'd been alone last night. Watching TV and then an early night. No alibi. That was important.

When the police sit Jake down in the interview room and ask him if he knows a woman by the name of Jessica Lamb, I wonder what he'll say. Will he deny ever knowing me? Or will he try to explain? Tell them a crazy story about a woman called Hannah Fitzroy and a game she played to get revenge. It sounds crazy. Implausible. And he'll have a hard time proving any of it even happened. We were always so careful, setting up a company and renting the loft and the French farmhouse through that.

Besides, if he tells them everything, he's handing them his motive for murder.

'So Jessica Lamb tricked you and stole from you?' I imagine one of the detectives asking. 'That must've made you very angry.'

Then they'll show him their evidence from the file they made of my complaints and the phones they found in his apartment – mine, and the unregistered one the messages were sent from that I bought a month ago. They'll show him the crime scene photographs and the DNA analysis of my blood, matching the DNA from my toothbrush in my apartment. They'll find fibres of my hair and blood in the boot of the cheap car he'd bought a few weeks back to get to the nearby villages for the new scam he's running. And then they'll ask him where he was last night.

I've given the police everything they need. There's more than enough blood and evidence to point to Jake killing me and hiding my body somewhere. There might not be a body, but there's plenty to prove Jessica Lamb is dead. And in this, I've taken the last thing Jake cares about – his life. There's no way out for Jake. I've made certain. A life sentence. The prison cell Jake was so terrified of in France.

The engine starts.

'Ready to go?'

I turn to the driver and smile.

Neve grins back.

We've made a good team these past few months. After Jake had left the apartment that day, I remembered what Neve said to me in the courtyard. *'When this all goes wrong, give me a call.'*

I found her number on Jake's phone, and when I was ready, I called and asked if she fancied another trip to England. She landed the following week. After we shared our stories of Jake over a bottle of wine, we started planning. Neve is as dedicated and relentless as I am, and we've made a good team.

While I was working at the café, setting up a life here, she was learning about blood splatter and crime scene analysis. While I was crying in the police station, she was shadowing Jake, learning his routine.

We talked about killing him. It would've been easier. I think I could've done it. I think I had it in me to kill him and walk away without a shred of guilt. But death is so final. I wanted Jake to spend the rest of his life in prison. I wanted him to spend every single day of his miserable nothing existence thinking about me and how I'd won our final competition...

A LETTER FROM LAUREN

Dear Reader,

Thank you so much for reading *For Better, For Worse*. If you want to keep up to date with my latest releases and offers, you can sign up for my newsletter at the following link. Your email address will never be shared, and you can unsubscribe at any time.

www.bookouture.com/lauren-north

I'm so thrilled to be sharing another thriller with you. *For Better, For Worse* was so much fun to write. I loved the points of view of Jake and Hannah as they found themselves in a nightmare that kept getting worse.

I've written about marriages and families, and mothers and children, but I've never written a thriller from the point of view of a couple madly in love, counting down the days until their wedding. I wanted to paint the picture of a perfect relationship, a perfect moment in their lives and then detonate a series of plot explosions that would push Hannah and Jake – and their relationship – to the max.

To arrive home from a walk in the picturesque beauty of Southern France and find a dead body in your hall is shocking. But then to realise you've been framed for the murder, and your perfect life is about to come crashing down, is pretty horrifying. What would you do? Would you call the police and hope they'll see past the mountain of evidence against you and believe your innocence? Or would you hide the body and protect your perfect life?

I really hope you enjoyed *For Better, For Worse*. I love to hear from my readers, whether through reviews, tags in posts, or messages, it never fails to brighten my day! My social media links are below, and I can be found most days popping in to Bluesky, Instagram and Facebook. If you enjoyed this one, then I'd be so grateful if you would leave a review on either Amazon or Goodreads, or simply share the book love by telling a friend.

With love and gratitude,

Lauren x

- facebook.com/LaurenNorthAuthor
- instagram.com/Lauren_C_North
- tiktok.com/@Lauren_C_North
- bsky.app/profile/laurennorthauthor.bsky.social

ACKNOWLEDGEMENTS

My first thank you is to the early readers and bloggers who put so much of their energy and time into supporting authors. Please know that I'm so grateful. A special mention to Sarah, Kate and Suhky and all the admins of The Bookload on Facebook for always supporting my books. And Sam from My Cosy Book Nook blog who is so generous with his time.

At the very early stages of this novel, before it was even an idea, in fact, I had the privilege of spending two weeks with a work experience student, giving her a taste of what the day-to-day life of an author is really like. Merry's passion for books and writing shone through every day. And when it came to developing an idea for a new book, Merry's understanding of story structure and fresh ideas played a huge role in the development of this novel. Without the 'what if...?' questions we threw at each other, this idea would not be what it is today. Thank you, Merry. I look forward to reading your books one day!

And while we're talking about shaping this novel, I must also thank my editor, Lucy Frederick. Your insights and ideas have made this book so much better. It really is a team effort, which is why I'd like to say thank you to the entire team at Bookouture. Please do take a moment to read the credits page at the back.

Thank you to my agent, Amanda Preston. You're spinning a lot of plates for a lot of authors, and I'm extremely grateful that you don't bat an eyelid when I suggest throwing another plate (or entire dinner set) into the mix. The dedication and energy you bring to my career is truly amazing! Thanks also to the entire LBA team.

I'd like to thank Anna Wallace for her input at the final stages, as well as Sarah, Carol, Catherine and Kathryn, who have to listen to me talk about my stories *a lot*!

And would it even be an acknowledgements section if I didn't thank Zoe Lea, Nikki Smith and Laura Pearson? You keep me going, listen to and support me through all the big moments and the little ones too. I'm grateful every day for you all.

A final thanks must go to my family. My father-in-law, Tony, who brings us treats and is a constant cheerleader. 'I don't know how you do it, girl,' you say to me often. I don't know myself most days. One word at a time and the unwavering love and support from Andy, Tommy and Lottie. Thank you!

PUBLISHING TEAM

Turning a manuscript into a book requires the efforts of many people. The publishing team at Bookouture would like to acknowledge everyone who contributed to this publication.

Commercial
Lauren Morrissette
Hannah Richmond
Imogen Allport

Cover design
The Brewster Project

Data and analysis
Mark Alder
Mohamed Bussuri

Editorial
Lucy Frederick
Melissa Tran

Copyeditor
Donna Hillyer

Proofreader
Laura Kincaid

Marketing
Alex Crow
Melanie Price
Occy Carr
Cíara Rosney
Martyna Młynarska

Operations and distribution
Marina Valles
Stephanie Straub
Joe Morris

Production
Hannah Snetsinger
Mandy Kullar
Ria Clare
Nadia Michael

Publicity
Kim Nash
Noelle Holten
Jess Readett
Sarah Hardy

Rights and contracts
Peta Nightingale
Richard King
Saidah Graham

Printed in Dunstable, United Kingdom